FIND YOUR WAY
TO MY
GRAVE

FIND YOUR WAY TO MY GRAVE

A Carrie Lisbon Mystery

Chris Keefer

First published by Level Best Books/Historia 2024

This novel is entirely a work of fiction. The names, characters and incidents portrayed in it are the work of the author's imagination. Any resemblance to actual persons, living or dead, events or localities is entirely coincidental.

Chris Keefer asserts the moral right to be identified as the author of this work.

Author Photo Credit: Creative Imaging Photography

First edition

ISBN: 978-1-68512-800-5

Cover art by Level Best Designs

This book was professionally typeset on Reedsy.
Find out more at reedsy.com

To my whole family, near and far. My cup runneth over.

Praise for Find Your Way to My Grave

"A stunning peek into a vivid past replete with burgeoning feminism, the development of mortuary science, and early photography capturing the seamy corruption of a repressed age. A winner. Bravo!"—Gary Earl Ross, author of the Nickel City mysteries.

"Keefer continues the adventures of Carrie Lisbon, one of the most extraordinary characters in historical fiction today. Carrie—a woman undertaker in rural New York in 1900—investigates a suspicious death, discovers a blackmail scheme, and negotiates an adulterous affair—in ways that will surprise and impress Keefer's readers."—Marlie Parker Wasserman, author of Inferno on Fifth

"Awash in period detail and replete with indelible characters, including a street urchin of Dickensian aspect, a dogged but ethically compromised sheriff, and an irrepressible if well-meaning muckraker, *Find Your Way to My Grave* is both a taut murder mystery and a deftly drawn character study of an imperfect heroine. As Carrie Lisbon fearlessly peels back layer upon layer of evildoing to solve the heinous crime, she must also come to terms with a lapse in moral judgment that threatens not only to undermine the investigation, but permanently damage herself and those she holds most dear."—Norman Woolworth, *The Lafitte Affair: A Bruneau Abellard Novel*

"Keefer has created a unique and unconventional character in Lisbon, a woman with intelligence, talent, and courage at a time when a female working in forensics was frowned upon. I loved the period detail, setting, and ambiance in *Find Your Way to My Grave*. As a writer of historical fiction myself, I also enjoyed learning about how things were done in Victorian America, particularly the embalming procedure and the art of photography in which the protagonist excels. Keefer's tale is a cleverly crafted and intriguing read."—Skye Alexander, author of *Running in the Shadows* and the Lizzie Crane Jazz Age mystery series

Prologue

Ransom Butler sneaked down the embankment of the Duncan, feeling his way in the dark, finding tufts of grass to wedge his bare feet. He kept an eye on the guard shack at the top of the old abutment. The hired man fell deeply asleep in the early morning hours, and Ransom made his forays into the construction yard then, when the man's snores could be heard, even this far below. Still, Ransom was careful not to make a sound. He didn't need a beating from anyone else.

During the day, the bridge project was a hive of activity, with men swarming and shouting, mallets pounding, and the massive crane squealing and belching. Its black smoke blended with the dust from an endless parade of wagons hauling lumber, barrels, and iron girders down Main Street, filling Hope Bridge with a hazy cloud. In the earliest hours of the day, before the sun rose, the place was deserted, and Ransom had only that brief window to forage.

In the darkness, the ten-year-old slithered the last few yards to the creek bottom and paused, rabbit still. A tiny cascade of dirt pattered down behind him. He regretted not taking the time to pull his shoes out of the bin at the shack. The stones were cold. Indian summer was over, and a light frost gathered in delicate shards. But he'd been barefoot all summer; it was hard to get back into the habit.

He started forward, placing his toes carefully on the wide stones, and began scanning, head down like a sniffing dog, eyes wide, looking for anomalies among the rocks and scrap wood. Any glint meant a meal.

The creek bed was nearly dry here. They diverted the water when they built the caissons to drive in the new pilings. A pool of standing water and slick mud seeped in around the massive wooden walls.

He wished he'd seen the old covered bridge collapse last spring. The flood took it, and that lady with it. Some of the kids said they heard her screaming as she was carried away, and Ransom didn't want to believe it. But sometimes the willies made his belly flutter and the hairs on his neck stand up, and then he'd skip a day, reasoning that the dead lady had warned him, somehow, that he'd be caught prowling. Last night was Hallowe'en, and ghost stories had prevailed all month. With all those tales of spooks and phantoms, it was easy to believe the lady's specter could linger here.

He had seen the creek's destruction the next day, though, when the water was still unbelievably high and downright terrifying with its speed and volume. Later, the remnants of the bridge had been pulled down and carted away. Now, the state was putting up this new bridge, a 'monstrosity' his father called it. Only his father would bitch about such progress. Everyone else regarded the new bridge as a boon, a constant source of discussion, a marvel of engineering to watch go up, and a gold mine of income if you could hustle. Ransom had no problem with the building of the new iron bridge. He could hustle.

He raided the worksite almost every day in the early hours, before the sun came up, while the man in the guard shack slept. He came before his father woke up; his pa never knew he was gone.

That's where Ransom's luck held. In the barest light of those pre-dawn hours, he managed to find what the workers dropped each day. Buttons, rope, tools, a tobacco pipe. Luck kept the watchman asleep. Luck kept Ransom trading his finds on the sly with the peddler who came by the dump once a week. And luck kept his father drunk and unable to find the Mason jar of coins Ransom had buried under the house.

A rock tipped beneath his calloused foot, and he froze. The hollow sound didn't stir the man in the shack above. Ransom tread more carefully, fully exposed, until he got below the emerging trestle. He could just make out the boxy skeleton reaching across the gap as dawn advanced. He'd have to hurry.

He resumed his search, bent over, peering into the darkness for anything remotely salvageable, remotely gleaming. He timed his forays for that moment of the day when the night let go and a smudge of dawn lightened the sky. It gave just enough light to see coins, which were hard to find in the dark, unless they were silver. That had only happened once.

He spotted the handle of a pair of pliers stomped into the muddy gravel. He grubbed them out and slid them into his pocket. The weight of them sagged his thin trousers. A few feet beyond, a bolt formed a geometric pattern among the water -smoothed rocks. He pocketed that, too. Then he spotted a pale round object a few feet from the edge of the caisson where the slurry of mud and water settled around the pilings.

Ransom knew better than to venture onto the mud to pick it up. He'd leave footprints, and that would be the end of his nightly bonanza. He was also scared to death of quicksand. Everybody knew the really softest, slickest mud had no bottom, and he'd be sucked down, screaming in despair, before anyone could help him. The lady's ghost might hover over him, watching. He shook his head to dispel the ghastly thought and looked around.

He'd seen workmen rearranging planks when they needed to push wheelbarrows over the stones. Why, he could use a board from the pile right over there!

Carefully, slowly, Ransom picked up one end of a plank. He slid his hands down the length until he felt it balance. He hefted the weight, swung it toward the mud, and tiptoed forward. When he was near enough, he laid it down gently, straining to keep his efforts silent. He pulled his fingers from beneath it, wincing as the weight pinched his skin. A rooster crowed on the opposite bank. He surely had to hurry.

He minced onto the plank. The object was only a few feet beyond the safety of the creek stones. Ransom slid his foot onto the board with caution. He heard this was how to cross quicksand and thin ice.

He took another step. The plank held. He could see faint ripples where the end bounced a little on the mud. He hoped it wasn't a sign anyone could recognize. The rooster crowed again.

With his next step, he was close enough to discern the silver gleam of a pocket watch. Thrilled, he snatched downward, recognizing the value of such a thing.

The watch came up, but the chain stopped his tug. It was affixed to a vest, and the vest buttoned over a belly. A man's pale hand—hairy knuckles and bloodless white fingers—came up out of the water, as if protesting the theft. Ransom dropped the watch and stiffened upright like the plank he stood on. He didn't care if the night watchman heard him screaming.

Chapter One

The first thing she put on was her grim face. Not the face with which she greeted mourners. That was the solemn, kindly face. Not the frown of concentration that crept over her when she inserted the embalming syringe, or applied lamp black to a woman's eyebrows with a light touch. Not the sidelong, cynical look reserved for those who doubted her professional acumen, either. That look preceded a thorough recitation of her credentials, followed by the look of pride.

The grim face was for the business of dealing with the dead. For the corpse: of stripping away whatever dignity it had left; for laying it out, revealing all its vulnerability. The grim face coincided with the donning of the full-length apron, the cloth mask when the situation called for one, and sometimes, the long rubber gloves. Although they cost a great deal and impeded her sense of touch, they kept her bare hands from touching decayed and slippery flesh. The grim face was devoid of emotion because the business of laying out an individual was solemn, and, in this case, forensic.

Suited up and grim, Carrie Lisbon peeled off the first layer of muddy clothing from the stiffening body. The woolen coat was soaked. It weighed a ton and smelled of oily water. The dead man's arms had floated, and rigor had posed them into a half wave. The elbow bent up, and the wrist bent down. She had to wrestle with the limbs to pull them from the sleeves.

"Be sure to remove all the clothing laterally, Mrs. Lisbon," her boss's measured voice murmured from across the cellar. "It will minimize the turning back and forth."

She shot him the cynical look. She knew what she was doing; he knew it, too. "Standard procedure," she said, just as evenly.

Arthur Worley moved smoothly across the floor to the other side of the preparation table. With his apron tied on tight, accenting his tall, stick-thin frame, he, too, wore his grim face. "My apologies," he said in his trademark monotone. "I meant no disrespect regarding your process. I must admit to some trepidation about him being under my care."

Carrie understood. Worley's unique admission to having emotions threatened to set off her own nerves. She was listed in the "Double AFD," the Association of American Funeral Director's annual Index, the same as he. The new, 1900 edition was on her desk at home, as his copy was in his office. She'd completed her coursework in mortuary science and her apprenticeship under her father's tutelage, then obtained her embalmer's license, as had Worley. They could claim decades of mortuary practice between them, and they both adhered to the professional ethics of their craft.

But before them lay a public figure, and they had been called to collect his body, document his injuries, and determine how he died. Worley was an assistant to the county coroner. It was his job to discern the cause of the otherwise healthy man's death. A crowd was already clamoring outside Worley's house, eager for news of the deceased and what it meant. She stepped back and took a breath.

"You're right. We should proceed with the utmost care." She turned to the other occupant in the room. "Are you sure you're able to witness the preceding, Mr. Morgan?"

She always called him by his formal name when addressing him in public. The Sheriff of Duncan County stood near the stairs. His height and heavy shoulders took up a lot of space. His pebble-colored hair nearly grazed the ceiling. There was a slight tremor in his hand as he waved them on with a 'carry on' gesture. Carrie recognized his attempts at keeping his handsome face as grim as hers.

"We'll be going slowly, so as to document every move we make," Worley said gravely.

Carrie had prepared a clipboard earlier, as Worley and a church sexton stretchered the body into the preparation room through the coffin doors at the back of Worley's cellar. His backyard sloped away from the house, exposing the foundation, allowing for a pair of double doors and two windows on either side. The clipboard was only one of the amenities Carrie admired about Worley's facility. He'd parged and painted the stone-walled chamber, wired in a bar of four electric lamps directly over the sturdy Passmore cooling board, and hung convenient shelves for his embalming materials, makeup, and dressing supplies. The cement floor had a large enamel sink embedded in it, so bodily fluids could drain away under the stream of water from a big brass faucet. Heat from a little pot-bellied stove dispelled just enough November chill to make working on the dead comfortable for the living.

Curtains were drawn across the doors and the shades were pulled down on the two windows. Concealing their work from prying eyes warranted more lamps to dispel the gloom. Carrie's papers, snapped into place, would catalogue the undertakers' progress of initial identification and examination, the witnesses present, removal and enumeration of the clothing, the list of personal effects, and the condition of the body, including injuries. Worley kept impeccable records of his bodies.

The man's jacket and vest came off next. The shirt was unbuttoned, and the sleeve wrestled off the same arm. Worley hefted the torso up by the shoulders, and Carrie bunched and tugged the clothing under and around the man's back. Blood leaked from the broken skull. Worley packed more rags around the wound. Morgan shifted on his feet, emitting a small grunt.

Once the dead man's chest and belly were exposed, the two undertakers snapped a sheet over his face and drew it down between his reaching arms. The shoes, although caked with mud and soaked to the point of swelling, were hand-tailored Italian loafers, beautifully made and stylish. They were nevertheless tugged off the feet and set aside. Carrie paused over the socks and their garters. They appeared to be two different colors, but upon a closer inspection, she saw one was filthy with dirt and mud, the other a pristine black. Without another thought, she pulled the socks off, and, turning, dropped one. It plopped with a wet splat onto the floor.

Worley paused. She murmured an apology before retrieving the sock and setting it aside with the other clothing. They resumed disrobing the man, wrestling with the trousers, alternately tugging, hitching, and lifting, exposing the buttocks and pallid, hairy legs.

In the presence of two men, one of whom was remarkably squeamish with bodies, decorum required shielding the male corpse from a lady's view. Both men knew Carrie had been an undertaker all her life, and assumed she'd seen lots of dead men laid out naked before. Nevertheless, she would maintain the body's dignity and her reputation to the letter. She positioned herself at the man's head and held up the sheet that covered the torso, high enough to shield her view from Worley's final removal of the man's shorts. She walked the sheet down the length of the body, carefully keeping the cloth between her face and the man's crotch, then dropped it over his feet.

The room smelled of blood, fishy creek water, black oil, and wet leather. The undertakers went through the man's pockets, enumerating the contents. Carrie scratched notes on her clipboard. They searched for hidden recesses and pressed on the seams of his clothes for sewn-in objects. Carrie cataloged each article of clothing, before stacking them into a heavy wet pile. She'd hang them later on a clothesline near the woodstove. In their current smelly condition, they'd be no use at the wake, but she would never return a decedent's clothing to the family in such a state. Working with the clammy garments made her fingers ache with cold. A more robust fire would have been a comfort, but an increase in heat would hasten decay.

Worley turned to the dead man on the table and lifted the sheet that covered the face. "Sheriff, if you'd be so kind as to provide a positive identification to this man."

"We all know who he is."

Morgan's gruff response was met with an apathetic glance from the mortician.

"I believe you can appreciate the gravity of our position, Del," Worley's normally reserved voice was not without a note of warning. "We need your formal declaration."

Carrie stood with her clipboard and pencil in hand, watching Delphius Morgan breathe in, reset his own grim face, and approach the table. The electric lights lit up the dead man's face harshly. *We do know who he is. But everyone here needs to be impeccable with the handling of this.*

"It's Martin Evans. His outfit is building the new bridge over the Duncan," Morgan said with a sigh, as if resigned to some sort of fate. Carrie didn't look at him as she wrote down his words.

She still tingled from his touch. They'd taken a huge risk last night—really, the early morning hours of today—and she was dismayed when this body was discovered, and she and Morgan met again over a dead man, instead of over a set of crisp sheets in the darkness. She had to remain aloof and impervious to her feelings while she carried out her duties as assistant mortician to Art Worley, Hope Bridge's established undertaker. She had planned to linger at her house in a languid state, at least for a little while today, sated, reviewing lurid details of their lovemaking. But she was an undertaker, called out to attend a person who had come to an unnatural end. She was going to have to perform her duties while cloaking her affair with Del Morgan behind an iron-clad mask—the grim face. Worley spoke, and Carrie focused keenly on the events in the cold cellar.

"What we're going to do next, Mr. Morgan, is examine and photograph his wounds," Worley said. He stood as tall as Morgan, but his long face and narrow body seemed unhealthy next to Morgan's hefty frame and color, although Morgan was becoming paler every time Carrie looked at him. "Doctor Wells should be here any minute to determine the cause of death, but I think you can see, his head has been struck."

Worley's sangfroid description downplayed the nature of the wound. The back of Evans' head had not just been struck, it collapsed under the impact. The occipital bone that cradled the back of the brain sunk inward like a toothless mouth. Wet hair emerged from the ragged gash. The skull bones were stained with blood. Morgan barely glanced at the grayish material leaking out of the wound before he shied away. Carrie saw him swallow hard and wrestle himself back under control.

"That's obvious," Morgan said, stepping back toward the stairs. "Is there anything you can do about his arms?"

Evans had lain in shallow water before being discovered at dawn by a young boy snooping around the construction site. His arms had risen slightly, buoyed up by the water, and rigor had begun. He seemed to be reaching out for something, except his limp hands had dropped before they could make the grasp.

"As you know, a body stiffens shortly after death," Worley said. "His rigidity will progress, then release over the next twenty-four hours. We'll be sure to shield him from public view until he is pose-worthy again."

"What more should I do here, Art?" Morgan asked. "If I'd eaten breakfast, I'd be losing it right now. I need to get some fresh air." He glanced with meaning at the cellar stairs.

"I'll have you sign Mrs. Lisbon's forms, and write a statement—in my office, of course—that you witnessed our initial examination, and identified this body. We'll provide a list of Mr. Evans' possessions shortly. That should do for the time being." Worley made a minute gesture at the escape route behind Morgan, and the big man took the papers Carrie held out, turned quickly, and went up the stairs without a backward glance.

Worley turned to Carrie with the slightest of smiles. There weren't too many things that turned their stomachs in regards to a deceased, nor the sights, sounds, and smells that accompanied a body. They were also quite aware of the discomfort of others. The bigger and tougher the witness, the more likely they were to puke.

Chapter Two

I t began that morning.

The summons had come from a shoeshine boy who plied his trade at the foot of the Chester Inn, the grand hotel at the edge of the Duncan Creek in the rural village of Hope Bridge. A traveler, seeing the hotel's pillars and gleaming white paint as their horse and buggy exited the old covered bridge, would be cheered by the sight. But the wooden bridge was gone, and its replacement was under construction. The grand Chester had become dingy with dust and scuffed with hundreds of passing feet. The shoeshine boy was either paid well to leave his trade, or, his errand must be extraordinary.

Carrie had just finished washing and dressing. Her movements were slow. She and Morgan had satisfied each other in the darkest hours of the waning night, and she was still feeling replete, her eyelids heavy. As a result, her hand, while fixing the morning coffee, was dreamy. The urgent rapping on the front door was followed immediately by an insistent pull on the bell string.

"Coming," she called and heard the rushed summons from the excited boy before she'd fully opened the door.

"Thesheriffwanstsyoudownbythebridge!" the boy rapid-fired. "There's a body! And he sent me to fetch you! You have to come along. Now!" He turned and ran off the porch. As he left her yard, he spun around and yelled again, "*Now!*"

No longer languid, and slightly alarmed, Carrie closed the door and composed herself. If he was asking for her assistance, Sheriff Morgan needed her as his 'keen observer.' There was a body. It belonged to a person who had not left this mortal world as a result of illness or natural causes. This person had died under circumstances that generated a lot of questions.

Undertakers are accustomed to being summoned and ready in a few moments. She only needed to remove her cooking apron, collect her mortician's bag, and walk to the site of the new iron bridge.

She hurried along the flagstone sidewalk, stepping over smashed jack-o-lanterns. During last night's Hallowe'en revelry, she had heard the hoots of roaming groups of teenagers, using clackers and whistles to make their mischief through the streets. The shenanigans were greeted by the barking of dogs and the yells of irate neighbors when the revelers continued their fun well past midnight. She'd been pleased that the country custom of noisemaking crowds and bonfires allowed Morgan's entrance and exit from her house to go unnoticed.

The sharp smell of crushed apples rose in the morning air. Stacks of baskets towered next to cider presses, where boys, already shirtless under a crisp blue sky, cranked the crusher wheel, sweating and laughing. By evening, their exhaustion would not save them from their other chores, but for now, they showed off their stamina for their neighbors who gathered with their bushels and jugs, waiting their turn at the press.

The morning was chilly. Carrie had pinned back her dark hair, put on her plum jacket, her workaday gray skirt, blue cotton blouse, socks, and brogans. Her winter coat, a black scarf, and heavy gloves would keep her warm. She preferred to wear sturdy clothes that wouldn't get in the way of her photography or embalming. She kept her skirts hemmed just above her ankles, eschewing fashion, and some would say modesty, in favor of cleanliness. One never knew what fell to the floor during an embalming, and she wasn't going to trail blood behind when she finished up. The cotton held up to repeated washings in boiling water and didn't hold the smells of death and chemicals.

Hiding her affair with Morgan meant she also needed to put on the grim face, the expected look of an undertaker. People tended to give her a wide berth anyway. Who wants to chat up a woman who habitually touched dead people?

She approached the town center, and joined a throng of curious onlookers who hurried toward the construction site. The new span over the Duncan Creek was to be an iron trestle, and the town's population had swelled since the project began.

The work site dominated the east end of town. The landscape was scraped bare of vegetation and trees. Parallel iron beams stretched unconnected over a gaping creek bed twenty feet below. A black steam engine hung its shovel—ominously silent today—from a crooked arm. Blackened steel cables hung limply from a massive derrick. The steeply angled pile driver wasn't banging away at the bedrock. The barricades couldn't be seen. A crowd had formed like a hedge of thick bushes in front of the wooden fence, everyone talking and pointing and straining to see the gruesome discovery below. Dozens of unfamiliar workmen in muddy trousers, oil-stained hats, and heavy boots idled among the townsfolk.

On the outskirts of the crowd, not deigning to gawk or gossip, was Morgan's rival for Sheriff of Duncan County, Howard Clowe.

Tall, self-absorbed, and crafty, Clowe leaned his crossed arms on one of the barricades, watching the scene below with both amusement and boredom. Several supporters for his election—supplicants, really—hovered behind him, awaiting his word. He turned from the barricade, straightened, and ran his hand smoothly through his thick, pale hair. He murmured a comment which garnered a hushed laugh from the hangers-on.

Election Day was less than a week away, and both candidates had come to Hope Bridge, where a rich voting block of men, who either worked on the bridge, or supported those who did, had assembled. Clowe had taken a room at the Chester. Of course, it was a smaller room, but Carrie heard that he'd displaced an assistant engineer by offering to double the hotel's usual rate. The engineer had been forced to bunk in with a junior accountant. Their room was crowded with a second bed, and stuffed with books and tools, making the housekeepers give up trying to clean the room or change the sheets for fear of disrupting the precarious stacks of mechanical paraphernalia, files, and clothing.

Clowe and Morgan had managed to circle each other like gladiators. Clowe threw barbs at Morgan from the newspaper, and sniped at him with murmured deprecations to his supporters. Morgan didn't dignify the childish assaults on his character with any response. He and his son Eddie quietly campaigned from town to town, shaking hands with old friends.

Carrie made for Thomas Bale, Hope Bridge's permanent deputy, who watched over the crowd from the top of the wooden staircase that led to the creek bottom. Just like those surrounding Howard Clowe, folks closest to Bale maintained a yard's distance from his intimidating pose. As deputy, he was a natural, but grudging choice. Competent, in his prime, and familiar with everyone in town and beyond, Bale knew his business and yours. And the general misgivings caused by the idea of a Black man with such authority were overcome when Bale simply crossed his arms and stared everyone down. Like he did now.

"Miss Carrie," he said, offering a hand. "Thank you for coming." His sharp eyes warmed when he addressed her, but she picked up on his formality. Bale lived in an apartment he'd fashioned above her uncle's unused carriage barn when he'd been burned out by drunken vigilantes a few years back. He'd lost his carpentry shop, and everything in it, but refused to leave his hometown, refused to be intimidated. He preferred to walk down Main Street with confidence and purpose. Savoir Machin, Carrie's late husband's uncle on his mother's side, with whom Carrie lived, gave Bale carte blanche with the barn, and Bale established himself again as a master carpenter. He often took his meals with them. More than a boarder, he was Sav's best friend since childhood. There, they were family. Here, he was boss.

"Not at all, Mr. Bale. I received Mr. Morgan's summons, and I came right away. What's the trouble?"

"We found a man at the site this morning. Work's been delayed today. The workers are not happy about it."

"Who found him?"

"The Butler boy. His name's Ransom. He does what the English call 'mudlarking' down at the site, and he pulled up a pocket watch. Turns out it was still attached to the owner."

Carrie winced. The poor boy must have been scared out of his wits. But she hadn't been called to minister to a frightened child. No doubt he had a mother for that. "Where's the body?"

"On the river bank. Covered. Del's down there. Night watchman heard the kid screaming. He came and got me. I had the guard cover him up. I sent for Del. He sent for you. Art Worley's bringing his hearse. I kept everyone away. But the watchman knows who it is. Now everybody does."

"Can you please take me to him?"

The general public was not permitted beyond the barricade. A speculative murmur rose as soon as Carrie and Bale stepped beyond the wooden fence and onto the top of the plank stairs. Carrie looked over the embankment that dropped abruptly away. The staircase slanted down a sheer face of rock and dirt. Chipped and covered with dried mud from the countless footsteps it endured each day, it was nevertheless solidly built.

The Duncan was classified as a creek, only two hundred feet or so across, and always filled with quick -flowing water. It widened or skinnied along its course. It rushed through steep cliffs or slowed through rich bottomlands, but here it was a manageable span, the perfect crossing place for a bridge. The Mohawk and Hudson Rivers to the north and east were ten times larger by comparison, but the Duncan proved to be as raging as those last spring when the town's only conveyance over the waterway had been destroyed.

Carrie had seen the steam crane arcing and belching over the gap. She'd heard the daily clanging of iron and steel and tools from her home on North Street, at the west end of town. She'd watched the progress from a distance, but she and the rest of the populace had never been allowed anywhere near the construction. Down here, in the belly of the site, the sheer magnitude of the project was frightening. Iron bars, upright posts, and massive beams hung without support overhead. The smell of oil, grease, and mud permeated the hollow under the iron skeleton. The creek murmured and sped around a wooden caisson that diverted the water away from iron piers. Each rose like a towering stump. Overhead, the tableau was ringed with curious faces.

Someone had pulled the corpse out of the muddy water and laid it on the stones. The sun and wind had dried a wide smear of blood from the water to the body's present location, but it was still garish, gory, and unmistakable. Carrie and Morgan greeted each other with a single nod, the body and the tarp between them. "Do you want me to have a look at him *in situ*, Mr. Morgan?"

Morgan's face was immaculately blank. *His grim face,* Carrie thought. And rightly so. He must be feeling as many conflicting emotions as she. The residual guilt and glory of their coupling, the intense scrutiny of the crowd above, and, in Morgan's particular case, illness from the proximity to a dead person.

He was running for Sheriff of Duncan County, a position to which he'd been appointed by the former sheriff barely two years ago, upon that man's retirement. The crowds above—voters who had mixed feelings about him— would be judging his every move. With election day this coming Tuesday, he now had to juggle his campaign, alongside the investigation of a sudden and spectacularly public death.

Morgan took a step back. "Yes," he said, and with that single word, and the calmness of his hazel-gray eyes, she saw his emotions and his abilities, his dignity and his conflicts were all well under control. Like Thomas Bale, Morgan was competent, and he knew it.

They had stumbled into an acquaintance last spring, when she discovered a woman, whom she was called to lay out, had not died in the manner reported by her husband. Morgan had been reluctant to accept her observations, but when he came to realize the truth of her theory and her value as an ally, he offered his first compliment, dubbing her a 'keen observer.' As an undertaker, and a woman, she saw things he didn't. Their affair had begun unintentionally in the aftermath of a prolonged storm and a disastrous flood that had nearly killed them both.

Morgan motioned for two men nearby to hold up each end of the tarp vertically, shielding the body from the crowd above. Carrie approached and took a long look at the dead man. Since becoming Morgan's occasional associate, she'd learned that a broad view helped to discern anything out of place. Minute examination was for the morgue.

The man on the stones was middle-aged with dark hair, salt and pepper at the temples, and a clean-shaven face. He was fully clothed, from his sprung-open collar to his shoes. He wore a shirt, vest, suit coat, woolen overcoat, and cuffed pants that clung wetly to his legs. His face and hair were covered in dried mud, the same gray color as the stones. The pocket watch lay on his deflated belly. One of his pallid hands hung in the air, arranged by rigor mortis in a gesture of surprise. A halo of watery blood circled the back of his head.

Carrie gathered her skirt and crouched beside the body. Parted lips revealed a mouth full of silty water and muddy teeth. Carrie lifted an eyelid and peered closely. "There's no petechiae," she murmured, dimly aware of an outburst of surprise from the onlookers above. They were seeing the "lady undertaker" as she was known, examining—*touching*—the man's body!

"He wasn't under strain before he died," she said quietly to Morgan. She was used to the sensationalism her actions brought on. She used a thumb and forefinger on the man's chin to turn the head gently away from her, but rigor prevented the movement. The attempt caused a small gush of bloodied water to issue from the back of his head.

"Was he found on his back?" she asked. Morgan conferred with the men who stood to the side. He turned to Carrie and nodded. She stood and motioned him closer. Stiffly, he leaned his ear toward her and she caught the warm scent of him. She lowered her voice even more.

"If this man fell from the bridge, he would most likely have suffered a head wound to the front of his skull as he fell forward, not the back, unless he twisted around trying to grasp something to stop his fall. We can examine him for other injuries when we get him to Worley's," she said. "But, there's a good-sized wound here. It may be what killed him. Can we find out if there's any blood, or bits of skin or hair on the bridge? Something to show he hit his head on the way down?"

For all the gains he'd made in mortuary terms since his acquaintance with her began, Morgan still blanched and swallowed heavily when she mentioned things like "bits" in regard to the remains of people. She spoke with no more sentiment than if she was referring to buttered toast. He suppressed an ill shudder and addressed Bale.

"Can you go up and take a look around the girders, Tom? See if you can find something that might indicate he hit his head up there?" Bale looked up at the skeleton of iron beams and struts, nodding.

"Can you look at the place where he was found, Mr. Morgan?" Carrie asked. "He might have hit his head on the rocks. That might explain the caved-in skull." Carrie wiggled her fingers as if exploring the back of the man's head. This time, Morgan turned away so he wouldn't see anymore.

Bale jogged up the stairs and onto the bridge. Some of the crowd swayed in his direction. He walked out past the abutment and onto the girders that stuck out over the creek. The iron beams ended abruptly, having not yet reached the mid-stream pier. Bale lay down on a girder and examined the end of the structure. He shifted his position, paused, and peered again. He leaned out, holding the I-beam with his hand, and curled over to look underneath. There was nothing below him but thin air and the creek bed. He repeated the process with the second parallel beam. He looked down at Morgan and shook his head.

The body was covered again when Bale came back. He turned at the sound of a horse and wagon pulling up.

"Worley's here," Bale said. Carrie glanced up to see the skinny, impeccably dressed undertaker peering over the top of the stairs. His impassive eyes met hers. His displeasure that she was down there with the body before him was communicated to her with the lift of an eyebrow.

Worley and three men descended with a litter and stood quietly a few yards away. Carrie conferred with him about blanketing the body. There was no need to have the grisly remains of the man in charge of the bridge project displayed for all. The scandal of his untimely and mysterious death was going to be hard enough to navigate. Worley gave her a baleful glance; the reproachful look said, of course, he had already thought of that. He didn't need her reminder to be discreet.

As the undertakers bundled the body as best they could around the stiffened, upraised arms, Bale and Morgan stepped out onto the set of planks someone had used to cross the slurry and retrieve Martin Evan's body. They looked into the scummy water pooling on the surface of the mud. Bale handed Morgan a shovel. He probed repeatedly where Evans had lain in the shadow of his emerging bridge. There were no rocks there at all.

15

Chapter Three

Amos Butler seized his son's shirt in one hand and shook him savagely. The boy, still dazed from pulling a dead man from the water, started crying, further enraging his father.

The senior Butler woke up mean this morning, called for his boy, and when he got no response, had hurled an empty bottle across the cabin. He struggled upright, pissed off his stoop, and shambled into town to find a drink and his boy, in that order. Instead, he found the town in an uproar, the steam shovel silenced, and Ransom, the center of attention.

"You cryin' now?" he sneered, sending foul breath into the boy's averted face.

Ransom sniveled and tried to wriggle out of his father's grip. The night watchman had confiscated his pliers and the bolt. Even without the weight of the contraband, his thin pants nearly slipped off his skinny hips under his father's thrashing. He grabbed at his backside, trying not to have his ass exposed in public.

"That's enough, Butler," Morgan said, as he and Carrie walked past. He didn't raise his voice, but it carried over the murmur of the crowd. "I need the boy to come with me. Not you. I'll get him home later."

Butler glared at the sheriff and dropped his son in disgust. With his mouth turned down in a nasty bow, he stalked off, hitching up his own pants. Ransom came to Morgan with his head down, his fist clenched around the bunched-up corner of his threadbare trousers. They ended raggedly halfway down his shins. His skin pebbled with the cold along his bare feet and legs. He rubbed the raw part of his bony chest where his father's calloused hand had abraded his skin. Carrie beckoned the boy to her side, but when she attempted to slide her arm around his shoulders, he jerked away.

Morgan kept a small office in several towns. He rode to each one on a regular schedule and spent a day or so there, hearing complaints, getting reports from his deputies, managing affairs. In Hope Bridge, Clevinger's Grocery leased a tiny spare room beyond the shelves and counters and the pot-bellied stove. Morgan brought the boy through the store without looking at any of the patrons who suspended their trading to watch. Carrie paused to ask the woman behind the counter if she could have something for the boy to eat and drink, and confirming the addition of the items to her own household tab, she followed Morgan and his scrawny witness into his office, carrying a store bottle of milk and some molasses cookies. She closed the door with her foot.

The child sat in a spindle back chair, hunched and shivering. His tender face was streaked with old dirt and new tears; his hair so stiff and crusted, she couldn't tell what color it was. Carrie set the food on Morgan's desk and pulled a blanket from the cot in the corner. When she offered it to Ransom, the boy shied away. Morgan said "put it on," and

Ransom wrapped himself up immediately. Morgan gestured to the food. Ransom grasped the heavy bottle, drinking half of it down before wiping his mouth and gasping. Then he gobbled the cookies.

Morgan leaned on his desk, with his hands held loosely together. "Ransom, you're not in trouble. You were at the bridge early this morning, and you found Mr. Evans. I want you to tell me what happened."

"I didn't take nothin'," Ransom murmured.

"Yeah, you did, but I don't care about that," Morgan said. "Tell me how you found Mr. Evans."

The boy swallowed hard, and his voice thinned. "I saw his watch. In the water. I put a plank down so I wouldn't get sucked into the quicksand."

Morgan nodded, as if to show the boy his decision had been admirable and wise. Ransom's teeth started chattering. "I pulled him up," he whispered. "Next thing I know, the watchman hauled me outta there."

"Did you take anything from Mr. Evans? Go through his pockets?"

The child's mouth fell open, and he shuddered in horror. "No!"

"Did you see anyone else there before you found him?"

Ransom shook his shaggy head. "No, sir."

"Did you hear anything?"

"Nothin.'"

"Think about it, Ransom," Morgan said slowly. "Take a minute and think about it."

The boy stared at Morgan. The big man stared back. He made a show of taking a deep, slow breath. The movement seemed to relax the boy as well. Carrie wondered if Ransom was seeing Evans' waterlogged face rising out of the water, or if he was mesmerized by the calm authority of Del Morgan. She watched his thin shoulders slump. Morgan's voice led him through his memory.

"Think about when you first went down the hill…climbing down the stones. You must have been really quiet… so you didn't wake the guard."

The boy nodded. "I tipped a stone. It knocked, but not so bad. I heard a rooster. I had to hurry up."

"What did you pick up?"

Owl-eyed, Ransom hesitated. Then he dropped his eyes and mumbled. "I found a pair of pliers. And a bolt."

Morgan didn't speak. The night watchman had shown both tools to Morgan earlier. Nervous in the tall man's silence, Ransom said. "They was in the mud. Likely to be lost underfoot anyway." His shrug was only the tightening of one shoulder. "Nobody would miss 'em."

Morgan waited a moment more, then slipped off the desk. He sat behind it and looked around the room. "Where do you live?"

"By the Banks."

Carrie knew the place. An impoverished lot, on the outskirts of town, where the soil was mucky and reeked like sewage. The ground sloped away from the road, and a scatter of dying trees and heavy undergrowth made the perfect place for dumping the town's refuse.

"How long have you been there?"

Ransom shrugged. "Fer-ever."

"Can you read, son? Tell time?"

"Some," the boy said solemnly. "I don't like school too much."

Morgan nodded. "When was the last time you were down at the bridge, Ransom?"

"Yesterday. I go about every day, unless…" A thin shoulder lifted in another shrug.

Morgan waited. Carrie knew that the big man's silence elicited nervous speech from those treated to it. She had succumbed to the tactic herself.

"Unless pa ain't had a bottle," the boy yammered. "Then he don't sleep too good. I got to give him my raft money, but sometimes if I find a quarter or something, I'll leave it for him to find, so he gits good and soused. Then he sleeps. Then I can go." Ransom's face took on a smidge of craftiness. A rare and faint smile crossed Morgan's face.

Good thinking, Carrie thought to herself, *for one so young.*

"But that ain't happened lately," Ransom added. "He's been flush lately."

"Everybody has, with the bridge going up," Morgan said. "And how about your mother? I take it, she's not with you and your pa?"

"No, sir. She ain't." The boy's chin lifted. Carrie saw the flicker of hurt cross his face. She was familiar with the loneliness of growing up without a mother. Hers had died when she was no more than three. She'd used that expression herself. Ransom was trying to show that it didn't hurt.

"Where is your mother?" Carrie asked.

Ransom shrugged. Carrie considered the boy's indifference. If the mother had died, Ransom would have said so. Children never forget when a parent dies. But one who goes away? Betrays the family? Abandons the children? That sin is explained with a sullen gesture to ward off the immense pain. She'd ask her uncle when he returned from Albany. If the Butlers were a local family, Sav Machin would be able to tell her the lineage, the whereabouts, and the origins of each and every one of them throughout the county, possibly throughout time itself. The tall, bony scholar had an immeasurable memory, and was as immersed in genealogies, civic associations, and social affairs as any man alive.

"All right then, Ransom," Morgan said. "You can go. Best avoid your pa today."

"I will, sir," Ransom said and stood. He draped the blanket over the back of the chair, and Carrie saw again how raggedly he was dressed. But there was no help for that. Charity in the form of new clothes or shoes, even a bite to eat, was not well-received by people like Ransom. The cookies were the only goodwill he'd accept.

When Ransom slipped away, Carrie left the door open and put herself in plain sight of the onlookers who peeked down the short hallway, eavesdropping as best they could.

She was relatively new to Hope Bridge, having arrived this spring. A widow who lived with her somewhat eccentric, bachelor uncle. A city woman with a career, a woman who worked on the dead. She was known to have some special association with the sheriff.

If they only knew, she thought and held her jacket in front of her waist, waiting for Morgan to sum up his interview and give her instructions.

"He may remember something else later," Morgan said, joining her at the door. "I need to head back to the bridge and talk with the watchman. Was he sleeping the whole fucking night, or just when Ransom was there? Can you get to Worley's? I don't want to keep him waiting. I'll be there soon."

Chapter Four

That afternoon, Martin Evans' body continued to stiffen as they worked on him. Washing the mud from his face and hair allowed them access to the terrible wound on the back of his head. Their aprons became smeared with mud, blood, and wash water. All the while, they were aware of a commotion overhead, the low buzz of a gathering crowd.

Carrie took the lead, and Worley became her assistant when it was time to photograph the fatal wound. Thomas Bale had brought her camera and tripod, and the box of dry plates she kept at the house. She had been taking and developing *memento mori* photographs for many years back in Nanuet, her former hometown. Her artistic compositions had garnered accolades in the paper, as well as extra income for *Lisbon & Shay, Undertakers*. She and her late husband, Phee, had set up a formal studio off their funeral parlor, where families could have a picture taken of their dead. If they wanted to be in the shot, there was plenty of room for that, too.

In this instance, she was taking pictures to document a fatal wound that may have been caused by another person.

Worley shaved around the gash on the back of Evans' head, while Carrie held aside a portion of hair, in order to conceal the resulting bald spot when they put him back together for his wake. She switched places with Worley, directing him to keep the hair out of the shot. She adjusted the light and shortened the tripod's legs. She murmured more directions, and Worley tipped the corpse's head up to the camera lens. When she was satisfied with the position of the head, and Worley's hands didn't alter the shape of the wound, she pulled the lens cap off and exposed the glass.

Presently, Thomas Bale knocked on the cellar door and slipped quietly down the stairs. "Evans' aide de camp wants to be let in," he said. He met Worley's eye with a shade of defiance. Worley's face hardened a little at Bale's presence.

"We are at a point where he may be admitted. Do you agree, Mrs. Lisbon?" Worley said.

"Certainly," Carrie answered. "We've got him cleaned up, and we've photographed as much as we can. I'll set the camera aside. What's the man's name?"

"Warren Maxwell," Bale said. "He's on the front porch, along with your friend Mr. Bemis, Miss Carrie, and a whole bunch of town elders. I saw three supervisors coming in from Duncan and Charles Town. They're not too happy I'm barring the door."

"I believe Mr. Maxwell can be admitted, if you please, Tom," Worley said without turning to address Bale. "I'd like to make arrangements for the disposition of the body, if he is the appropriate authority for such a transaction."

Carrie watched Bale's retreat, saddened again to see how cold he and Worley had become to each other. They were both smart, accomplished, and effective. Both were longtime residents of Hope Bridge. At one time, Bale's skills as a master carpenter met Worley's standards for exquisite caskets. Bale had saved Worley's life while they served in Cuba in 1898. Worley had reciprocated this past spring. But Thomas Bale had committed an act that disrupted Worley's household, and threatened an irreplaceable reputation in the nascent profession of mortuary science. The two men had been at odds ever since.

Warren Maxwell came down the cellar stairs hastily at first. A young man, in his late twenties or so, with a clean-shaven face and a high celluloid collar, he slowed as he took in his surroundings and his employer's stiffened remains. Although still covered in sheeting, Evans' knees bent up and out, making it look like he'd been frozen in a squat, in addition to the ghoulish reach of his arms. Carrie watched Maxwell's cheeks drain of color and his eyelids flutter. She hurried to his side.

"I'm Mrs. Lisbon, Mr. Maxwell," she said loudly, catching his elbow. The cloth of his suit was fine, but she felt his muscles slacken beneath. "I'm going to stop you from falling." She eased Maxwell backward as his knees buckled. A few words sloughed out of his mouth.

"…gonna do…" He sagged onto the stairs, his eyes fixed on the body. Carrie motioned with her chin to Worley, who wordlessly pinched a cotton boll between the ends of a long forceps, and dipped it into an apothecary jar of ammonium carbonate. He wet the boll and waved it under Maxwell's nose.

"*Buh!*" Maxwell jerked away from the acrid assault. His eyes flew open. Carrie held onto his sleeve.

"You're fine, Mr. Maxwell," she said. "Take a moment and collect yourself. Mr. Evans is cleaned and prepared. Only you will see him like this. The rigidity will pass, and we'll pose him more naturally before he's seen again."

Maxwell shook his head and gestured for another whiff of the smelling salts. He stood, clenched his shaking hands briefly, and took a deep breath. He stayed at the bottom of the stairs.

"Mr. Evans was your employer?" Worley asked.

Maxwell nodded, but Carrie thought he was not yet fully aware of the conversation. His eyes darted over the length of the body. He glanced around and honed in on the pile of clothing that Carrie hadn't yet hung to dry.

"If you are the person in a position to do so," Worley said, "I'll need to make arrangements with you for the dispensation of his remains. He does not need to stay here. I understand he originally came from Saugerties? He may be returned there, to be interred, if that is the family's wish. But I will certainly prepare him and install him in a casket for transport."

"I'm in a position to do so," Maxwell said curtly. "Are those his things?" He waved a hand at the clothing.

That's an odd first question, Carrie thought as she studied him. *He asks about the clothes?* He had fainted at the sight of Evans. Perhaps he was trying to evade the impact of his boss's remains by asking a question about something much less gruesome.

Worley seemed to sense the incongruity as well. Carrie detected the slightest hesitation of his response. "They are. We've documented a complete list of articles of clothing and personal effects. We will retain them for the time being. The sheriff will need to review them during the course of his inquiries."

Maxwell's expression sharpened. "His watch is valuable. He always carried some money. Has that been accounted for?"

"Certainly," Worley said. His eyelids dropped ever so slightly, the only indication of his offense at the young man's insult. He gestured to the items Carrie had laid out on the counter.

"Was he carrying anything else?" Maxwell demanded.

"The body was transported by me personally from the site to this room. Mrs. Lisbon and I are the only people who have touched his things. The watch and the pocket change he carried were the only personal items we removed."

Maxwell frowned and stepped around the embalming table where Evans lay. He beelined to the pile of clothing, picked up each article, rummaged through the pockets, and dropped them in a heap on top of the sodden socks and shoes. He stepped to the counter, grabbed up the watch and coins, and jammed them into his own trouser pockets. He turned to Worley.

"Very well," he said. "What kind of arrangements do we need to make, Mr....?"

"Worley," the undertaker said tightly. "We'll go up to my office to discuss the details." He still wore his soiled and bloodied apron. For a moment, Carrie thought he might leave it on just to reciprocate Maxwell's dismissive and demanding comments. But Worley was too consummate in his business persona to appear upstairs draped in the uglier attire of his work. He did, however, make a slow show of removing the cloth in front of Maxwell.

Maxwell didn't spare Carrie a glance as he went up the stairs. Worley followed him with deliberate dignity, throwing a look of peevish tolerance over his shoulder at Carrie.

Alone, she lay the clothes and socks out to dry near the woodstove, annoyed that Maxwell had the bad manners to mess up her neat work. She added a few pieces of wood to the fire, closed down the vent, and placed the beautiful shoes on the floor near the stove. They were clotted with mud inside and out. Evan's woolen socks stank of his feet and creek mud. She wrinkled her nose, pulled them into shape, and lay them next to the shoes.

Still annoyed at Maxwell's behavior, she realized he didn't ask how Evans had died. In her experience, the first question most people had when faced with the body of a loved one, or at least a close associate, was 'what happened?' The next thing on their mind was 'did he suffer?' Then, they all exhibited a sense of confusion and disbelief and then, as she knew well, the plunge into grief.

Yet, Maxwell didn't behave like that. When he recovered from his faint, he insulted them both—forgetting Worley's name, ignoring her, and practically stealing the dead man's effects before they had a chance to indicate he could rightly take them. He hadn't even acknowledged Carrie's kindness by assisting him when he fainted. *I should have let him hit his head.*

Maxwell had focused instead on Evan's things. That kind of behavior elicited only one question: *What was he looking for?*

Chapter Five

Among the crowd of curious residents who assembled that afternoon on the sidewalk in front of Worley's funeral home was a short, red-haired man, covered in freckles and topped with a round bowler hat. He hailed Carrie the moment she appeared on the walkway leading from the back of the house late that afternoon.

She had known Bill Bemis for years. She and Phee had befriended the tenacious reporter when Bemis was investigating a series of murders back in Nanuet, and she had laid out one of the victims. Last spring, they'd both emigrated to this rural upstate county. She, to escape the despair of mourning and depression, and he, to follow stories for his newspaper, *The Nanuet Daily.* He stayed after finding even more exciting opportunities for his scribbling. The county paper had hired him immediately, banking on having a 'big city' reporter enhancing their paper, and the editor had gambled well. Bemis's ready skills and numerous articles had boosted subscriptions, so much so, *The Duncan Herald* had grown from a weekly to a daily.

While she trusted Bemis, his presence meant he was after a story, and she knew he would be as tough as a bulldog once he got his teeth into something as juicy as the sudden death of the head man building the first iron bridge in Duncan County. She held up her hands as Bemis and the rest of the crowd hurried toward her.

"I am in no position of authority," she said firmly, heading off the barrage of questions. "Yes, it's Mr. Evans, and no, I cannot say any more. I'm not the sheriff nor next of kin. Please, excuse me. I'm going home."

"Of course, Mrs. Lisbon. Let her through, folks," Bemis said loudly, shooing people away and taking her elbow. "Let me escort you."

Carrie knew Bemis's gesture of chivalry wouldn't come without a price. She had been right there with the body while it lay under the bridge. She had examined, prepared, and photographed Evans for hours down in Worley's mortuary. Bill Bemis knew this. She was the ultimate source for a reporter.

"Bill," Carrie warned as soon as they cleared the crowd, "you know I'm not going to say a word."

"You wound me, Carrie!" Bemis said happily. "I haven't asked a single question."

"Uh, huh," she responded drily. "But you've already got your headlines, don't you? You already know the who, what, when, and where. No one knows the why. And I'm not going to jeopardize Mr. Morgan's investigation by disclosing anything right now."

"Ah! So, there's hope," Bemis teased, undeterred. "No matter. I'm headed for the telegraph office to file my exclusive. I've got enough for tomorrow's edition."

"Do you think this will influence Mr. Morgan's election?" With her hand tucked into his elbow, Carrie could feel the reporter's excitement thrumming through his body.

"How could it not?" Bemis said. "Del's only got half the county on his side, what with Clowe's mudslinging about his skills. But he'll be the man of the hour if he figures out how Evans met his demise. And he wins big, if he does so *quickly*. People don't want to be worried about killers in their midst."

To win with only half the county's support, knowing that the other half voted for an out-of-towner, would not sit well with Morgan. Especially since his rival was playing an underhanded campaign, buying ads in the paper with bold headlines disparaging Morgan, and worse. Knowing him as she did—not as a lover, but as a capable, working man—Carrie knew Morgan would be conflicted about that. He'd prefer to win, of course, but it was unreasonable for people to expect a conclusion to a death investigation in only five days. Unless someone stepped forward and declared their guilt, Morgan would be methodical in his pursuit. He wouldn't be worried about winning his first election. He'd be more concerned about getting to the bottom of Evan's death. And was it murder? Even if he brought in a killer on Election Day, would that eleventh -hour triumph sway votes?

But Bemis implied a huge story line. And knowing *him* as she did, she refused the bait.

"Killers?" Carrie asked. "What makes you say that?"

Bemis scoffed, and his freckles stretched with a wolfish grin. "How does a guy who builds bridges fall from one? What's he doing up there in the middle of the night? There was no lantern found up there, or near the body. Why would he go up there in the dark? There was no moon last night, either. It was pitch black! And the night watchman didn't see anyone all night long."

"You spoke to the watchman?"

"Indeed, I did. The guard shack stands on the old abutment. From there, it looks out over the whole site. The guard swears he saw no one going out onto the bridge all night."

"He was also asleep when the boy was stealing things down below. He was probably asleep all night."

"Oh, really?"

"Damnit!" Carrie huffed a laugh, acknowledging Bemis's skill at getting her to disclose information.

She could rely on her friend's discretion when it came to a newspaper article of this nature, but she felt a sharp, sobering fear. If her affair with Morgan was discovered…if it ever came to light—and they'd taken such a risk last night! —Bemis could never ignore *that*.

Bemis grinned devilishly. "I never cite my sources, Carrie, especially if they're in delicate positions." He resumed the topic of Morgan's bid for election. "Those ads Clowe's been running are taking their toll. There're folks that get taken in by that bunkum. Still, I'm not going to underestimate Del's chances. There are plenty of folks who don't like an outlander coming in and disparaging their man. Del keeps law and order well enough. And he's a county boy. Why rock the boat with a new captain?"

"I'm sure he's not worried about it," Carrie said. "But it's grating to read all that drivel about him. And me."

Not only was Morgan's election rival maligning his abilities as sheriff, the bastard was printing anything that could be misconstrued as scandalous, including Morgan's reliance on a lady undertaker for expertise when there were plenty of educated and far more experienced men who could—and should—be called upon for such dreadful tasks. Carrie had been horrified to read Clowe's insinuation in the paper just last week. *'One should wonder what other appeal Mrs. Carrie Lisbon has for our fair sheriff.'*

They made the turn up North Street. The cement sidewalks gave way to squared flagstones. Cider presses still churned, and the spicy scent of crushed apples drifted through Carrie's neighborhood. The sun had passed its zenith, and the scant warmth of the late autumn day was fading quickly. A hard frost a week earlier snapped the leaves from the maples and elms. Their dark limbs scored jagged lines against a vivid blue sky. A hog squealed far off in the distance. Butchering was underway.

Bemis pulled his arm from beneath her elbow when they reached her door. Being a newspaper man, he knew the power of the pen. He tried to downplay the impact Clowe's print campaign was having on her.

"Don't let the ads perturb you. Everyone who knows you knows anything scandalous is ludicrous."

Carrie smiled warmly. Her expression of appreciation for his kind words hid the stab of guilt in her chest. "Thank you, Bill. Come on in and get something to eat. Then you won't be hungry staying up to write your articles all night."

"Capital idea! I had to skip breakfast."

Carrie watched her friend's eyes take on a crafty gleam. If Sav was here, instead of collecting the charter for the new Hope Bridge Library, Bemis would ply him for every fact he knew about the deceased, the current sheriff, and his malingering rival. Her uncle would be more than happy to provide a wealth of minutia about all the players. As it was, Carrie would be his only, albeit reticent, source.

"And I'm not talking about Evans or anything else." She cautioned with a wagging finger.

The house was fragrant with the scents of fresh bread, savory beef, onions, and apples. Carrie and Bemis groaned with pleasure, hung their coats, and hurried down the hall to the kitchen, where a deep, cast-iron skillet sat on the cook stove.

"Mmm! Mrs. Woodruff just delivered our supper," Carrie said, pulling off the lid. "You'll stay and eat with me?"

"I'm not walking away from whatever *that* is," Bemis said decisively. He crowded in with Carrie and breathed deeply over the escaping aromas.

Carrie took a pitcher full of water from the warming basin on the side of the stove, excused herself, and went to her two-room suite. She occupied a pleasant sitting room with a writing desk, and a few framed photographs on the wall. The adjoining bedroom had a charming back door that opened onto a tiny porch. It was a practical combination for the master and mistress of the house when it was built thirty-odd years ago. Although the suite's proximity to the kitchen might have encouraged another woman to make that her daily focus, Carrie found the back door more enticing. The domestic arts, especially cooking, were not the strongest of her suits. She was delighted that Sav insisted they continue to retain Mrs. Woodruff as the supplier of their dinner meals after Carrie had moved in. A clever man, he understood her limitations as well.

Freshened with a quick sponge bath and clean clothes, she rejoined Bemis in the kitchen. He'd helped himself to the bread and butter, and had the courtesy to slather a piece for her. She chewed the fresh slice as she set out plates. Bemis tucked his kerchief into the neck of his collar and picked up a spoon. His freckles stretched, and his spotted ears flared as he grinned in anticipation. Carrie ladled stew into bowls and sat opposite him.

Bemis started the conversation. "Honestly, I was surprised when Clowe announced he was running. A man from downstate? Why would he do that? He must make more money in the southern counties than here. And his campaign has been to simply run down Del for having no experience, not his own record."

Carrie blew on her spoonful and shrugged. "It's what they all do, isn't it? I can't believe people still fall for it."

"We all know Del's done all right. He kept the peace through the flood, even after his own brother's murder. He's fair with folks. I like how he keeps offices in all the big towns. Duncan County knows he's competent. And for pity's sake, he's not a braggart. I don't think it does Clowe any good to act the mudslinger. No one appreciates that."

Carrie agreed with Bemis's assessment of Morgan. She *and* Sav were on the receiving end of Morgan's bravery and reticence. Both their lives had been threatened earlier this year. Morgan knew what had happened, and kept the circumstances to himself.

"But it works, unfortunately," Carrie replied, trying not to wince at the thought of her own reputation being a target of Clowe's. She steered the discussion away. "I've always had the impression Clowe's expertise pertained to city crime. You know. Street gangs and thugs. Brothels. Organized thievery all over the docks on the Hudson. We have a very different set of lawbreakers here in the country."

"Oh, indeed," Bemis rolled his eyes. "Only a few murders this year. Plus, kidnapping. A little extortion. Not to mention the looting that went on after the flood this spring. I'm sure Clowe hasn't encountered any of that downstate."

Carrie pointed a spoon and said, "I'm saying the scofflaws in a densely populated city are unending, whereas this spate of misfortunes in our county is an aberration. This doesn't happen all the time. We're a law-abiding people for the most part, and a lawman from downstate, accustomed to a different set of crimes, may find our community somewhat boring, once things settle down. So, again, why does Clowe want the job?"

Bemis blew a derisive sound. "In a week, he may be in charge of a murder investigation. Nothing boring about that!"

"Who said anything about a murder, Bill?" Carrie chided, catching the reporter in one of his verbal sleights of hand.

Bemis squinted at her, sidelong and sly. "I'd like to know how a man who builds bridges—which are naturally high and placed over thin air—falls from one in the dark of night. I'd like to know why he went up there in the first place, seeing as how he is supposedly afraid of heights."

"Afraid of—*what?*"

"Afraid of heights, yes. Bizarre, is it not? To be a bridge builder and not be able to stomach the chasm over which your project is being erected? I heard that he needs to hang on tight to even a porch rail, or else he experiences vertigo and breaks into a sweat."

"Where did you hear that?"

Bemis's face wrinkled into a perfect smug. He leaned back. "Sources."

Carrie laughed. "Then how did he inspect the work? Did your sources disclose that?"

"No need to. We all saw how it was done. Evans used a telescope! Even you've seen him with it, no doubt."

"I have," Carrie conceded thoughtfully. The whole bridgeworks operation was a novelty. She had on many occasions stopped to watch the men at work, to catch a glimpse of the engineer with his complicated brass equipment. Everyone paused in their errands to watch the massive crane gouging great clots of earth from the land, and the hundreds of men toiling above and below, hammering, hauling, pounding, and yelling. "I just thought it was the usual thing an engineer would have used. Isn't there another tool? Mounted on a tripod?"

"A transit, yes. He used that, too."

"But he was afraid of heights?"

"Rumor has it."

"If that's true, the last place he'd go is up there, especially at night. He would have been even more disoriented."

Bemis lifted a red eyebrow.

"Which means, he was disoriented and fell, Bill. Not that he was murdered."

"Think about it, Carrie. Did you ever see Evans on that bridge? Ever see him anywhere near the edge?"

"Of course…well, no, but then, I haven't been observing all day, every day."

"I interview all day, every day. I haven't talked to *anyone* who's seen Evans take a step onto that platform, onto those girders, or look over the edge. I *have* seen him gripping the handrail of the steps and, as white as a ghost, go down those stairs to the creek bed. He turns his face to the bank the whole time. I've seen his condition with my own eyes."

Carrie had no response. Bill was an observant fellow as well as tenacious.

She'd have to concede to his firsthand knowledge. The fact that Evans had a fatal wound on the back of his head—an injury that suggested he had fallen backward—may or may not be consistent with hitting his head on the way down. But Bale had found no human bits on the girders overhead.

"Why would he be murdered, Bill?"

"Why, indeed?" Bemis leaned forward. "Everyone thinks bridge builders are gods, like Roebling or Buck—civil engineers *extraordinaire.* But as the project engineer, Evans had to be ruthless. He had to keep on schedule. He had to run the operation with an iron fist, from the laborers to the accounting. I'm sure he aggravated more than a few suppliers. It's a theory. You know how my mind works."

Bemis paused and took a big bite of bread and butter. With his eyes closed, he groaned as he chewed. "When does Betsy deliver again?"

"She delivers our suppers four times a week. She has another bread van, now, and two people under her. She sells lunches down by the bridge. It's been lucrative for her with so many extra men in town."

"She's a goddess," Bemis mumbled.

Carrie agreed, thinking of the heavy, big-knuckled woman who never stopped moving and always spoke as if everyone were hard of hearing.

"I'll be sure to interview her," Bemis went on. "I'll bet *she's* never seen Evans on the bridge. Did you know it's going to have a macadam deck? To accommodate automobiles."

"That's wonderful," Carrie said. "I'd love to ride in one of those. I saw them all the time in Nanuet. And Lord knows Duncan County can do with smoother roads."

After another mouthful of stew Bemis said, "Anyway, what *did* bring Clowe to Duncan? That's my angle. I could understand if he were here for Betsy's cooking, but you're right. Most men, especially a city man like Clowe, wouldn't want the job. Why settle on this Podunk backwater?"

"I protest your insult, sir!" Carrie laughed. "If Sav were here, he'd be appalled." She straightened her back and did her best impression of her gangly, scholarly uncle's recitation of Duncan County's progressive nature. "Our county seat has an opera house and a library with an extensive genealogy collection. We produce milk and cheese for Albany by the ton, and that train, good sir, has increased its scheduled runs by a quarter more than last year to accommodate that commerce. Our schools have a ninety-four percent graduation rate, and soon, we'll have an iron bridge!" She crossed her arms in mock offense. "Podunk, indeed!"

"I rescind my criticism, Mr. Machin," Bemis played along. They resumed their own characters and ate in affable silence. Bemis circled back. "But the question has become a burning one for me. I have some friends in Albany, and back in Nanuet who can do some digging. Meanwhile, tell me, what did you make of Mr. Evans' mortal remains?"

"Give it a rest and enjoy your dinner, Bill."

The reporter waved a hand in concession, then spied a plate next to the blue-checked food boxes that trademarked Mrs. Woodruff's deliveries. "Can we get started on that pie?"

Chapter Six

As soon as the covered bridge crossed the Duncan Creek in 1816, the Chester Inn was built on its western bank. A squat wooden building, low and dark, it lasted for forty years until a fire gutted the second floor. The son of the original owner razed the place and built the current, much grander hotel. His investment paid off. Travelers heading west, jostled on hard wagon seats over alternating sections of plank road, dirt road, and disastrous mud holes, found the gleaming, white, three-story Chester a godsend of comfort. Now, it boasted amenities like a billiards room with a private bar, a dining room, its own telegraph service, and real Turkey carpets in the corner suites. It was the place for public announcements and grandstanding from the pillared façade.

The porch and steps buzzed that evening with an overflowing crowd. The same boy who brought Morgan's summons to Carrie that morning struggled to get the lamps lit among the laborers who muscled into the lobby. They'd lost several hours work this morning, and the head man was dead. They were anxious to hear if their livelihoods were in jeopardy.

Townsfolk crammed into the lobby, ready to hear the news firsthand, so it could be passed on and on and on. The remaining management of Evans Bridgeworks occupied the dining room on the right. They wanted assurances from the county sheriff that construction would continue immediately. Town elders from both Hope Bridge and neighboring hamlets stood in small knots, murmuring to each other, speculating under knitted brows. The air inside was stifling despite the cold November chill seeping in from the wide-open doors.

Bemis left Carrie at the door to the dining-turned-conference room. He identified the mayor of Hope Bridge, grousing with the other town board members, hurried into their midst, and proceeded to fire off questions.

Carrie spotted Mrs. Ina Barnstable, the town's society columnist, who wrote about shopping trips, travels and visits, and the illness and fortunes of her neighbors for the *Duncan Herald.* Her weekly report on Hope Bridge's social happenings had grown over the years from a single column to nearly half a page. Not only was there news of who called on whom, and who shopped in Duncan, or the more distant city of Albany, (a trip that always garnered interest), Ina had gotten creative about reporting the details of new home construction, the scene at Town Board meetings, and the attendance at social clubs. Readers knew what refreshments were served, the type of lighting in a host's home, and who recently installed one of those new-fangled telephones. Ina herself had purchased one recently for her Elm Street home, taking advantage of the new lines that had been erected to accommodate the Bridgework's needs. She was usually the one listening in on the open party lines.

The plump correspondent stood alert, just outside the door to the dining room, waving a fan near her face. Carrie caught her eye, and Ina waved her fingers with a delighted smile before realizing she shouldn't be so excited about this ghastly turn of events. Carrie squeezed in and stood between the doorjamb and a potted fern. Cigar smoke hung just below the ceiling. No one sat.

Del Morgan stood resolute next to his deputies, Thomas Bale and Leo Lamont. Standing tall and broad, he raised a hand, and the hubbub quieted down.

"Martin Evans was an industrious man," Morgan began in a voice no louder than a conversational tone. "I'll express my condolences to his family and his staff."

He paused, his gaze steady. "We'll be looking into how and why he died. This is Tom Bale and Leo Lamont, my deputies. You all know them. They'll be asking questions and following up with developments. I'll expect cooperation from everyone."

Lamont was a steady man of middle years, with a thick, precisely trimmed, spade-shaped beard, and a reluctance to speak that surpassed even Morgan's. Bale, the only Black man in the room, stood with his arms crossed and looked everyone in the eye.

Bill Bemis called out. "How did Evans die?"

Morgan focused on the reporter. "We're not giving those details yet."

"Was he robbed?" Bemis shot back.

"We don't believe he was robbed."

"Does that mean it was an accident?"

Morgan shook his head, keeping up with Bemis. "We can't be sure right now."

Someone shouted rudely, "It means you have no idea!"

Morgan's face gave nothing away. "No, it means we are still collecting evidence."

"Sounds like you don't know what you're doing!" the shouter responded. Agreeing murmurs rippled throughout the crowd. At this, Morgan smiled thinly. Carrie felt a chill. That was not a smile one would want from this man.

"You're from Mr. Clowe's camp, aren't you?" Morgan said. "Please give him my regards. I'm surprised he's not here, providing assistance, since he's so much more experienced than I."

Laughter and applause scattered through the spectators.

"What do the undertakers say?" This abrupt call came from someone close to Carrie.

There was an expectant pause, and Carrie held her breath as more and more people turned in her direction. Art Worley, known for his disdainful dignity, hadn't come to this informational gathering. *I shouldn't have come, either!* In the spotlight, pinned against the wall, unprepared, and rigid with sudden discomfort, she froze.

Then Bemis called out. "I asked them that this afternoon! They have as much to say as their customers!"

The crowd laughed at the old undertaker joke, and to Carrie's intense relief, they turned back to the lawmen at the front of the room.

"Are you still running, Morgan?" A different heckler called from another part of the room.

"This is not a political stump," Morgan reprimanded. "This is a public announcement regarding the untimely death of Martin Evans, the bridge builder." His glare was subtle, but did the trick. He turned back to his message. "We've concluded our examination of the ground around the bridge. The crew can resume work tomorrow."

Cheers erupted in the crowded room, and as word spread throughout the hotel, more shouts of approval went up. The oily-smelling men in work clothes who got as far as the hotel lobby, joined in. *Clever of him to announce that bit of information,* Carrie thought. The laborers had come from all over Duncan to get work this summer, and they would cast their votes this Tuesday. By reassuring them of their job security, the incumbent sheriff would likely get their vote.

Morgan concluded his announcements by asking again for cooperation from witnesses, and then refused to answer any other questions. He and Lamont pushed their way toward the door. The clamor in the room increased. People shook Morgan's hand, shouted follow-up questions, and began the inevitable speculation. Morgan paused at the door to shake Carrie's hand. She was still rigid. The public greeting made her one of Morgan's inner circle.

"I'll be at Worley's in the morning to get his report," Morgan said. "Thank you for coming, Mrs. Lisbon."

Bill Bemis sheared off from his current targets and hurried after the exiting lawmen. As he passed, Carrie leaned toward him.

"Thank you," she whispered quickly.

"Not at all," he said happily, his red freckles stretching with his smile. "No one cuts in on my exclusive!" He winked and spun away to catch up with the main story.

Beyond Bill Bemis, she caught sight of Howard Clowe in the billiards room across the lobby. With one foot on the brass rail, and his elbows on the bar, he was watching her. He raised his glass, tipped it slightly in her direction, and then was lost to view as the crowd in the hotel swirled and shifted.

* * *

"I'll see you home, Miss Carrie," Bale said, joining her at the door.

"Thank you, Thomas, but don't you have a duty to Mr. Morgan?"

"I have a duty to see to law and order in town," Bale said. "And that means getting out of here and walking you home."

When she moved in with her uncle eight months after her husband's death, she considered herself independent of a male chaperone. While Sav had fretted nervously about her integration, Bale looked after her with much more subtlety. He didn't hover; he was companionable. She'd come to terms with it.

Yet, with the influx of workers to their small town, a formerly pleasant stroll along Main Street had become a gauntlet of workmen and administrators, delivery men, more wagon traffic at all hours, and its resulting horse dung. An auto car on one festive occasion had caused a commotion that disrupted the entire village. There was a general confusion of noise and impediments day and night, that sharpened tempers. While the swell of men created a windfall for those with spare rooms and outbuildings to rent, an unescorted woman in this once -sleepy village felt more than a little hesitant to walk home in the dark by herself.

"Let's escort Mrs. Barnstable as well, Thomas," Carrie said, and hailed the plump correspondent. Ina waved in return and hustled toward them, asserting her matronly status as a means of getting through the crowd. Her powdery scent arrived a moment before she did.

Bale stepped in front of them and cleared the way without a word. A Black man didn't take the arm of a white woman. In fact, there were those who thought a Black man shouldn't be in the Chester with white men, shouldn't be wearing a deputy's badge, shouldn't look a man in the eye. But Bale had a confidence that allowed him to walk wherever the hell he pleased, a badge that backed up that confidence, and a reputation as a man not to be trifled with. His friendship with the county sheriff, his wits, and his lightning-fast boxer's fists made detractors stand aside.

"Well, that's certainly an encouraging turn of events," Ina warbled, taking up Carrie's arm. Her fan was replaced by a small notebook and pencil. "I'm partial to our Sheriff Morgan. I'm so glad he'll get to the bottom of this. He's done remarkably well for us this past year or so."

Carrie held her tongue. As with Bill Bemis, in the social columnist's presence, the less said, the better.

The chilly night air was refreshing after the stuffy hotel. They turned off Main and took Elm, heading south toward Ina's house. The receding shine of gas lamps provided just enough light to see. Ina chatted up Carrie and ignored Bale. She waved a plump hand for emphasis as she spoke, her reticule swinging wildly from its velvet braid on her wrist. Bale strolled quietly behind them.

"I'm so disappointed to not be able to attend poor Mr. Evans' wake," Ina said. "I'm sure your artistry will preserve his handsome good looks. Tell me. Will you be using LaBlache face powder? Even on a man?"

Ina was known, *soto voce,* as a funeral crank. Her society column featured effusive details about funerals, burial rites, descriptions of the deceased, the bereaved family's attire, and the carriages used in the cortege. She often portrayed more pomp and circumstance than was actually the case.

"I use the same treatment for men as for ladies, Mrs. Barnstable," Carrie said, comfortable with disclosing what had already been publicized.

"He's from somewhere downstate, isn't he?" Ina asked. "Will you perform an embalming?"

"Yes. It's necessary if the body is to be transported any distance."

She'd throw this bone to Ina as well. The columnist would chase it instead of asking more questions about her work. So many people, especially Ina Barnstable, were fascinated with embalming. The practice of preserving and sanitizing bodies for wakes and funerals was construed as a method to make the body appear lifelike for eternity. Ina thought of it as a craze. Carrie was annoyed with the morbid curiosity. It discredited the medical operation which undertakers had been perfecting for close to forty years. If she were honest, she took a small measure of satisfaction knowing Ina would be denied the glory of Evan's downstate funeral.

Ina bussed Carrie's cheek at her front porch steps. She gave Bale a brief glance of acknowledgement and hustled into her house. *No doubt she'll be writing into the small hours of the morning.*

Bale walked beside Carrie in comfortable silence and they started for home. They didn't need to discuss Ina's slighting of Bale. Her dismissal was commonplace. Bale didn't lower himself to challenge it.

The din from the Chester Inn still hovered over town. Sharper, louder voices could be heard on various streets as the crowd dispersed, and without the fatigue of a hard day's work, those voices seemed to take on an air of revelry.

"Hallowe'en was last night," Bale muttered. "Any decent man would go home; go to bed. I'll be moving people along all night."

Farther off, a man shouted, and Bale stopped short. Carrie did the same, listening intently. Their little, ten-road town was not tranquil these days, and the Hallowe'en revelry that went on last night *did* seem to be resurrecting itself tonight. She wondered why that particular shout drew Bale's attention. When the drunken voice came again, Bale turned around and walked toward the outskirts of town.

"We won't be a minute, Miss Carrie. That sounds like ol' man Butler is taking his problems out on his boy."

Chapter Seven

They left the streets and fading house lamps behind. With not even a sliver of moonlight, the darkness was immense. Flagstone slabs and boardwalks ended. Unable to see a clear path, they were forced to walk in the road. They stumbled over ruts on the half-frozen track, and Carrie pushed Bale aside to avoid a pile of road apples she saw at the last moment. Bale led them toward the Banks.

When they arrived, Carrie could hear the murmur of the Duncan Creek. A rotting stench was pervasive. Amos Butler had stacked wagon parts, metal pieces, bricks, rocks, and household trash like an abatis of garbage all around his house. The shack was a patchwork of slab wood siding and decaying shingles, plugged here and there with rags and mud to keep out the drafts. It teetered on a frost-heaved, stone foundation.

Butler had kept up his disjointed shouting the whole time. He stopped, as if he had paused to take a drink, remembered what he was yelling about, and started up again. Carrie didn't hear a sound from the little boy. She stayed on the road above the scrap yard while Bale maneuvered silently down the steep drop and around the piles of junk.

"Ya stupid, goddamn sonofabitch," Butler slurred. Carrie heard thumping sounds. "Ya can't keep yer mouth shut? Yer useless and stupid, and now ya blabbed all over the place!"

Bale stepped onto the creaking boards Butler had nailed together to act as steps. He pounded on the rickety door. From where she stood, Carrie saw the flimsy thing shaking. Dim lamplight shone through the cracks.

"Mr. Butler!" Bale said loudly. "I need to see your boy."

Amos Butler yanked open the door, shouting, "Wha' da ya want?" He stood there, swaying. His shirt hung, half-buttoned. A single suspender held up his sagging trousers. His rheumy eyes glistened like his slack lips.

Then he recognized Bale and his badge. Still blustering with righteous anger, Butler hesitated, momentarily torn between compliance with the law, and the recognition that a Black man, to whom he held a wisp of superiority, stood on his porch. Butler paused, then made a bad decision.

"Get offa ma porch, boy."

Thomas Bale's hand shot out and yanked Butler forward. The other hand spun him around, and Amos Butler was flat on the floor within a second. He woofed out a surprised grunt, struggled briefly to free an arm bent painfully behind his back, then cried out as Bale's knee pressed on his spine.

"I think you meant to say *deputy*, Mr. Butler," Bale said, crouching over the man's ear. "I've got most of my weight on the other knee, but I can exert a bit more pressure on your drunk ass if I need to. Understand?"

"Yes!" Butler shouted. "Get offa me!"

"In a minute," Bale growled into Butler's ear. "I said I want your boy. He's a witness, and you'll stand aside. Are we in agreement on that?"

"Yes!"

"*That's* the right move," Bale said conversationally. "Ransom. Run up to the road. Now. Go on. Your papa ain't hurt."

Ransom appeared from inside the cabin. He stepped around his father and Bale, his eyes like saucers. As he passed, Butler roared at him again. "Keep yer mouth shut—" Butler finished the sentence with a yowl, signaling a tweak in pressure from Bale.

Ransom bolted up the path, nimble in the dark maze of junk. He stopped short in front of Carrie. She put a finger to her lips and flicked her other hand toward herself. Bale had not mentioned she was there. Butler would not know she was involved. She pulled Ransom to her side, and they watched Bale rise and step away from his father.

Bale snarled to the gasping man. "Stay down 'til I'm clear." He walked away. Butler lay there, moaning.

When he joined them at the top of the bank, Bale took Ransom's hand,

and they walked quickly back down the dark road. When they were clear of the dump, Bale crouched in front of Ransom and put his hands on the boy's shoulders.

"I didn't hurt your papa," he said quietly. "And you're not in any trouble. Understand?"

Ransom nodded, owl-eyed and stiff.

"You've seen me around town? You know I'm the sheriff's deputy? Good. My job is to help Sheriff Morgan figure out all sorts of things, and to keep the peace. Do you know what I mean?"

The boy shook his head. It was no more than a shudder. Behind them, Butler had resumed his ranting. Something glass shattered against the wall inside the shack. Carrie could hear Ransom's ragged breath. She put a hand on his shoulder, too. He was trembling.

"Keeping the peace means saving you from a beating I'm sure your papa wasn't finished with," Bale said. "So, I'm going to have you spend the night at Miss Carrie's house. We're going to get you a bath and something to eat. And in the morning, I need you to tell me all the things that happened when you found Mr. Evans."

Ransom swallowed hard. His head bobbed up and down, but it was hard to tell if the movement wasn't just a giant shudder. Bale steadied him over the ruts, his arm providing warmth to the ill-clad boy. When they finally reached Carrie's house, Ransom was stiff and stumbling. Bale carried him into the loft above the carriage barn.

Carrie warmed the leftovers in the stew pot, and collected the rest of the bread and a crock of butter. She bundled the food and a small bottle of brandy into a basket, as well as one of Sav's old shirts for the boy to sleep in. They still had some fresh cider, cold in a jug on the back porch, and she hooked a finger into the handle on her way by.

She seldom had occasion to enter Bale's home. Since her uncle owned no horse or carriage, Bale had rebuilt his shop in the empty lower level. The barn retained a slight smell of horses, but now the aroma of pine shavings and tung oil dominated. Thomas Bale carried the same scents. The three of them often met in the barn on late afternoons, with the door wide open and a summer breeze drifting by. She shucked peas, or trimmed greens, or attempted not to stick herself too badly while mending a shirt. Sav told stories, and Bale worked the wood. Here they may be family, but propriety still dictated that his apartment on the upper floor was off- limits.

This time, it was different. She climbed the stairs along one wall of the shop, rapped on the door, and entered Bale's home. His kitchen table sat between two curtained windows, which were themselves framed with bookshelves. A good-sized woodstove pumped out heat with two overstuffed chairs nearby. A single hutch was heavy with crockery, tins, and utensils. Across the room, Bale had built a wall for his bed and bureau. Not spartan, but efficient, warm and comfortable.

Ransom was wadded up, knees to chin, in a big, square laundry bucket near the woodstove. He clutched the sides and held his breath as Bale poured water over his head. Ransom took up the soap and scrubbed it through his hair. Carrie laid out the meal as Bale murmured instructions and gave the boy a final rinse, sluicing off the rest of the grime and dump smell. He wrapped Ransom in a towel and pointed to the bedroom. Carrie saw a dark bruise on the side of the child's mouth as he scuttled away.

When he crept back with Sav's shirt draped to his knees, Bale motioned for him to take a seat at the table. Ransom sat timidly, looking like a mouse caught in sudden lamplight in the middle of the floor. Carrie rolled up the shirt sleeves for him, and ladled stew. Ransom gobbled it down the instant she stepped away. She settled into one of the two upholstered chairs. Bale poured pink-hued cider, then held the glass to the lamplight, examining its color. He glanced at Carrie and winked. He refilled Ransom's bowl and buttered another slice of bread.

"You can come and go as you please, Ransom," Bale told him. "You don't have to stay here. But I want you to. At least for tonight. I know your papa isn't kind, but he's your family. And that's your home. You go back there anytime you want. Do you remember how to get *here?*"

Ransom nodded, still chewing.

"Good," Bale said. "If ever he comes at you like he did tonight, all drunk and bent on beating you, come here. That door is never locked."

Ransom was all eyes. He stopped chewing and stared at Bale. Carrie thought he was going to bolt, bare feet and shirttails flying out the door and into the night.

Bale grinned at him. "Don't think I won't want you to do a few chores for me. There's always some wood to carry, or my shop to sweep. In fact, I have some tools that need sharpening. There's always a call for a good sharpening man. I can show you how to use that whetstone tomorrow. Why was your papa so mad at you?"

Ransom looked down at his plate.

"No one here is mad at you, Ransom," Bale soothed.

"My raft is gone," the boy murmured. Tears welled in his eyes. "I went to git it this mornin', after…" he swallowed and looked away from a ghastly memory. "…after I found that man."

"I've seen you ferrying workers across the creek," Bale said. "What happened to your raft?"

"I always tie it up good. Ain't no way it slipped off." Ransom defended himself with a frown. "I think someone stole it. Pa was mad, cause now—"

He cut himself off and glowered. His hands closed, and he pulled them off the table like he wanted less of his body exposed.

"Cause now your papa doesn't have a means to get his drinking money," Bale said quietly. "You think someone took it? Why?"

Carrie saw defeat mixed with the boy's exhaustion. The kid was destitute. *And his father was beating him for it?*

"That Joe Allen over in East Hope?" Ransom said angrily. "He wants all the fares for himself. He's got his own raft, *and* he's got a shoe shine right outside the Chester! All's I want is a few fares, for chrissake!" His hand shot up to cover his mouth. He stared at Carrie, horrified that he'd cussed in the presence of a lady. Carrie smiled and waved a lazy hand, assuring him he'd come to no harm because of it. Ransom dropped his hand and nearly shouted with pent -up emotion.

"Now, I got no raft. They'll put up *two* guards at the bridge. I won't be able to pick no more. I got nothin'!"

"Tell you what," Bale said. "Finish your cider. You get some sleep. We'll get you situated in the morning. I can look for your raft on my rounds. If that Allen kid took it, I'll be sure he gives it back."

They made up a bed for him on the floor between the woodstove and the door. Ransom burrowed under the blankets wordlessly and settled down. They talked about mundane things while Carrie cleaned up the dishes and washed Ransom's clothes in the laundry tub. She and Bale twisted the shirt and pants from opposite ends, carefully, so as not to further tear the pathetic garments. After a while, they heard Ransom heave a sigh and go still.

"Have we just kidnapped a child?" she whispered.

"Yep, so his papa didn't beat him to death. There are a few laws that allow for the removal of a child in that circumstance."

"How do you know that?" Carrie asked.

Bale shrugged. "I read. Del gave me a badge. I figured I'd better know what I was doing with it. Did you just drug a child with brandy-laced cider?"

It was Carrie's turn to shrug. "I thought it was for the best."

Bale retrieved the cider jug and poured out the remainder into two glasses. He handed one to Carrie. They sat in his upholstered chairs and blew out a breath at the same time. Carrie regarded the pink cider in her glass. She was pleased with the results it had on Ransom. She toasted Bale and their kidnapping efforts.

"Do you think he knows more than he's already told us?" Carrie asked, looking down at Ransom's bruised face.

"Funny, I think he does. If he comes up with a single detail more," Bale said, "my actions tonight will be justified. I don't care if he says he heard a bird fly over. I really just wanted to get him out of that shack. And Butler's too stupid to complain about kidnapping."

"Do you want him in your shop, Thomas? I think he steals whatever he can."

"I mark my tools," Bale smiled. "I know where he lives. He's a smart boy. It's his old man I wonder about. Selling shit from a dump doesn't pay much."

Carrie didn't notice the epithet. Growing up without a mother, steeped in a male-dominated trade, tutored by her father and his associates, had all exposed her to profanity. She used it herself. She was comfortable with men's candor.

"If Ransom was stealing things from the site, his father wouldn't be stupid enough to try to sell them back, would he?" Carrie asked.

"No. There's a tinker—you've seen him. Old man with an old mule? He comes around once or twice a month. Buys and sells. Butler would sell to him first. But maybe he'd send *his son* to the site with a tool he 'found.' Ransom might collect a reward. More likely, he'd collect a beating. But you can't buy much liquor with a penny. I wonder if the old man sold the kid's raft."

"Why? I've seen those two boys ferrying workers from East Hope. They're at it every day. It must have brought in a steady income. If Mr. Butler sold it, he really is stupid."

Chapter Eight

Carrie hadn't slept well, and the fumes from Worley's embalming solution irritated her. She should have eaten before coming over. Coffee burbled in her empty stomach, adding indigestion to a headache she didn't need. She and Worley routinely opened the windows when they were embalming, so the smell of the chemicals could dissipate, but today, even the cold air dumping into the room didn't help her mood. Grumpy and wordless, she helped prepare Martin Evans' body, which had become flaccid during the night.

She concentrated on catching the dripping rubber tube in a basin as Worley removed the syringe from the brachial artery. A towel under the pan protected her arms. They both wore aprons and a cloth tied around their faces. Worley squeezed the bulb to increase pressure in the glass carboy and made incisions in Evans' belly. Carrie provided him with a clean trocar affixed to the rinsed tubing, and Worley began injecting the body cavity. Carrie would sew up the incisions with tiny sutures when he was done.

She had all but forced herself into Worley's mortuary business when she laid out the body of a child at her own home on the day of her arrival here. When the news of a lady undertaker performing funerals was gossiped all over in a matter of hours, Worley asked for her assistance with the preparation of a deceased young woman, since his own wife, who would normally have done the job, was too ill with consumption. Carrie would lay out Rosabel Worley, too, not long after. Since then, she and Worley had come to a loose agreement of sorts. While he acknowledged her competence and legitimacy as a qualified undertaker and embalmer, his long, laconic, and uncomfortably dubious looks at her, tended to undermine her confidence as his freelance associate. She stepped away from the body and looked around the preparation room. The pile of clothing and shoes was gone.

"Where are Mr. Evans' things?"

"Clara took them away last night," Worley said without a break in his concentration. "They were smelly. I had to put them upstairs and outside the door. She refuses to come into the mortuary."

Worley's third housekeeper in as many months was the worst one yet. The previous two had been unable to remain in the house overnight, citing "spooks" and "a presence," and quitting within two weeks. Clara had hung on, a dullard to the presence of spirits. She cooked terribly, swept occasionally, polished listlessly, and grumbled ceaselessly about the wash. Her dodging anything having to do with Worley's prep room, and her generally slovenly mannerisms grated on Carrie's nerves. She couldn't imagine how a fastidious man like Arthur Worley put up with it.

You regret sacking Marta now, don't you? Carrie thought unkindly. Worley's beautiful Irish housekeeper had been cheerful, competent, and hardworking. She even helped with the dead, crossing herself the way the Irish did, expressing reverence and kindness. She became his dying wife's personal nurse, and she befriended Carrie as easily as she drew breath. But 'Funeral Director' was a new category of legitimate tradesmen, and those who took the job seriously made sure they adhered to high standards of propriety. Worley had to distance himself once Marta's lover had been disclosed.

"His shoes are quite expensive," Carrie said. "I hope she didn't throw them out. I thought I could clean them and use them for the dressing."

Worley's expression didn't change. He was unconcerned with the fate of shoes.

When the embalming was complete, Carrie forced herself to be thorough with washing the tools and tidying the room. Her headache was making her ears ring. She wanted something to eat, before they got back to the business of dressing Mr. Evans. She scrubbed her hands and arms and went upstairs to face whatever Clara had prepared for lunch, and to ask her about Evans' clothing.

"All that stuff went into the rag bag," Clara said loudly, setting out lunch dishes. She plopped down in a chair opposite Carrie and served herself. Her dull blonde hair was constantly escaping its pins, and as she passed a plate of ham and biscuits, she chewed sloppily. "Somebody'll make use of it. But that muddy smell won't never come out."

"Where are the shoes?" Carrie asked, and took a bite of overcooked ham. She thought about suggesting to Worley that he consider using Mrs. Woodruff's chuck wagon like the rest of Hope Bridge. *Surely, he can't enjoy eating this?* She couldn't picture him queueing up for a plate of succulent chipped beef on boiled potatoes, with a side of apple pie, alongside roughly dressed and filthy roustabouts at the end of the day. But given the unappetizing meal she was currently presented with, she thought he might.

"They were sopping wet, and all curled up," Clara said. "And such thin things! Why would a man wear such dainty shoes? I like a man who wears a sturdy boot and ain't afraid to get his hands dirty." Clara popped half a biscuit in her mouth, chewed twice and spoke around the mash. "Them dandies at the Chester may be handsome, but they ain't worth half a day's work! Know what I mean?" she said, and crumbs flew.

"But, what did you do with them?" Carrie persisted, trying not to look down at the debris that encircled the other woman's plate.

"You want 'em?" Clara's jaw worked sideways.

Jesus, I just want to know where the hell they are! Carrie nearly barked in frustration. Her headache blared. Marta would never have yammered on about a decedent's clothing. She'd have had them washed, dried, and laid out already.

"Yes," Carrie said evenly and put her fork down. She lost the appetite that had plagued her all morning. "You're right, a man's shoes ought to be sturdy. But, if we put some clodhoppers on Mr. Evans' feet, his people will want to know what we did with the expensive ones."

Her patience thin, she gave in to a small measure of wickedness. Clara was a lousy housekeeper, and an awful cook. She tolerated the formal parlor where bodies were presented, but only when the room was empty. She absolutely avoided the cellar and their work down there. Carrie went for the sloppy woman's weakness.

"I need them for dressing the corpse downstairs."

Clara stopped chewing. "I'll get 'em," she said, and rose from the table. She returned with the odorous pair hanging from her fingers, dropped them by Carrie's feet, and returned to her meal without washing her hands. Wordlessly, Carrie picked them up and left the kitchen, too disgusted to even say thank you. She held the shoes away from her body. They stunk of foot odor and creek mud. She suppressed a retch, thinking of Clara picking up her sandwich. *Good lord, I miss you, Marta!*

She would at least clean off the mud, dry them by the wood stove, and dab them with mint oil, before attempting to fit them onto the dead man's feet. She had reached out for the cellar door latch, looking forward to the calm and quiet confines of the mortuary, when she noticed the leather footbed of one shoe had come unglued. It curled upward like a dog's tongue. Gingerly, she pulled on it. Beneath the smooth leather that shielded the foot from the metal shank inside was a crudely hollowed -out hole.

* * *

Worley took his meals in his office. Carrie found him ensconced behind his desk, with the day's paper opened wide and his dishes, mostly untouched, returned neatly to their tray. Clearly, he, too, was unimpressed with Clara's culinary skills. Carrie held up the ruined shoes.

"Did Mr. Maxwell make any claim to Mr. Evans' clothing?" Carrie asked.

Worley shook his head, without looking up. "He signed for the watch and coin, which he took with him."

"So, the clothing and shoes are abandoned?"

Worley flicked a gaze upward, suddenly intent. The question was unnecessary. Every mortician knew that clothing and items not taken by the family were deemed abandoned. Such items were donated to the poor.

"Yes." His slow reply was laced with caution.

Carrie showed him the hiding place carved into the footbed of Evan's dainty shoe. "I thought Mr. Evans should wear his good shoes, but I saw the leather on the inside had swelled with water and curled up. You remember Mr. Maxwell searched through Mr. Evans' clothing. Perhaps he was looking for this."

Worley observed the shoe's mutilation, thought for a moment, then nodded. "Yes, I'm quite sure the series of events concludes this to be abandoned property. I've written in my notes of Mr. Maxwell's decline to take the clothing with him before he signed for the other articles."

Carrie turned her head sideways and spoke evenly. "But we recognize that this is an item of a personal nature, and it's customary to return such an item to its rightful owner."

Again, Worley paused thoughtfully.

"Customary does not mean 'legally obligated,'" he said, folding his hands on the desk. "Mr. Maxwell indicated in no uncertain terms that he was the person responsible for dispensing of the body, and for the collection of personal items, which he did." Worley's eyebrows rose fractionally. "Everything else was summarily abandoned. Are we to proceed with the time-consuming efforts of attempting to return to the family lost buttons and shoelaces if they are to become separated from formally abandoned property?" He paused, sniffed haughtily through his thin nose, and concluded. "I think not."

"I'll telephone the Chester and ask about another pair of shoes for Mr. Evans," Carrie said. "And I'd like to put clean and dry clothing on him. We can't use the clothes he was found in."

"Agreed. I expect he'll have an adequate outfit. And, please make a call to Mr. Morgan about this discovery, as well," Worley said, and resumed reading the paper.

Carrie made her call to the Chester, using Worley's telephone, a handsome, polished oak model, with a brass cradle and black lacquered receiver, which hung on the wall between the parlor and the kitchen. Hope Bridge had added two more operators to deal with the constant connections between Evans Bridgeworks and its suppliers, between village merchants and the train depots in Duncan and Mariet, and among the growing number of households who proudly bought the expensive device to increase their gossip. The extra operators worked out of Ruth Nickerson's house on Elm Street. Ruth was generally irascible, but she had worked a deal with town elders, negotiating for the rental use of her sitting room, which had become an operator's exchange. Everyone had an angle for income while the new bridge was under construction. Folks rented rooms; Betsy Woodruff sold meals. Even Stockwell's, the confectioner in Duncan, had a standing order to deliver a lemon cake to Martin Evans every Tuesday. The innkeeper from Sussex Mill brought it to him on her way through, no doubt collecting a nice tip each time.

Three operators meant two more sets of ears listening in on conversations. The phone lines were plagued with eavesdroppers. Her request reached the Chester's operator and went straight to the major domo. He would arrange for Evans' clothing to be delivered within the hour. She hung up and was connected again to Morgan, relaying Worley's request to see him. She didn't disclose the reason why. Morgan, also savvy to the listening gossips, didn't ask.

She sneaked back into the kitchen, after determining Clara's whereabouts by her heavy tread upstairs. She took a handful of store-bought cookies from a tin in the pantry, noticing the dwindling supply of jams, canned fruits, and vegetables on shelves Marta had kept stocked and orderly. She found a milk jug in the cold cellar, but there were too many cobwebs to her liking—another state of affairs Marta would never have tolerated—and decided against it. She poured herself a glass of water, retreated to the empty funeral parlor at the front of the house, and munched her cookies, staring out the window. She closed her eyes against the cold pane of glass, and was relieved to feel her headache dissipating.

Her recovery was interrupted by a loud protest from Clara at the front door, a terse, masculine response, and quick footsteps stomping into the house. Carrie reached the door to the parlor and was about to step into the hallway when she was nearly bowled over by Warren Maxwell barging past. He shot her a nasty look, and marched into Worley's office, brandishing a scuffed valise like a shield.

Maxwell looked like he hadn't slept. His clothing was rumpled, his tie loose, his eyes red-rimmed and wild. He stomped up to Worley's desk, and shouted, "Where are his shoes?"

Carrie thought he trembled, but she was too taken aback by the man's invasion of Worley's sanctum to consider anything past her own surprise. Behind Mr. Maxwell, Del Morgan passed through the front door, still held open by a dumbfounded Clara. He came silently down the hallway, passing Carrie with barely a glance, intent on Maxwell and Worley.

"What has you so upset, Mr. Maxwell?" he asked, startling the distraught man.

Maxwell tucked his chin to slow his breathing, but his eyes darted about. He spotted the swollen shoes Carrie had left and snatched them up. "Mr. Evans had a key. I have searched everywhere for it. When the woman undertaker called just now and told me I needed to bring over another pair of shoes, I thought that's where he may have hidden it. I was correct." He held up the delaminating shoe, scraped his finger inside the footbed, and shoved it toward them. "I was right," he spat. "Where is it?"

Morgan remained unmoved by the man's display. "Why did he hide a key, Mr. Maxwell?"

"It's personal," Maxwell said curtly. He was breathing hard. "He has a right to keep his personal affairs under lock and key."

"You were his aide. His secretary. Is that correct?" Morgan said. "What things of a personal nature did he keep locked up?"

"Private matters, sir, unrelated to his death," Maxwell blustered. "What progress have *you* made in regards to the investigation? Not that I expect any kind of competence from a backwater lawman!"

"What investigation?" Morgan replied calmly.

"What investigation? You announced it yourself last night! His death, you idiot!" Maxwell threw out his hands in exasperation. "Why aren't you trying to find out who killed him?"

"Who said someone killed him?" Morgan said neutrally. He asked the exact question Carrie asked Bill Bemis. "And why would private matters be unrelated to his death?"

Maxwell babbled. "Well, I assume—it seemed like—there's no reason to assume he wasn't killed by someone, perhaps by accident!"

Morgan remained silent. Ransom had babbled when Morgan employed this tactic. Now Maxwell did. She glanced at Worley, who sat with his hands clasped, watching over the scene, motionless as a spider waiting patiently for a fly to exhaust itself.

Maxwell rallied, no mean feat when subjected to Morgan's silence. "Well? What have you been *doing?*"

"Since last night?" Morgan asked with sarcasm. "We've interviewed witnesses, searched the site where Mr. Evans was found, and secured his room at the Chester."

"Which I easily detoured," Maxwell snorted, "when I told that *bellboy* you put on guard to stand aside for the engineer's secretary. He was useless to barring my entrance."

Morgan didn't seem perturbed that Maxwell had breached his security. He responded without inflection. "What did you do in the room?"

Maxwell leaned forward. His chin rose in challenge. "I searched for the key and collected clothing for Mr. Evans' burial. I've also taken the liberty of settling the bill with the hotel and made arrangements with the undertakers to have Mr. Evans sent back to Saugerties for his funeral."

"You won't be going?" Morgan asked.

"I have pressing business. I need to find a new job."

"Why won't you stay on in this one?"

Maxwell snorted again. "I am Mr. Evans' secretary. Bloomfield will bring his own secretary!"

"You took that valise out of the room?" Morgan asked.

Maxwell didn't falter. "To carry his clothing."

Morgan picked up the bag, set it on a chair, and opened it. Inside was a tangle of men's clothing, thrown in and rumpled. The lining of the valise had been ripped away from the frame, and shreds of fabric cropped up around the clasps. "You tore it apart to search it?"

"Yes."

"Looking for the key."

"Yes."

Carrie was impressed by Maxwell's admission. He was cocky. Defiant. Did he have a right to circumvent a sheriff's order? *Why isn't Del angry about Maxwell's raid on a room he cordoned off and set a guard?*

Morgan asked. "Why would your boss hide this key, even from you? Don't secretaries manage their employer's personal affairs, too?"

Maxwell's frown deepened. "As I said, it's a proprietary matter—"

"Proprietary to whom, Mr. Maxwell?" Morgan scrutinized him.

"Never mind that!" Maxwell stabbed a finger at the discarded footwear. "I see that Mr. Evans hid the key in his shoe!" He turned on Worley. "Did you find it? Have you kept it from me?"

"No." Worley spoke with classic impassivity. Maxwell expelled a frustrated, desperate breath.

Morgan spoke again. "Do you know where Mr. Wheeler is, Mr. Maxwell? Tall, ugly man, striped trousers. Wears a bowler with a gray ribbon. I've been told he may have headed north. Maybe he took the train out of Mariet?"

"Wheeler?" Maxwell's voice thinned. Carrie watched him clench his shaking hands. "I haven't seen him for days. Did he even come to Hope Bridge?"

Carrie knew the man they spoke of. He was another stranger among the hordes of strangers that came to town for work. But he wasn't a roustabout; his clothing wasn't oil -stained, or dusty. He didn't enter the job site in the morning or leave it in the evening among the bone-tired men who formed a dinner line at Betsy Woodruff's bread van. She'd seen him lingering in front of the Chester; she was glad she didn't have to go by him. He was the reason women became timorous walking home alone. She'd seen him approach Martin Evans a few days ago, while the engineer was peering through his scope, or transit, or whatever apparatus was perched on the tripod that day.

She remembered the encounter because Evans had jerked away from his eyepiece when Wheeler spoke to him. Wheeler had given Evans an evil grin, and Evans stared at him like a lamb before a wolf.

"Came and went," Morgan said. "I keep an eye on all the ne'er-do-wells that have come into Duncan County since Evans Bridgeworks came to town. Mr. Wheeler seemed to be a man folks shied away from. People said he was a rough character. He was a body guard, wasn't he?"

"Mr. Evans needed no body guard!"

"I didn't say Evans' body guard," Morgan said. "He was described as being close to *you*, Mr. Maxwell. Not Mr. Evans. Was he *your* body guard?"

"I don't have any connection to him. My job was to run Mr. Evans' business transactions. That business is concluded." Maxwell glared at them. Carrie saw his heart thudding under his shirt. The veins in his neck stood out in effort. Without a word, he spun on a heel and made for the door. Morgan's words stopped him cold.

"Leaving town is out of the question," he said. "You were Evans' right-hand man. I'll need answers from you as questions come up."

Maxwell turned stiffly, giving Morgan a malevolent glare. Carrie, standing close, could see the tremble of anger in his chin. Then he stormed down the hall, left the front door open, and hurried out of sight. Carrie looked at Morgan.

They had developed a telepathy since they'd first met. Not the veiled look of desire between lovers. That had come later. This was the exchange of looks that told one the other had information.

Morgan took the cue, turned to Worley, and said, "Worley, did you find a key among Mr. Evans' possessions?"

"I did not," he said. "Mr. Maxwell collected and signed for Mr. Evans' personal effects yesterday. Everything else is legally considered abandoned. Mr. Maxwell *abandoned* the deceased's clothing and shoes. It's quite common. We clean the items and donate them to the church for rummage sales, or for the poor. It's a tenet of the profession."

Morgan caught on. Worley wasn't likely to have cleaned and disposed of the clothing himself. Strictly speaking, he hadn't lied to Maxwell. "So, who found the shoe?"

"Mrs. Lisbon. This morning, when she retrieved them to dress Mr. Evans."

Morgan glanced at Carrie but said nothing. He picked up the shoe with the hole in it and grunted. "Hm. It's the first place I'd have looked."

Chapter Nine

They left Worley's together, entered the steady stream of walking traffic on Main Street, and headed toward his office at Clevinger's. They kept themselves on the opposite edges of the sidewalk so as to maintain a prudent distance apart.

"I didn't think Mr. Maxwell could have gotten into Mr. Evans' room at the Chester, if you posted a guard," Carrie said. In spite of the public distance, she caught Morgan's scent of mild sweat, warm tobacco, and the cold freshness that comes from being outdoors on a brisk November day.

"The guard actually *was* a bellboy," Morgan said. "His job was to protest, but back down. I wanted to see who'd search Evans' room. I'd already been there. I didn't find anything that might indicate why he was killed."

"Do you think it was an accident?"

"Martin Evans appears to have fallen from the bridge and struck his head on something. The impact was fatal, according to Doc Wells. And Evans was carousing at the Chester beforehand. Doc Wells said he may have been quite drunk when he went up on the bridge."

They approached the dusty center of town, a hive of activity. The coming and going of stone masons, iron workers, teamsters, carpenters, and welders created a constant racket. Carrie walked beside Morgan, anticipating more. The 'more' was Morgan's speculation. The questions he had, that she was beginning to form as well.

"What I'd like to know is, did he go up there alone?" Morgan finally said. "Drunk and alone? Why? There was no moon. It was dark as hell. If he went with someone and fell, why didn't that person go get help?"

"Unless they were horsing around, and Evans fell by accident. It was Hallowe'en. The whole town was carousing," Carrie said. "Then the other person might run away. Scared."

"Or the other person pushed him and ran away. Scared."

"Bill said Evans was afraid of heights."

"I heard that, too. He used a telescope to check on the work. Just about fainted when he had to go down the stairs." Morgan's mouth pinched in at the corner, the barest slant of a smile on his lips. "Betsy Woodruff has nothing on Bill Bemis."

"You know, we didn't find any blood or hair on the bridge to show that he hit his head there. And you poked at the mud where he lay. There were no stones there either."

"Which makes me think—"

"—he didn't fall from there," they murmured together.

The glance they gave each other held the satisfaction of thinking alike, the thrilling realization of an advancement in the investigation, and not a small measure of desire. She dropped her gaze; didn't alter her stride. But she did suck in a breath to quell the bolt of excitement.

Morgan cleared his throat and said, "I've told Mrs. Morgan that I'll be staying here for the next few days. I can't campaign anywhere else with this going on."

Morgan and his wife, Katrina, lived in Duncan, the biggest village in Duncan County, home to the previously-touted opera house and genealogy-rich library. Mention of the kind and industrious woman they were both deceiving sobered them like an ice bath. The other sobering aspect of their conversation was Morgan's election bid. If he couldn't travel around the county garnering votes only a few days before the election, and with his rival besmirching his character at every turn, how was he to win?

"I need to call her to see if Eddie's home," Morgan went on. "He was supposed to meet me here yesterday, but he didn't show."

Carrie heard a touch of concern in his voice. "Didn't you say he's been putting up posters around the county?" Carrie knew the Morgans' sixteen-year-old son was responsible for putting up 'Vote for Morgan' posters on every bridge and barn he could find. With Morgan no longer able to travel the county, glad-handing supporters, Eddie's efforts would be crucial.

"He is, but he was finishing up in Charles Town and maybe Sweetwater, north of the Shun Pike. He should've come in Hallowe'en night. I was expecting him at Clevinger's."

Carrie's arched brow was her response. *But you were at my place Hallowe'en night.* If Morgan's son had arrived at the tiny office at Clevinger's in the early morning hours, Morgan was not there. Would Eddie question his father's whereabouts? What excuse would Morgan give? *We took such a huge risk!*

They were interrupted by a cluster of farmers, and their wives who declared their votes would be for him this coming Tuesday. Morgan took each work-roughened hand with both of his. It was his trademark, a gesture of genuine warmth and sincerity for his supporters, and an acknowledgement of his gratitude and friendship. Carrie stood a few paces away, giving the candidate space and distancing herself from any involvement.

When they resumed their conversation, Morgan shook his head. "He's been alone, riding around with posters. I'm sure he's fine. I'll bet he's been helping out at somebody's farm. He's like that."

"I'm sure that's what happ—" Carrie cut off the reassurance, frowning.

Howard Clowe, beaming in a crafty manner and well-dressed in a pale gray, wool suit, sauntered directly toward them.

"Delphius Morgan!" His booming challenge was cheerful. "And the lovely Mrs. Lisbon." Clowe leaned toward Carrie. "Again, we find you in each other's company!"

Clowe's hail produced the results he wanted. The flowing crowd stopped to listen to the impromptu exchange between the candidates.

Neither party extended a hand. Carrie didn't smile. "As befits colleagues," she said neutrally. "I see you still have some followers." She gestured to the hangers -on behind him.

"I do!" Clowe beamed. He paused and smoothed his hair. "And a great many more than my esteemed rival, according to newspaper reports. Tell me, Morgan. What progress have you made in regards the bridge builder's death?"

"No," Morgan said, as if denying a child a licorice. "You have no more right to the details of my investigation than any other member of the public, Howard."

Clowe smiled broadly. "By Tuesday night, I will! You'll need to turn over all your notes so I can assume the case."

"We'll see," Morgan said quietly. "If you'll excuse us." He stepped around Clowe. Carrie gave the smug man a parting glare and followed.

They pushed through the crowd that murmured disappointment at the lack of debate. Carrie fumed. She read the newspaper ads Clowe had purchased in the *Duncan Herald* over the last month with dismay and a healthy jolt of fear. He submitted regular opinion letters, too, not only demeaning Morgan's record and abilities, but insinuating something to the effect that Morgan, a married man, spent entirely too much time with a widowed undertaker who seemed to have 'beguiling tendencies.'

Carrie had never thought of herself as a woman who beguiled. The word suggested she used her femininity overtly to gain favors from men, an enticing wanton, trying to catch a husband. It was unbecoming. It was suspect. She had seldom questioned her comfort with men. She'd been brought up by her father. She wore the pinafores expected of a little girl, and gained womanhood by asking him the questions normally posed to a mother. He treated her as an equal, and her social perceptions were more aligned with how a man thought. She had always found herself being, well, herself, around men. With women, and with only a few exceptions, she'd always been on her guard.

Clowe's insinuation that she'd somehow entrapped Morgan was insulting. That's not how it happened. Not at first. They'd both nearly lost their lives, and when Morgan brought her back to her house to recover, they'd simply...well, simply comforted each other. The survivor's need to reassert life had simply gone its full course. They'd agreed to forget about it. They would never repeat it.

But the spark couldn't be smothered. The next time *had* been deliberate. They'd sought each other out. Had she been beguiling then? She'd been bruised and battered from an encounter that—*again*—nearly cost her life. Morgan had been there as a lawman; she as a witness to crimes he'd been investigating. An opportunity presented itself, and that spark flared.

Then, on Hallowe'en night, with no moon, and the hullabaloo of revelers, barking dogs, and the shouted complaints of interrupted sleep throughout town, with Sav gone to Albany to pick up his library charter and Bale patrolling elsewhere, Morgan had tapped on her back porch door, and she'd let him in without a lamp, without a word, and with need steaming off her body.

Clowe's suggestions were also dangerous. It was frightening that he had struck upon this line of disparagement in order to run down Morgan in the paper. Ads with thick black letters declaring "INCOMPETENCE!" listed trumped-up failures and Morgan's inexperience, while bulleting Clowe's years as a downstate monarch of law enforcement and achievement.

"BUFFOON!" was the latest headline, with a crudely drawn caricature of Morgan, his hat canted drunkenly and his eyes slightly crossed. Clowe's picture, by comparison, highlighted his waving crown of virtuous white hair, a confident lift of his chin, and an impressive badge on his chest. A letter to the editor included the same accolades and slurs in addition to a remark about Carrie.

> Why is our esteemed Mr. Morgan in such close association with the beguiling widow, Mrs. Lisbon of Hope Bridge? Must the current sheriff depend on the wits of a woman? One should wonder what other appeal the comely widow has for our beleaguered sheriff.

The cold dread that dropped into Carrie's stomach when she read those words was replaced by white -hot anger. *Comely?* In her everyday skirt and blouse? Wearing a simple straw boater and smelling of embalming fluids? Who was this man to ride into Duncan County and cast such aspersions on her and Morgan?

Clowe had arrived late in the summer, just in time to throw his hat in the ring. She had arrived in the spring, a widow in despair. Yes, she was from downstate like him, but she had family here. She intended to try to heal her grief here, melt into oblivion, not stir things up. Clowe had insinuated wrongdoing, made a caricature of Morgan, attempted to intimidate, and continued to behave in an overbearing manner. A man who attempted to pass off his hostility with charm. She may be comfortable in the company of men, but this one made her flesh crawl.

In Clowe's effort to win a small county election, he'd chosen to denigrate his opponent by targeting his associates. She felt her heart seize up in terror again.

He was right on the mark!

Chapter Ten

"If Evans hid the key in his shoe," Morgan resumed his line of thought when they were clear of Clowe, "where is it now?"

"If he had it hidden in his shoe for safekeeping, why would it be gone from there?" Carrie followed up. "What would prompt him to take it out and use it—then lose it?"

"We have to find the key, so we can figure out what it opens," Morgan said.

"So, we're in a race with Mr. Maxwell."

Morgan nodded.

"Getting back to what we said before," Carrie said. "Are you looking for the place where Evans was killed?"

"I'll get Leo to start looking here in town."

They arrived at Clevinger's, one of two general stores on Main Street. A hired boy, dressed in a grocer's apron, stood on the steps beside a barrel smelling of vinegar and dill, waving a pair of tongs and shouting, "Penny a pickle!" Carrie and Morgan paused for housewives coming and going through the front door, carrying sacks and baskets laden with their purchases. The bell clanged constantly.

Inside, the mercantile was crowded. The floor -to -ceiling shelves behind the counter were lined with big glass jars and wooden boxes with colorful paper labels. Sam Clevinger wrote one customer's tally in a ledger, while his wife and several ladies examined a bolt of cloth.

They had to weave through the crammed aisles that Clevinger had put up to accommodate the increase in customers in order to get to Morgan's office. Carrie stood just inside the room, in the doorframe, clearly visible to anyone looking down the short hallway. Morgan took a seat at his desk and picked up the receiver of the phone he'd had installed over the summer. He cranked the handle to alert the operator of his position on the line, gave a name and a number to connect, waited, and, after a moment, hung up.

He clenched a fist and looked down at stacks of papers and books on his desk with a frown. "Katrina's not answering."

Carrie didn't reply. Compartmentalizing Morgan as a business associate separated him from Morgan, the lover. The trick also served to isolate her feelings about his relationship with his wife. They both held Katrina in high regard; she was a wonderful woman. Neither bore her any ill will. Morgan had a happy, prosperous marriage, one they never meant to threaten.

She was the keen observer. She was to help Morgan get to the bottom of Evans' death, not nibble around the edges of his family life. She'd met Katrina over the summer. The Morgan couple got along well together. They loved their only son, and Morgan looked after his wife and marriage as any good man should. Morgan's was the greater sin. Having entered into an affair with Carrie, he had much more to lose than she. Still, she pursed her own lips in worry.

If Morgan was concerned about his son, even though his tells were subtle, there might be something to it.

Morgan stood, walked to the door, and called to a young boy out in the store. He assured the child's mother the boy was only needed to run to the telegraph office. The woman nodded, glanced at Carrie, and resumed her shopping. Morgan handed the boy a slip of paper, hastily scrawled with directions, and gave him a nickel from his vest pocket. The boy weaved through the aisles and disappeared.

"I want Katrina to call, or send a wire if Eddie's home," Morgan muttered as an explanation. "I hate to ask, Mrs. Lisbon, but could you stay for a while, in case she calls? I've got to talk with Lamont. Get him started looking for Evan's death site. I'll have Tom start looking for Eddie."

"Certainly," Carrie said. She stepped aside, and watched him nodding in friendly acknowledgement to the folks in the store. Then he was out the front door and gone.

Alone in the office, she debated where to sit. Assuming a position in Morgan's chair, behind his desk was rather presumptuous. The other chair was a wooden ladder-back, with a rock-hard seat, but she wasn't going to stand in the doorway, in plain sight of onlookers and invite conversation. Not that most people sought her out for chitchat in any case.

She took the hard seat and looked around the room.

Morgan traveled regularly around the county so as to make himself accessible. He kept small rented rooms in three of Duncan's largest towns. His intention was to have an office to work in, and to interview complainants or witnesses like Ransom Butler. His constituents liked the reliable schedule he kept with them.

The accommodations in each office were spare, but comfortable, like Morgan's conversation. A folding cot occupied a corner next to a small table and lamp. A trunk at the foot of the bed kept blankets and a pillow fresh and out of sight. Carrie imagined Katrina, efficient and serene and thoughtful, tucking fresh clothes and a hearty sandwich into a bag before he set out in his travels.

She didn't make her bed this morning, and she'd left yesterday's garments draped over the back of a chair, where a pair of long socks lay wadded on the rug. Housekeeping always seemed to fall into the category of things labeled *a matter for later,* as she hurried off to work at Worley's, or the garden, or the photography studio she'd set up in Sav's formal parlor. There was always so much more to do than tidy.

She huffed away the comparison of herself to Katrina, found a day-old newspaper, and snapped it open, deliberately skipping over the latest Morgan lampoon. At least she could read until the damn phone rang.

Twenty minutes later, the striker clanged between the phone bells. She scrambled for the handset, crumpling the paper under her arm. "Hello?"

"Call for Sheriff Morgan," an operator said.

"Thank you. He's instructed me to take the call."

"I'll connect you."

The line went dead, then Katrina Morgan's smooth and sure voice came over the wire. "Del?"

"No, Katrina. It's Carrie Lisbon. Mr. Morgan wanted me to wait in his office for your call."

"Oh, hello, Carrie!" Katrina said warmly. "So nice to speak with you. I just got a telegram from Del. He shouldn't have gone to the expense. He should have called."

"He did. He got no answer."

"Oh! It must have been just a little while ago? I was outside hanging the wash."

"He asked me to stay to receive your call," Carrie explained. "Can I bring him a message?"

"He wanted to know if Eddie had come home. He was supposed to meet up with Del yesterday in Hope Bridge. He's not there?"

"No. Not that we know of."

Carrie winced. She'd let slip the word 'we.' Would Katrina conclude she and Morgan had been discussing his family affairs? Certainly, that was beyond the purview of the keen observer. Was that simple term enough to raise suspicion? *And, dammit, how many people were listening on the line?* She pulled her racing thoughts to a stop.

Of course, Morgan would share his concerns for Eddie with one of his associates. He asked Carrie to take his wife's return call. *This is perfectly normal.* Carrie nudged her discomfort aside and chose her next words carefully. It wouldn't do for her to use Morgan's given name with his wife. The familiarity might say too much.

"Mr. Morgan thought that maybe Eddie had stayed somewhere else. Maybe to help out on someone's farm."

Katrina's voice faded as wind jostled the line somewhere between the two towns. "— so like him," she said. "But he hasn't come back here, either."

Carrie could imagine the stab of fear that might, at this moment, be plunging into Katrina's heart if her only son was unaccounted for. She took a breath and said firmly, trying to reassure. "There is so much of the harvest to get in. And the cideries are going 'round the clock. I'm sure that's what he's doing."

"And Eddie would want to help," Katrina said. Her voice was assured, not at all wobbly with panic. "He likely thinks it will reflect well on his father. He's been so excited about helping with the campaign."

"I'll let Mr. Morgan know right away, Katrina. He's called for Mr. Lamont to help him with his work here. I'm sure they'll keep an eye out for Eddie as well. Shall I have him 'phone you as soon as he turns up?" She had her verbiage under control. She was simply the secretary.

"Yes, please, Carrie. That would be so kind. I'll do the same." Having made plans that required no more details or pleasantries, they hung up. Carrie hurried out, hearing the door lock when she pulled it shut. She wove through Clevinger's, ignoring the lingering stares of customers who may or may not believe everything they read in the paper.

* * *

Where would Del be?

He didn't say where he was going, just that he had to put his precisely-bearded deputy onto searching for the place where Evans died. Where would that be? The Chester had been searched. The bridge had been searched. What was left? The two lawmen could be anywhere.

If Carrie was to deliver Katrina's message, she needed to find them. Although Hope Bridge wasn't that big of a town, aimlessly walking around was not going to work. She knew where Lamont lived. She'd start there.

It hadn't rained lately, and the early frosts had done little to tamp down the dust kicked up by horses, heavy wagons, speeding carriages, and foot traffic. On Main Street, a dirty haze hovered in rolling clouds behind each vehicle. It never settled back down. Carrie had become accustomed, like everyone else, to holding a kerchief over her face since construction began in August.

The Lamont's lived on a side street that wasn't directly under the cloud of dust. Still, every white clapboard was tinged with a fine coat of dirt. Carrie dropped her kerchief and stated her request when Mrs. Lamont opened the door. The smell of bread and onions, butter, and apples came with her.

The deputy's wife was bony and pleasant, with a cap of grey hair. Her clothes and apron were sewn well, and from the open door, Carrie could see the simple and orderly home beyond. Mrs. Lamont only knew that her husband had gone as soon as the sun came up.

"I have a message for Mr. Morgan, from his wife," Carrie said. While she could trust Deputy Leo Lamont with the message about Eddie, she didn't know Mrs. Lamont at all, and couldn't relay Katrina's message via Lamont's wife. She might gossip. "If you see him, will you tell him I need to speak with him?"

Mrs. Lamont agreed. She shifted in the doorway. A tiny movement, but one that accented the stiffening of her pleasant smile. Carrie hesitated, then asked directly, "Is there something else?"

The deputy's wife glanced around at her neighborhood, and stepped aside. "Come in a moment, won't you, Mrs. Lisbon?"

Carrie crossed the threshold with a familiar feeling. *She's going to impart a confidence.* Undertakers are always the recipients of family secrets. At least one family member revealed all, literally laid bare before them.

Mrs. Lamont closed the door but did not invite Carrie any further than the short hallway. She clasped her hands close beneath her bosom, then her smile faltered, and she stammered. "It's just that there was something in the paper about… you… and Mr. Morgan…?"

Carrie felt a sudden sense of vertigo. Her anticipation of receiving a request for confidentiality when the time came, and her reassuring response that undertakers practiced the strictest confidences, dropped away. She put a hand to her solar plexus, as if she'd felt a blow. She was aware that the skin of her face had become wooden. She dimly heard Mrs. Lamont's hasty backtracking.

"Oh, I'm sorry to have upset you, Mrs. Lisbon!" Mrs. Lamont reached out a bony hand. "We've all come to know you as a respectable, hardworking woman. Ina Barnstable talks about your talents all the time."

But Carrie stepped back from the compassionate outreach. Tears sprang to her eyes. *The insinuations are true!* Instead of confidence and indignation, she had to respond with lies.

"Ugh! That damn Clowe," she huffed, too angry to worry about swearing in polite company. "Suggesting Mr. Morgan and I have more than a professional relationship! The nerve of him! Just to win an election!"

"It's not that Leo and I—or anyone else—thinks it's true!" Mrs. Lamont waved her hands like signals flags. "We know you, and we know Mr. Morgan. I've met his wife. She's a perfect helpmate, a good housekeeper, and a Christian woman. He would never do such a thing. *You* would never do such a thing!"

The ringing in her ears nearly drowned Mrs. Lamont's words. When she stopped speaking, Carrie looked up, confused. In the pregnant silence, there was something more that wasn't being said.

"But…?" she asked, with more brutality than this good woman deserved. She knew what was coming.

Her camaraderie with men was comfortable, but she'd experienced rejection and ridicule from women for as long as she could remember. She'd been taunted as the child whose father kept dead bodies in the house, bullied as a schoolgirl who created floral tributes for funerals, and rejected as a young woman who not only *chose* an occupation, but pursued a ghoulish one! Carrie had learned to dismiss the hurt, to combat it with education and success, and to rely on the satisfaction of a life's work when invitations to ladies' societies dried up.

Mrs. Lamont swallowed, and offered a tremulous smile. "Well, it's just that you haven't been to church in a while. I know Mr. Morgan can't attend every Sunday. He has an excuse, what with him being so busy, and he never knows when he has to be called out to see to something. But I thought—if I could give you some advice—that is, Leo and I thought—"

Carrie's years of self-disciplined training kicked in automatically. Her chin lifted, her breath came and went. She instinctively drew herself up, shook her head, and smiled defiantly.

"I understand your thoughts, Mrs. Lamont. I'm used to this sort of thing." She felt a single unshed tear finally break loose and fall down her cheek. "I grew up as the child of an undertaker. I've endured more than my fair share of slings and arrows, simply due to my father's profession and mine. I get plenty of 'church' at each and every funeral I attend." She swiped her cheek with the dusty kerchief, leaving a streak of dirt behind. A surly line of war paint.

Mrs. Lamont reached out again, speaking quickly. "Oh, Mrs. Lisbon. I only wanted to let you know that Leo and I feel responsible—just a bit— for you, and for Mr. Morgan's election. Leo is so proud to be his deputy. Mr. Morgan is such a highly regarded man. And we wouldn't want his—or your—reputations to be dirtied. Gossip can be so harmful to one's standing."

Carrie stepped back. "I consider those who gossip to be crows, mobbing an eagle. Why should he be concerned? Why should I?"

She managed to dredge up some cordiality for Mrs. Lamont's 'advice' and to remind her that Sheriff Morgan needed to hear her message from Katrina. She left the orderly home to resume her mission, walking as if she were a woman on business, neither hurrying nor strolling. She picked up the pieces of her shattered emotions and put them back in their places.

Shame went to the deepest part of her brain. After all, she and Del might never bed each other again. It was too risky, too outlandish a crime to continue. Insecurity was brushed to the back of her heart. She hadn't been the rejected schoolgirl in fifteen years. That feeling had been thoroughly eradicated when she met Phee, her handsome and loving husband who cherished her, her talents, and her vocation. She considered, and discovered, she had no guilt whatsoever about her church attendance. Church services were uninspiring. She was not unique in her spotty attendance. She tithed on the high holidays and accompanied her Uncle Sav when he wanted to attend, if only for the social hour afterward. They always attended the fundraising suppers, since neither one of them enjoyed cooking.

But she held tightly to one emotion. She kept the anger bright and sharp in her clenched fist.

Damn you, Howard Clowe!How dare you expose me.

Chapter Eleven

She rejected the idea of leaving a spoken message with Sam Clevinger, the grocer, or his wife out of a newly sharpened sense of self-preservation. How would it look for her to leave a confidential word for the sheriff? How would it be interpreted? Her steps slowed with indecision.

She decided the best course of action—and something she should have done in the first place—was to simply leave a note for Morgan summarizing her conversation with Katrina. He needed to know his son was not home. She couldn't spend all day chasing him down to tell him.

Additionally, she wasn't sure when or why they might meet again. Her job had been to take one 'phone call and that was done. She had been given no additional responsibilities regarding the investigation of Martin Evans' death. The preparation of the body was nearly complete, and he'd be on his way for burial tonight. Her keen observations were over.

A note would conclude her duties, yet, she was cautious. In her case, it might smack of intimacy and witnesses would gossip all the more. She wanted no further fuel for *that* fire, but in the interest of maintaining a public distance from Morgan, it was her only choice.

But, *damn it,* she had locked the door to his office when she left. She'd have to stop by the store counter and get a key from Sam Clevinger, that is, if he had a spare key.

Or, she picked the lock.

She hadn't done so in years, but she could probably still manage. She and Phee had been able to get by any lock they encountered, especially when fueled by embarrassment. More than once, during their early apprentices, they'd closed a casket, naively satisfied with their final product, only to discover that the widower left instructions for a lock of hair to be snipped, or the crucifix wasn't supposed to be buried with the child. Later, fueled by desire, they'd broken into a linen closet at that picnic at the Methodist rectory...

She wasn't thinking straight. Mrs. Lamont's kindly advice had rattled her. She snorted at her thoughts. Clevinger's was always packed with customers peering down the short hallway toward the sheriff's office. Anyone seeing her crouched over the door knob would know what she was up to.

When she came to live with Sav, she'd been appraised by Hope Bridge's townsfolk as if she were a new species. She'd not been accepted right away, but she'd kept firm in her resolve to portray herself as a legitimate and talented business woman—which she was. Ina Barnstable's praises had helped her gain approval as well as a clientele. Carrie was shocked to learn that women were requesting her as their cosmetist upon their deaths. She wasn't about to lose that ground by getting caught picking a lock.

Mrs. Lamont's opinion that she and Morgan were innocent settled like a heavy internal burden. *My God! If we were ever found out!* The thought set her heart thumping again. *A matter for later,* she cautioned herself. Leaving a message for Morgan was the immediate problem. She'd relegate her entanglement with him to the back burner.

What would a man do in this case?

By the time she heard the pickle boy, the solution had come. She thought about the men she trusted—and who had trusted her. She saw Phee's handsome face first, loving, and mischievous, then Sav's bushy-haired, horse-toothed countenance. Open, blithely enthusiastic. Her father's face, kindly and intelligent. He'd always known what to do. He'd been a great teacher. She saw Thomas Bale, with his clever and sardonic grin. All the men in her life exhibited the classic traits of success: pride, mastery of their trades, and confidence. She'd do the same. It came easily. She wasn't going to let innuendo and nasty accusations impede her work. *It's no one's business.*

She was a professional. She was Sheriff Del Morgan's associate. She didn't have to explain herself. And she didn't have to behave as though her actions with him were anything less than legitimate. This town knew she dealt with the dead. She knew things only undertakers know. That gave her a level of confidence, even superiority. She'd use it.

She walked into the store, asked Sam Clevinger for a paper and a pencil, and, after she jotted the note, she folded it and, without a word, held out her hand for the key to Morgan's door. Simple as that.

She mimicked Morgan's imposing expression as she waited. Clevinger didn't bat an eye, but pulled a set from his trousers, selected one, and held it out to her by its pin. She thanked him with a wordless nod, delivered the note to the sheriff's desk, locked the door, and returned the key to the proprietor. Just like any man on business would.

Outside, in addition to the dust that coated everything from window panes to ladies' hats, a thick blanket of cloud covered the afternoon sky, washing all color from the landscape. Carrie held her kerchief over her mouth and nose. She was grateful for the disguise when she looked up to see Howard Clowe on the other side of the street. He was surrounded by a set of younger men, the idlers who woke late and played cards at the Chester long into the night. They listened to his speech and nodded to each other like agitators, buying the promise of better luck from this new hand. Putting distance between herself and them, she heard a burst of laughter, and guessed that Clowe had made Morgan the butt of a joke.

Up ahead, she saw Warren Maxwell walking quickly with his head down, furtively glancing side to side.

He had demonstrated some interesting behavior this morning when he railed against the sheriff, when he defied Morgan's guard at Evan's hotel room, and with his desperate need to know the whereabouts of Evan's missing key. Maxwell surely had something to hide behind his bluffing posture. Did he *not* concern himself with the nature of his boss's death, because he already knew how he'd died?

Carrie maintained her pace, keeping an eye on Maxwell as he resolutely marched up the street. She stepped into the dirt road to avoid a wide group of women and their packages and craned her neck to watch Maxwell push open the door to Hope Bridge's post and telegraph office.

The place was a hub of communication. Everyone purchased penny post cards to keep in touch, from the men working on the bridge, to the farmwife sending news to kin a mile up the road, to the traveler noting his latest stop. She and Sav had a pigeon hole for their letters. Emmett Cross, and sometimes Sav, operated the telegraph, which was expensive, but more reliable than the telephones with their flimsy wires.

Did Maxwell keep a post office box? To correspond with his family? Did he have a family to correspond to? Did Evans have a box? That would make sense, if Evans needed to maintain contact with his suppliers and his downstate office. But the Bridgeworks management had their mail delivered directly to the Chester, where they all stayed. *Was Evan's key stored here?*

Perhaps she might witness Maxwell retrieving the key. She could follow him to where he might use it. That would be helpful information for Morgan. Maybe, her keen observations were *not* done.

A ghostly cloud of dust entered with her when she pushed open the heavy door. The lobby's stone floor was powdered with residue and dappled with footprints. From behind the postman's brass bars, Emmett Cross glanced up at her. His thick fingers held a stubby pencil. Maxwell stood at the counter, dictating a telegram. He spun around at the sound of the door, cutting off his words immediately. He and Carrie locked eyes.

He took a step toward her. "Are you following me?" he demanded.

"What? No!" Carrie was unprepared for his attack. Her surprise was genuine. "I came to buy postcards."

Maxwell glanced at Emmett and scowled. "Never mind!" he snapped at the telegrapher and stomped out, glaring at Carrie on his way by.

The postmaster shrugged and drew a single line across the paper he'd been using. Needing to complete her ruse, Carrie stepped up to the window and asked for a dozen cards. Emmett glanced around at both sides of his cluttered desk and grunted. "I gotta go get 'em from the store room. I'll be right back."

When he left the counter, Carrie slipped a hand under the brass bars and turned the notepad so she could read the messages that had been dictated that day. The veteran postmaster wrote each message on paper before sending it, a common telegrapher's method of avoiding errors. Cross thriftily used a single line to eliminate the recited words after he'd sent the message, or in Maxwell's case, when the message was canceled. Carrie easily read the message Morgan had sent earlier today to Katrina. "Is LR there/Call me/" She felt an unexpected catch in her throat. It was Morgan's pet name for his son. She remembered standing at his shoulder on a blistering hot day last summer when he told her he'd always called his boy 'Little Rascal,' or 'LR' for short.

She also read Maxwell's aborted message.

"Complications. Need more time. Plea—"

She spun the notepad around and withdrew her hand a second before Emmett came back, unwrapping a bundle of post cards from a wide paper strap.

"I like these pictures of the old bridge," he said, before handing one to Carrie. The postcards showed a photograph of the old covered bridge, taken from the east side, looking west. Beyond it were the orderly rooftops of Hope Bridge, and the pointed steeple of the Methodist Church poking through a ruffle of trees.

The pretty scene triggered a terrible memory. Carrie heard the squeal of the wooden structure as it collapsed into the deafening roar of flood water, and the despairing screams of the woman who went with them. She shook her head, realizing she had missed something Emmett said.

"What?"

"How many do you need?"

"A dozen, please," Carrie murmured. "Oh! I'm afraid I don't have my purse with me. Could you please add these to my account?" She took the cards and pressed Emmett for one more favor.

"Can I use the back door?"

Emmett nodded, his expression knowing. He ushered her out the back door to the delivery yard beyond.

"Lots of pressure these days, ain't there," he said quietly. He looked around. The gravel lot was bordered by the back yards of several houses. No one, especially Maxwell, was about. "The coast is clear."

She thanked Emmett for the assistance and set off with a new purpose. She needed to find Morgan with even more compelling news than that of his missing son.

She'd snooped. She wasn't ashamed. Not in the traditional sense of nosiness; she wasn't going to gossip about what she'd learned. It had served her and Morgan well in the past, especially when she discovered information—by snooping—about things that had been important. This time, she found out three things that suggested Maxwell *was* up to something.

First, everyone dictated a message to the telegrapher with the understanding that the word STOP would be inserted between each sentence instead of a period. Punctuation in a telegraph was likely to be misinterpreted. If you wanted a period, you paid more for it. Morgan had adhered to this convention, as evidenced by Cross making a slash between each sentence, which would translate into the word STOP when the actual code was sent. But Cross placed a period between Maxwell's words. Maxwell was spending money on punctuation. The words, therefore, must be very important.

Secondly, Maxwell dictated three sentences, or rather two, and a plea. "Complications" meant he was telling the receiver that plans had gone awry. Evans' death was certainly a complication. But Evans' Bridgeworks already knew about that. Was the lost key a complication?

Maxwell indicated he needed more time. For what? To circumvent the complications? To search for the key? To straighten out affairs at Evans' office? Surely there was a great deal of documentation to pass on to the new administrator of the project. That was a given. Why wouldn't he wait to bring the next man up to speed in person?

It was the aborted word "please" that had the most impact. Carrie was sure that was the unfinished word on Emmett's notepad. It was the word Maxwell cut off when Carrie came in.

Telegrams were sent to inform, and to do so succinctly, as in 'Arriving Chicago STOP 11 January STOP Union Station 3 PM.' They were like commands in that they were worded in a blunt manner. No frivolities, like please, or thank you, were used. Each word cost the sender, so it was customary for polite words to be omitted. They were understood.

Yet Emmett had written it down. If it was on Emmett's dictation pad, Maxwell must have insisted on including the word. It was an important word. It was necessary to the message. It was a plea. Why would he plead for more time?

Lastly, the Chester Inn had become the hotel of choice for the Bridgeworks management ever since the project started. Their business team, engineers, quartermaster, and foremen needed lodging, food, a ready room, and other amenities. To meet the needs of its guests, as well as the increase of its own supplies for those guests, the Chester had installed a telegraph line in addition to its current phone line. A guest wishing to send messages, orders, questions, and itineraries could simply send them from the Chester. It saved time, and the Chester billed voraciously.

Carrie presumed Maxwell was still employed by Evans Bridgeworks and, therefore still staying at the Chester. If he was still an employee, and he was still a guest at the hotel, why was he using the town telegraph office to send his pleading message?

That was simple. He didn't want anyone at the Chester to know about it.

Chapter Twelve

Mulling over Maxwell's unsent message, Carrie walked to Worley's to help him finish up with Evans. It was late afternoon, and she was so hungry that even Clara's over-salted cabbage and pork tasted like heaven. She ate standing up in the kitchen, grateful that Clara wasn't chomping and smacking along with her, then hurried down into the mortuary, endured Worley's subtle scowl, and got to work.

They dressed and leveraged the corpse into the casket from the embalming table. She fussed over the tie and collar. Although she was prepared to apply cosmetics, Worley shook his head, indicating that a treatment of lotion was all that was necessary to present Martin Evans to whatever family awaited his remains in Saugerties. The casket lid was closed, and Worley carefully nailed it shut. There was a transport wagon waiting in the yard. Carrie left the teamster and Worley to the business of loading up. She strolled home in the dim evening light.

At home, Bale was not in his apartment when she called up. Nor was Ransom. She was impatient to tell Bale or Morgan her information about Maxwell's telegram. She ate leftover bread and butter, washed it down with tea, and to keep busy, she started on developing Evan's death pictures.

Morgan asked her to produce them as soon as she was able. She had documented the grisly evidence of his death from all angles. There were pictures of his clothed body, his naked body (with a chaste sheet across his groin, of course), the stiff-armed pose, the mud in his mouth, the fatal wound. There was no mistaking the cause of death. If Doctor Wells hadn't declared Martin Evans dead from a massive head wound, then the photographs she'd taken made a compelling statement to that effect.

She'd been so focused on the chemical process, paying careful attention to the mixtures and timing when the doorbell jangled. She pulled aside the burlap panel she'd installed as a darkening curtain and saw stars in the sky. *What time is it?*

Undertakers are called upon at all hours. She was never surprised to answer the door and find someone requesting her services. People called on Sav Machin for his expertise on civic and scholarly subjects even more. Carrie made sure that despite the neglect of her personal suite of rooms, the porch and front hallway were always swept and tidy. It wouldn't do to have an undertaker greet callers with a messy first impression. This time, she may need to explain the smell embedded in her clothing was from her photography hobby, not embalming chemicals. She opened the door.

Mr. and Mrs. Delphius Morgan stood on the porch, bundled against the sharp cold, with ruddy cheeks and apologetic smiles. A suitcase sat at Katrina's feet like an obedient dog.

"Oh! Hello," Carrie stammered, quickly applauding herself for not blurting Morgan's first name.

"Hello, Mrs. Lisbon," Morgan said. "I'm sorry to bother you so late, but I hope you can help us with a problem."

Carrie looked from husband to wife and back. Business would bring Morgan to her home, to the front door. But the Morgans lived in Duncan, the county seat, almost twelve miles away. Why was Katrina here?

"Of course. Please come in." She stood aside and ushered Katrina into the hallway. Morgan picked up the suitcase and followed. He closed the door and stood near it, hat in hand.

Like Morgan, Katrina was only a few years older than Carrie, but her bearing—her assured competence—made her seem older. She wasn't as tall as Carrie, or her husband. She was stoutly built, a work horse, ready and willing to perform all tasks. Her elocution was modest. Her clothing reflected an excellent aptitude for sewing. Her shoes and coat were sturdy, but dulled by a film of construction dust.

"Don't mind the scent of chemicals," Carrie blathered, trying to overcome her uncertainty. "I was putting together some photographs. It's a pleasant surprise to see you, Katrina."

"I surprised Del, too," Katrina said. "I'm afraid I've acted rashly, and it's backfired."

"You still haven't heard from Eddie?" Carrie said warily. *Oh, no! Was this a call for the undertaker?*

"No. But I'm sure he's fine," Katrina said, followed by a firm nod of her head. "This is a problem of accommodation, I'm afraid."

Carrie looked from husband to wife again, and then the meaning of their appearance at her door after dark, bearing a suitcase, became clear.

Hope Bridge had one hotel, the Chester, and two inns, the Valley Star on the west end of town, and an old drover's inn across the Duncan Creek in East Hope. Every room was filled. The hoteliers had squeezed extra beds in their rooms, alcoves, and hallways. Every resident in and around town with a room to spare had rented them out with breakfast to boot. Unused carriage barns and chicken coops had been remodeled and furnished to accommodate the workers.

Katrina continued. "After our 'phone call, I admit to being quite worried about Eddie, so I came here, on my family's behalf, where I thought I could be of some help." She looked into Carrie's eyes with apology and something else—entreaty? She went on. "I came without consulting Del. The cot at his office is not adequate, and when we discovered 'there's no room at the inn,' I thought of you." Katrina glanced up at her husband. "He agreed right away. But if I'm imposing—"

Carrie covered the sudden clutch in her throat by waving the Morgans forward with both of her hands. "Not at all! Of course, you can stay here. It's the perfect solution. My uncle is away on business. You can have my room. I'll stay in his."

"That's so kind of you," Katrina said and grasped Carrie's hands. "I won't be a bother. I'll make myself useful to you. Oh, your hands are so cold! Are you sure I won't put you out?"

Carrie clasped her icy fingers around Katrina's like they were long -lost friends. She leaned in, smiling warmly. "It's no bother. I'm so pleased you thought of me. I want you to make yourself at home. Come on. Please. Mr. Morgan can get on with his work, and you and I will settle in and wait for Eddie to come."

Carrie gestured to Morgan, who looked on with a slightly incredulous expression. "Come in, come in, Mr. Morgan! Put her bag down there." She waited primly while the Morgans said their good-byes, dropping her eyes when Morgan bent to kiss his wife's cheek. Katrina held his hand a moment more and reminded him to contact her as soon as he heard from Eddie. Morgan nodded a simple thanks to Carrie and closed the door behind him.

She turned to Katrina, took up her bag, and led her to the two rooms at the back of the house. "I'm afraid I've neglected my housekeeping, with all the fuss over the bridge man's death," she said, quickly snatching up discarded undergarments, a stained apron, and socks. Her eyes darted around the room, imagining evidence of Del Morgan everywhere. "I'll just be a minute tidying."

"What a lovely suite, Carrie," Katrina said, graciously ignoring the frantic cleaning, the tented books on the floor, and the unmade bed. Instead, she complimented the artful arrangement of birch twigs and pressed leaves in a chipped crock. Then she took up position on one side of Carrie's bed and helped snap the bedding into place.

"I've just laundered the sheets!" Carrie chirped. She felt her voice thin with alarm. At least that detail had been done after Morgan left her bed *only yesterday morning!* Tamping down panic at the thought, she smoothed the heavy quilt over the blankets, hiding her blushing face.

"That's a lovely quilt," Katrina said, fingering the stitching.

"I can't take any credit for it," Carrie said. The roaring in her ears had stopped when Morgan left the house, but—*my god! Is that his scent on my pillow?* She smiled maniacally. "I believe it was one of Sav's auntie's who pieced it together. I can't sew a stitch."

They finished tidying, then toured the kitchen, walked outside to the outhouse, and climbed the stairs to Sav's room and library. Katrina praised the wallpaper, the many books and maps Sav kept, and the magnificence of Oscar, the yellow-breasted azure macaw Sav had rescued from a drunken sailor in his youth. Oscar had his own room upstairs, secure behind a screen door. Carrie warned Katrina that Sav's beloved pet was likely to make noises that sounded remarkably like cursing. That, and Oscar was quite possessive of his seed bucket. A bite from the nearly four-foot bird was likely to be very bad.

Oscar pulled his head from beneath his wing, turned a gimlet eye to them, and swore most profanely.

Back in the kitchen, Carrie put the kettle on for tea. She had harvested a quantity of chamomile this summer, and wanted to at least serve her guest something. She apologized for not having anything to go with the tea, but Katrina went to Carrie's room and returned triumphantly, cracking open the lid from a tin of cookies.

Of course, she would have thought to bring cookies.

Carrie hoped the brew, steeped to the point of bitterness, and sweetened with a generous portion of honey, would ease her nerves, replace the wooden smile on her face, and provide some stability under her feet.

* * *

Her thoughts were wild that night. She lay in Sav's bed, surrounded by his scent of ink and mild sweat, staring at the ceiling, rigid and remembering.

Was there any evidence of Del in her room? Had she washed the sheets thoroughly? Could Katrina smell any residual scent of him? Of his warm tobacco? *Good God, what was she thinking, bedding him here!*

She hadn't been thinking, that was the problem. Neither of them had. Blind lust had taken over. As soon as Morgan was in the back door, their hands and lips were all over each other. She didn't remember how their clothing came off, just the delicious sensation of cool air on her bare skin, his hands on her breasts, his weight, his scent, the joyous parting of her willing body, and the intense elation that repeated itself over and over. *Jesus!* It had been Morgan's word, whispered harshly in her ear as, he, too, was overwhelmed.

And now Morgan's wife lay in the *same damn bed!* Carrie wanted to jump up and run screaming. At least pace the room. But the floorboards creaked, and Katrina would hear it and know a guilty mind was at work. Deep breaths didn't help; tossing and turning only twisted her blankets around her legs, ensnaring her even more tightly. She flung the bedding aside and stood in the cold.

Katrina doesn't know, she reminded herself firmly. *You cleaned up. There is no scent of him. You covered your tracks.* She pursed her lips in disgust.

After Phee died, she had clawed her way up and out of a pit of despair, getting up each morning with a mantra that helped her simply put one foot in front of the other. She clung to it now, hoping to settle down.

Just get up. Just get that far. Then we'll see.

Carlin Sophia Shay married Ephesians Michael Lisbon, her father's protégé, when she was nineteen years old. They had been good friends, happily wed, successful morticians. Her father made both of them full partners, creating *Lisbon & Shay, Undertakers* of Nanuet, New York. They'd been innocents on their wedding day, but their satisfaction in their marriage bed increased with experience. And they'd had some very gratifying experiences.

When the train pulled away from the Nanuet platform in August of 1899, she waved good-bye, missing him already, but resigned to make the trip to visit her aging auntie in Port Jervis. He had waved back, and she didn't see his grimace of pain, nor did she see the progression of acute appendicitis knifing through his body with agonizing swiftness. She ran into their house after pacing the return train, after screaming in the streets for a cab. Two doctors had begun surgery right there in the bedroom. She would never forget the stink of blood, antiseptic, and bowels, or the sudden plunge into disbelief at the sight of Phee. Cold. Dead. Gone.

Just get up! She had cried to him, as the surgeons sewed him up in silence. *Don't leave me, Phee. Don't leave me!*

After a month of fuzzy memories with Sav presiding over her affairs, she'd agreed to go live with the aging auntie to begin her widowhood. But before the darkest winter of her life had ended, she rebelled against the pain of her loss, against being buttoned up in odious black clothing, cooped up with her auntie and her smelly little dog. Carrie bolted back to Nanuet just as the white tulips Phee had bought her years before were emerging from her kitchen garden.

The black crepe was torn off, and a tear-stained letter was written to Sav. Could she come live with him? He had been the only buoyant thing visible from her place in despair. She longed for his inky scent. He was an intellect, not a harpy like her aunt, who was consumed with dressing Carrie 'like a proper widow.' He had no dog. He lived in a quiet, little country town. She came to Hope Bridge in May of this year.

Just get up. Just get that far. Then we'll see. She had used that phrase to carry on, step by leaden step, to resume life, such as it was, in the aftermath of losing everything she'd ever loved. Now, she employed the soothing phrase in a heinous reassurance that her transgressions were well hidden, that she was still getting away with adultery.

With a disgusted huff, she threw on her house coat and left the room. She stepped onto the landing and tapped for the handrail at the top of the stairs. She had all but fled, forgetting to light the finger lamp that would have illuminated the way downstairs.

There had been no moon on Hallowe'en night, and two nights later, there was still no offering of illumination from the night sky. She tiptoed down the familiar stairs to the front door and peered out the side window into blackness. When she saw her reflection, with its wide, haunted eyes and messy dark hair, she spun around. The reflection was the result of light from a lamp, turned down low, in the kitchen.

"Katrina?" she whispered from the kitchen doorway. Del Morgan's wife had revived the cookstove fire. She sat at the kitchen table with her hands clasped on the tablecloth. She appeared to be praying. In a flash of guilt, Carrie pictured Katrina confronting her with accusation. *'Why does your bed smell like my husband?'*

But Del's wife looked up at Carrie and smiled softly. "Did I wake you, Carrie? I'm sorry. I was trying to be quiet."

"No," Carrie answered. "What's wrong? Are you all right?"

Katrina smiled again, and her fingers flickered over each other before resuming their clasp. "I can't sleep. I'm worried about Eddie."

"Oh," was all Carrie could manage, as relief washed over her. She spoke softly, "I can't sleep either. I'll make us an old-fashioned posset. My father taught me the recipe. It helps." She quietly set about collecting a pot, the jug of milk in the ice box, and a bottle of brandy from the pantry. The dim light of Katrina's lamp and the warmth of the wood stove compelled her to move gently, slowly. She didn't want to disturb Katrina's need for peace.

"Del is often away from home," Katrina sighed. "Of course, he has to be. I don't begrudge him the time he spends on his job. He's quite honored to be county sheriff."

Carrie said nothing, stirring cinnamon and honey into the milk, grateful that her back was turned, that the fire warmed her chilly hands. She had the strangest feeling, talking about Morgan with his wife. She knew the same man. She knew a completely different man.

"We never know what will happen, what sorts of things he has to go and take care of. Eddie and I are so proud of him," Katrina went on. "When he comes home, Eddie always asks about his work. This past year, he's been going with his father, sometimes. To help. They get on so well together."

Katrina's shoulders softened. The talking was doing her good, Carrie thought. It's relieving the pressure of worry that was, no doubt, building inside her. *More will come. She'll get to it in a minute.*

"Eddie's such a good boy. And he's turned into quite a fine young man," Katrina said, smiling like all mothers smile, when they think of their sons. "He's intelligent, like his father. He's always so helpful. And so hardworking. Do you know he saved up for that horse he's riding? For years. Oh, how he *worked.* Everywhere. Earning a few dollars here and there. His father and I couldn't stand it. We wanted to buy him that horse for his fifteenth birthday, but he wouldn't hear of it." More pride strengthened her voice in the lamplight. "That's the way it should be, I expect."

"He's a credit to you and Mr. Morgan," Carrie said softly. "Children don't come out with virtues. They're taught by example."

It was a trite thing to say, but true. She met Eddie Morgan last summer, at the Annual Sheriff's Benefit Ball, an event Morgan and Katrina had redesigned to resemble a barn dance, complete with banjos and fiddles. Eddie was a fine-looking, sixteen-year-old, with his mother's brown hair and eyes, and his father's height. Lanky, and formally dressed, he stood dutifully next to his parents in the receiving line, greeting her and everyone else stiffly. They met again when he was called upon to drive her and Marta home from the county poorhouse a week later. More at ease with that task, Eddie handled the family horse and carriage with skill.

Katrina smiled modestly. "We only have Eddie. I didn't lose any others. They just didn't catch. I've often thought the good Lord gave me just the one, so I could raise him well."

"And you have," Carrie murmured. She tapped the spoon on the edge of the sauce pan gently, and concentrated on pouring the steaming, spiked milk into cups. Katrina stopped the unconscious wringing of her hands and wrapped her fingers around the warm china. Carrie slipped into the opposite chair and sipped her drink. She felt her own shoulders relax. There was a moment of contentment, a moment when the fellowship of women facing their fears together, eased them.

"Mr. Morgan will keep looking for him in the morning," Carrie said. "He has Thomas looking for him, too. It doesn't seem right that Eddie hasn't arrived where he's supposed to, or that he hasn't called or sent a telegram."

"But he may be in a place that has no phone lines yet, or a telegraph office."

"Then he's not too far away. There aren't many places without a line these days. And if he can't get ahold of you that way, there's bound to be someone who's seen him. We'll hear tomorrow, for sure."

"You're right. Del will take care of it." Katrina tsked and shook her head, admonishing herself. Her hair was down for the night. It softened features that had the potential to become stern as she aged. She had the open and honest face of a woman who spent time on her family, not herself. Now, with Carrie as confidante, Katrina's face appeared to be just shy of careworn. "I've just added to his burden. I shouldn't worry. I shouldn't have come."

Carrie smiled tenderly, reached across the table, and took Katrina's hand. It was warm, calloused. "He's your boy. Of course, you'd be worried."

"Del is grateful that I don't nag him with worries. It does no good, anyway,"

Katrina sighed. "When he proposed to me, I made the mistake of asking him to not smoke. I meant that I didn't want him in an early grave like his father. He told me never to worry about that. He carries tobacco now, only to offer it to others. I've come to love the way it smells on him."

God, me too! Carrie closed her eyes and smiled warmly, envisioning not only Morgan's warmth, but the scent that emanated from that simple pouch of chew he kept on him. It had seduced her.

She conjured Katrina's life, a childhood cradled in a household with two parents, happy siblings, plenty of friends; an appropriate upbringing, with schooling and rituals, holidays, and milestones. She saw Katrina as a young girl mastering sewing and cooking, all things Carrie had hated doing, took no pleasure in, and still eschewed whenever possible. Katrina probably had an appropriate courtship with the young Del Morgan, an appropriate engagement period, and a well-fêted marriage. She produced a spotless household and a child for her husband, a boy they could be immensely proud of. She was a model mother, a model wife, a model helpmate to the county sheriff, a supporter, and a companion. Throughout it all, she may not have tripped up or offended anyone, anywhere, ever. She did not deserve a terrible fate for her only child.

"Del always has so much to contend with," Katrina said. "I make sure he has a happy home. I see to it that he's ready for each day. It wouldn't do to have a man of his stature come home to a shrew. I refuse to complain."

She unleashed Carrie's hands, and sat back. "We live a steady life. I keep right with the Lord. I plan ahead. I try to do what's best. I keep a good house. I'm content. If I'm going to sin, it will be with pride. When you find your way to my grave, my stone will say, 'the good wife of Delphius Morgan.'"

As she listed her contributions, the explanation of her life's work became an appeal to God. An offering. A bargain. In exchange, He would provide her with his blessings and the continued safety of her son and her husband.

"I rock no boats," Katrina concluded in the softly lit kitchen. Her prayer ended; her appeal sent.

Carrie stared at her, unable to do anything else. The appeal hadn't gone to God. It shot like a bullet straight into her own heart and soul. The impact flattened her reserves. She felt immense fatigue. Either the posset was working, or the weight of her burdens wore her down. She had one startling thought for Del Morgan's wife.

And I am your leviathan.

Chapter Thirteen

When Thomas Bale walked through town, he did so with the graceful confidence of a man who knew his business, knew his neighbors, knew the lay of the land. He knew who had his back, and who did not.

Carrie watched him approach, marveling at his demeanor. Compact and beautifully proportioned, of African descent, the great-grandson of freed slaves who'd come to New York before the War of Secession. His parents saw to it their children could read and write, regardless of their exclusion from schools. Bale rarely showed any perturbance when confronted with public doubt about his legitimacy as a deputy, or when enduring the undercurrent of racism that simmered in so many. He'd been threatened with lynching, burned out of his home, maligned, and ignored. Yet, his friendship was steadfast; he saved lives in two countries. Carrie had seen him handle a dead child with reverence, and saw to it that her surviving family were cared for.

Morgan had given Bale the badge off his own chest and ordered him to organize, conscript, and generally bully menfolk into securing the town after the bridge disaster. Bale never gave it back. He had sewn it onto the lapel of his coat when the weather turned cold, displaying it at eye level. Thomas Bale's confidence had a challenging edge. He arrived at her porch with the mail and a newspaper under his arm.

"Good morning, Thomas," Carrie stopped sweeping the porch clear of last night's leaves and dust. She could see her breath, but the cold air was a relief from the heat generated by Katrina's cooking. The woman had gotten up before dawn and returned from Clevinger's Grocery and Bookhoudt's Dry

Goods laden with a twenty-pound box of supplies. Carrie was genuinely glad to have Bale arrive to distract her houseguest. *Here, he's family.*

"Come on in. I've got a treat for breakfast."

"Oh? What would that be?" His voice was warm with humor.

"I'm not cooking."

Bale's laughter carried them inside. The house was thick with the scents of bacon, cinnamon, yeast, and coffee. In the kitchen, Katrina dunked a slice of bread into egg and cream, and dropped it into a fry pan slick with butter. A pound of bacon lay crisscrossed on a warmed plate on a back burner. Rising bread bulged from another bowl. She turned to them expectantly.

"Mr. Bale, how nice to see you," she said, putting down the spatula and extending her hand with a wide smile.

Carrie watched Bale's expression change when he locked eyes with Katrina. *Less confident. More sympathetic. He's brought bad news.*

"Mr. Morgan asked me to see if I could find your boy. I've been out since yesterday afternoon. I didn't find him."

Katrina closed her eyes, deflated, sucked in a quick breath, and put on a shaky smile. "Thank you for looking, Mr. Bale."

"But let me tell you what I did find," he said, taking a cup of coffee from her. "I went up north, all the way to Sussex Mill. It's a tiny little town, nothing but a post office and an inn. Willie's Tavern. Nice folks. I saw where Eddie put up posters all along the way. Now, I can't say if he was traveling north or south when he pasted them up, but he was there. I also traveled west.

"I thought if I was Eddie, I'd make sure my papa's poster was on every bridge and barn in Duncan County, and I'd put it right over that ugly mug of Howard Clowe's. But that's not how the Morgan family operates. If I was Eddie, I'd put my posters up *before* the bridges, so folks would see my papa's face *before* his competition. There are two bridges that cross the Little Duncan and Cole Creek west of here, and all the hop barns next to the road *before* both bridges had your husband's posters on them. Just like I thought."

Katrina flipped the cinnamon toast without taking her eyes off Bale.

He continued. "I found posters all along the Shun Pike. The next town over is Bitter Hay. There were new posters there, too. I thought maybe he'd gone west, back toward Duncan."

"I should have stayed home. What if he's gone there? I didn't think to leave a note!"

Bale held up a cautionary hand, arresting Katrina's worried comments. "He's supposed to ask if he can hang any promotional bill on someone's barn." He inclined his head toward Carrie. "Another law I've been reading about. You have to get permission from the landowner before you install any signage.

"I asked the Wrights on the Shun Pike when Eddie had been by. They said Thursday. Late afternoon. He stayed and had supper with them. They said he insisted on getting back on the road after sundown. Old man Wright thought Eddie came south."

Katrina stared hard at him. "He was headed south?"

"Possibly. Right down North Street."

"He was headed for Hope Bridge? He was so close. Why wouldn't he have gone straight to Del's office?"

"I asked Mr. Wright again, but after some reflection, he couldn't say for sure which direction Eddie took, and there's a few little roads he might have taken between here and Hope Bridge, in order to hang posters—"

"In the dark?" Katrina interrupted.

Carrie lifted an eyebrow. It was unlike Katrina to be rude.

Bale turned up his palms. "Or he could have just bedded down at someone's house. He could have stayed the night and then worked off his room and board in the morning. He might be headed west to cover another part of Duncan."

Katrina tightened her lips. Her hands resumed whipping eggs and cream and cinnamon. "It's not like Eddie to not leave word. I don't see why he didn't let us know where he was going. And he was so close to Hope Bridge."

"But if he rode west along the Shun Pike," Carrie put in, "he'd be farther away. Finding a place to stay makes more sense than traveling the roads at night. It's been very dark lately. No moonlight."

Katrina spoke quickly. "I don't think he knows anyone personally in that direction. It's not like him to just ask someone unknown if he could stay the night. But I could be wrong. He's a friendly boy. He may have made friends that I don't know about. He *has* been working all over the last couple of years. Saving up. To buy that horse." She looked earnestly at them, then turned back to cooking. "In any case, thank you for trying, Mr. Bale. I'm sorry I was short with you. We're back to waiting."

She pushed things around on the stove, piled spongy cinnamon bread and bacon on a plate, and handed it to Bale. He looked at the other plates and bowls and pans that Katrina had laden with cooked food, with still more being prepared, then traded dubious looks with Carrie. He passed the first plate to her and took another one from Katrina. She made a plate for herself and pushed the frying pan onto a cold burner. She offered a short prayer and passed a jug of cider. The tiny clacking sounds of forks on plates sounded awkward. Bale broke the silence.

"I'm not done looking, Mrs. Morgan. I'm supposed to keep the peace, but I can interpret that order in any number of ways." He smiled with encouragement. "Finding your boy will bring some peace. I'll be back out, right after I finish off this plate." Katrina only nodded and offered another tight smile.

He's so much better at consoling her than I am, Carrie thought. She was only good for changing the subject.

"I want to look in on Ransom Butler today, Thomas. Do you think that's a good idea?" Carrie asked.

"That little waif can take care of himself," Bale said, dabbing a napkin to his lips. "But I'll bet he'd appreciate some of this breakfast."

Katrina smiled again in acknowledgement of his compliment. For all the cooking she'd done, Carrie noticed she'd eaten only a few bites. She wondered if Katrina was forcing food past a mouth as dry and useless as her own.

Chapter Fourteen

Bale offered to help clean up after breakfast, but Katrina shooed him away and asked him to continue the search for Eddie. They both saw the slightest tremble in her smile as she wrapped a sandwich the size of a book into a towel and handed it to him. She gave him another one to deliver to her husband. Bale couldn't fit it into his coat pocket.

Carrie took Katrina's hands in her own, stopping her from beginning another meal. She struck the damper to close down the stove, leaving behind the dishes and the towels and the mess (which was the usual condition she left her house in) and explained her mission to find Ransom Butler, the 'little waif' who had become somewhat of a ward to Bale. She pulled Katrina from the kitchen and thrust her in the direction of her hat and coat.

They walked south and west toward the edge of town. The dominating roar and clang of construction faded. November's chill was crisp on their cheeks. Thin light filtering through a layer of clouds washed the color from the sky, the remaining foliage, and their clothing. Katrina carried a small basket, heavy with food. She chatted politely about Hope Bridge's homes and municipal improvements. Carrie filled her in on Ransom's discovery of Evans' body and Bale's rescue of the child. Their chatter dried up as they approached the Banks.

This end of town lacked the perfume of pressed apples. The smell of wet metal and sewage pervaded the slope that pitched down toward the creek. A garbage cart from the Chester Inn was backed up to the bank. A young man scraped refuse out of the back end with a square shovel. They heard the clatter of broken dishes and the plop of a wet, malodorous mash hitting the ground. Below the dump site, barren trees stood among weeds and iron rust bleeding into the creek.

Amos Butler stood next to the Chester's cart, besotted, swaying, watching the garbage slop over the bank. He held out a grimy hand for a coin, chucked a burlap bag on the back of the wet cart, and sat down on it. The young man put a hand on the halter of the horse and led it away. Butler bounced drunkenly as the cart passed the women. He didn't look up.

"Well, that's a small favor," Carrie said, eyeing Butler, and turning toward Butler's shack. "I didn't really know how to ask him about the welfare of his boy."

Katrina followed Carrie down the muddy path to Butler's shack with her skirt held high. Broken metal and splintered wood threatened to snag their clothing. They reached the steps to the shack without mishap, and Carrie saw the damage Bale had done to the door when he kicked it open two nights before. No repairs had been made.

"Ransom?" she called. With no answer, she pushed open the door, glanced around, and retreated. "Ugh. There's only one room, and it stinks to high heaven. The boy's not in there."

"Do we dare look around?" Katrina asked, looking dubiously at the stacks of things that had been laid up, like cairns to mark the trail through the rubbish. One path led down to the creek. She picked up her own skirt and navigated carefully to the water's edge.

The Duncan was wide and straight here. She could see ripples in the center where the water flowed faster. A child could launch a raft in still water, ride it down on one side, hook it to the tow line that crossed the creek, and pull it back and forth, carrying workers who rented sleeping space in East Hope. He couldn't pole it back upriver each night. Poling against the current was impossible for a child as scrawny as Ransom. She remembered he and another boy—Joe something—kept their rafts tied near the bridge abutments. Ransom said he'd tied it up good; no way it came loose.

Ransom's a clever child, she thought, looking out over the water. With his raft and his pilfering, the boy from the dump utilized what resources he had. Her next thought was accompanied by a spike of anger. *How dare his father beat him when he was only trying his best to survive in his shitty circumstances!*

"A child lives here?" Katrina murmured, "and that drunken man we just passed is his father? I think I'd like to beat him myself."

Katrina's departure from equanimity was startling. Carrie glanced quickly at Morgan's wife, who grimaced, not going so far as to scowl. *We better find her boy—and soon—or she's going to blow.*

Katrina gestured for Carrie to continue upriver. Upstream, the smell of garbage blew away from them. The sandy mud was cratered with footprints. Farther along, they came to a place where a dense stand of burdocks, switchgrass, and brambles had been beaten down to form a small corral of sorts. Inside, hidden from view, was a new barrel, a repaired pail, and a full pot of mechanical grease. Two wagon wheels leaned against a tree, looking quite serviceable. Her immediate thought was that Butler may be pilfering as well as his boy. She saw a length of railroad track, spotted with rust, one end disappearing into the burdocks.

The other end stuck out into the yard, its exposed end covered in what looked like the rust that pervaded every other metal item in the dump. Carrie drew herself upright in alarm at the same time, barring Katrina from moving forward. Not rust. It was dried blood. Below it, the crushed vegetation was blackened. Dark stains spattered the frost-bitten leaves.

"Don't come any closer," Carrie said quietly, already scanning the ground for the source.

Beside her, Katrina gasped. "Is it Eddie?"

The breathless question made Carrie spin around. "No! No, Katrina. There's no body."

Katrina backed away with her hands pressed over her mouth. Her shaking fingers pointed up in prayer.

"Can you find your way back to town, Katrina?" Carrie said sharply. "Send Del, then go back to my house. You'll find my camera and tripod in the parlor. Bring it back here. Don't say a word to anyone."

She listened to Katrina hurrying back along the riverbank and then waited until silence resumed. She crouched, leaned closer, not moving her feet from the spot. What was it about this scene that said something terrible happened here? This was a dump, a place where garbage was dropped and left to rot. Out of sight, out of mind. All manner of awful things might be found here. Household detritus, unusable even for the thriftiest housewife, offal from the butcher. Castoff, broken, unidentifiable things.

But the general garbage was dumped well away from this spot. These items had been set aside. They were of greater value than the piles Butler had stacked up elsewhere. How had he obtained a pail of mechanic's grease? The new barrel? Those wheels? He may have stolen them, then left them out in the weather to age them, as a means to disguise them, so he could sell them later. What did he intend to do with a piece of railroad track?

More importantly, why was one end covered in blood? Butler didn't use this spot to slaughter a chicken. There would have been feathers. No one struck an iron rail with a hand ax. A wooden chopping block threw no sparks or iron splinters that invariably aimed for one's eye. The pigs being slaughtered at this time of year were hung up first, not killed on the ground. Something else had been killed here.

She stood and looked around. Ransom said his father had been flush lately. Everyone was, with the influx of workers. He was surely selling things, like everyone else. But what was he selling that involved this much blood?

The silence was broken by the rhythmic clang of the pile driver back in town. She envisioned Katrina hurrying along the road. She hoped the normally composed woman would pretend nothing was wrong and slow her steps so it looked like she was taking in the sights, instead of hurrying to alert her husband. It's what Carrie would do. She hoped Howard Clowe wouldn't intercept Katrina. She hoped Katrina had no trouble finding Del. She hoped Del would come right away. He'd understand what puzzled her about this scene.

She stared at the cut off end of track. The steel had twisted upward when it was cut apart. The cut end had a wicked, jagged edge. She leaned closer, peering at the wash of blood on iron, and at the tiny dab of skin that glued shafts of dark hair into place.

* * *

Perhaps it was the combination of stressors Carrie knew to be roiling about under Del Morgan's otherwise neutral façade, combined with the sight of the 'bits' she pointed out, that caused him to turn away and heave the contents of his stomach into the bushes. She waited patiently as he leaned against a sapling for a moment, sweating, and getting his breath under control. Then he spit several times and wiped his mouth with his handkerchief before turning to look again at the bloody piece of rail.

"And you think what?" he said in a tight voice. A light sweat glistened on his pale forehead.

"I think a person struck their head on the end of this rail. The impact caused a significant injury, hence all the blood. I'm willing to bet the shape of Martin Evans' head wound matches the end of this rail. Worley's already sent him to Saugerties, but I can wire the undertakers and ask them to send a sample of hair, so we can compare the two. I'll collect this bit of scalp—oops, sorry—"

Morgan spun away to vomit again. Carrie pressed her lips together and waited. Either she must learn to cease the gory descriptions of her trade, or he must learn to conquer his queasiness.

"I'll take some pictures of all this when Katrina gets here," she resumed when he had recovered. This time, he stood with his back to her and stared out over the Duncan's placid, gray surface. He nodded, but didn't say anything.

"I can develop them this afternoon," Carrie went on, reciting a list like he often did. "I'll wire the Saugerties undertaker. I have to tell Art Worley. The sample will come to him."

Morgan nodded, addressing the water. "Do you know where Butler is now? Or Ransom?"

"Katrina and I saw Mr. Butler getting a ride to town on the Chester's garbage cart. Where does he usually buy his hooch? You'll most likely find him there."

Morgan shrugged without turning. "He'll be easy enough to find. But I want the boy. Tom said the kid lost his raft. He and I should go looking for it."

Chapter Fifteen

arrie walked with Morgan back to the main part of the dump. They met Katrina on the road, lugging Carrie's oak-legged tripod under one arm, the Star View camera by its leather strap, and a small bottle of cider. She greeted them cheerfully, puffing for breath, and scrutinized her husband's pallid face.

"I thought I'd make it look like I was on a picnic," she said, handing the jug to Morgan. "But it looks like you might really need this."

Morgan took the bottle and walked a few paces away. He took a swig, swished it around his mouth, then spat quietly into the bushes. Carrie gave Katrina a weak smile and took the camera equipment. They made plans to reconvene at the house after Morgan found Ransom. She watched as Katrina slid her arm under her husband's elbow and patted it sympathetically. They started back together.

I'm such a fool, she thought. The miserable idea haunted her as she picked her way back through the dump, back along the creek, and through the underbrush to Butler's hidden yard. *They are such good people!* How could she even think of getting away with an affair? A sickening bolus of guilt threatened to make her spill her guts, just like Morgan, but not with disgust over human remains. Her self-loathing served that purpose.

What have we done?

She was angry with herself. She *liked* Katrina Morgan. The woman was nothing but kind to her, competent and compassionate to everyone else. Morgan was a fine man with a good future and a great deal to lose. She felt like a lackey, left behind to do a grubby task, while he walked away with his wife, acting as if he wasn't unfaithful.

Resigned to photograph this evidence with the same expertise as she used to lay out her cadavers, she put on her grim face. She set up the tripod, mounted the camera, and began the adjustments.

Concentrating on the work helped her to simmer down. She took her time adjusting, repositioning, calculating the light, framing. She had to be careful. If she were photographing a deceased back in Nanuet, or even here, in Worley's funeral parlor, she'd have the luxury of taking a number of shots. She hadn't thought to tell Katrina to retrieve the box of dry plates from the pantry. She only had one glass plate loaded into the camera. She held her breath, opened the lens cap, exposed the plate to the grisly bits of Martin Evans' head, and counted to thirty before covering the lens again. The one shot would have to do.

She pulled a kerchief from her skirt pocket, inserted her fingers into the material, and gently pried the scrap of scalp and its fringe of hairs from the metal. She stopped herself from bringing up the image of Morgan being sick in the bushes as she folded the remains into the cloth. She remembered Katrina's ministering to her ill husband. Like Thomas Bale, her comforting came naturally. Anger threatened to well up again. She wanted to be a comfort to Del, and to Ransom, even to Katrina. Instead, she was engrossed with human remains. She stuffed the kerchief in her pocket.

She unscrewed the camera from its mount and was retracting the legs of the tripod when she heard drunken singing coming from the dump. She froze, then swore. Butler had returned.

She'd forgotten about him. She'd been wrapped up in her tangled sentiments, concentrating on the picture. Now, she was trapped here, with the gore from a human being at her feet and her heavy equipment weighing down her flight.

How was she to justify her presence? Should she saunter along the river bank, pretending to be out on a stroll, taking photographs? That wouldn't work. This stretch of creek was ugly, strewn with refuse, and with no foliage this late in the fall, there was no lovely bucolic scenery. And, she'd be coming from Butler's stash of contraband—if that's what these things hidden in the weeds truly were. He'd be suspicious if she came from that direction, to say the least. Then what would she do?

The drunken singing came closer.

Carrie grabbed up the equipment and flung herself through the weeds. She pushed past stalks of dead burdocks as tall as herself, and spun around behind a giant cottonwood. The tree hid her and the equipment, but the deeply grooved bark scrubbed against her jacket, making a harsh sound. She heard Butler enter his secondary yard. Footsteps on dry grass. His tune became interspersed with pauses and grunts. He was moving something that took a lot of effort.

Did we leave any tracks? Does he see them? She peeked around the tree.

He huffed and sang as he dragged loops of heavy chain into the yard. He dropped them into the bushes. The links rattled to the ground, leaving a swatch of rust across his sleeves. Carrie pulled back behind the tree. When the singing stopped, she risked another look.

He was much closer, bent over near the railroad track. Carrie winced at the hairy cleavage where his shirt pulled up, and his trousers pulled down. Butler straightened and looked around, swaying a little.

"Goddamn you," he muttered.

Just before he turned his head in her direction, she darted back behind the tree and held her breath, hoping he was too inebriated to recognize the imprints of the tripod's pointed metal feet, or the swath she'd trampled through the burdocks.

A cold chill washed over her. She expected Butler to grab her from her hiding place any second. He didn't. Instead, she remained rigid for the next half hour, peeping out, while Butler used his own shirt, soaked with creek water, to wash away the blood from the rail. He made several trips, dropping the shirt in the creek, hauling it up, and wringing it out over the track. He went down on one knee and scrubbed, then stood and kicked dirt and dead leaves over the saturated ground.

Carrie watched the fishy white skin of Butler's neck and shoulders pucker with cold where his filthy union suit gaped. He was soaked when he finally turned and walked back to his hut. He carried his ragged shirt, with his suspenders straining to hold up his sodden pants. He was no longer stumbling drunk.

She crept out of her hiding place and examined the rail. There was no longer a gory mess to indicate a possible death scene. She had the only evidence of it on a frail glass plate in her camera.

Why had Butler washed it away? He put in a great deal of effort and discomfort—a combination he didn't seem the type to endure—to hide the place where someone had hit their head and died. He had not hesitated, not gone to his hut and come back with a rag, but had taken off his shirt, in November no less, and washed away the blood. And she was alone with that knowledge and with him nearby. She had no choice. She had to get away.

She couldn't go through the dump. To avoid Butler, the only choice was to bushwhack up the bank and get to the road without making a lot of noise. The heavy tripod would have to stay, but she couldn't risk leaving the camera and its one glass plate negative behind.

She set out, hoisting her skirt over her knees in order to climb over the dense weeds and branches. Earlier, she'd descended the same bank into the dump, using the established paths. She hadn't realized how steep the bank was. Here in the bushes, the incline was sharp, not mashed down from traffic or shored up by garbage or cut into steps. She had to climb hand over hand. She rested the camera above her as she hoisted herself up the bank, cringing as she set the polished oak box down in the dirt. Her skirt became scuffed and covered with leaf litter. Despite the chilly weather, she was sweating with exertion and fear that the single precious piece of glass in the camera would jostle and break. Eventually, she saw the vegetation clearing several yards ahead where the road opened up. She wasn't far from the entrance to the dump. She hoped Butler had retreated into his house and that he was indulging in another bottle of rotgut.

A wagon approached from the west, just beyond the last screen of trees and bushes. She stayed hidden as it drew near. It was driven by a man holding the reins of a single horse. He wasn't in a hurry; the horse walked at leisure. The wagon was a flat bed, used to transport lumber, beer, or ice blocks. Loading and unloading was a simple matter of pushing or rolling the freight on and off the flat surface. Except this wagon didn't carry logs or blocks or barrels. Her jaw dropped in astonishment.

The casket of Martin Evans rode in the back. And Bill Bemis sat next to it, legs dangling off, scribbling in his reporter's notebook.

Chapter Sixteen

Carrie bolted from the weeds, hailed them desperately, and the startled driver pulled the horse to a stop. Like everyone else in Duncan County that fall, the teamster was more than happy to stop for a passenger and another coin for his trouble.

She climbed into the bed next to Bemis and they bounced back into town, exchanging incredulities about the circumstance.

"What are you doing with Evans' casket?"

"Writing an article, what else? What are you doing with burrs in your hair?"

Carrie reached up. That maddening itch in her scalp was, in fact, a wad of burdock seeds. She pulled at them, and discovered the impossibly tangled mess was going to need more than just fingers to fix. She snugged her camera securely between her hip and Bemis's.

"I was taking pictures. I got turned around and lost. I had to climb out of a ditch."

"Not buying that for a second," Bemis said, and tugged a ball of prickers from her hair. "Pictures of what?"

"Nothing—ouch! —that would interest you." Carrie laughed and stopped him from pulling more of her hair. He gave her camera a sly look.

"There is no doubt something tantalizing on that glass. Another body in the woods?"

Anything anyone did was a potential story for Bill Bemis, especially her. She loved her friend, but instinctively held back her discovery. If she were right about the wound matching the rail, she and Morgan had found the place where Evans died. But no one could pick up a length of railroad track and wield it. It was the other way around. Evans had fallen backward onto the track and hit his head.

So, was it a deliberate act or an accident?

Morgan would not appreciate her indiscretion if she told Bemis anything. She was good for changing the subject. "What are you doing with Evans' casket?" she repeated.

"Ah, well, in my pursuit of the details about the good man's untimely death, and given the reticence of our esteemed sheriff, last night, I decided to escort the remains down to Saugerties. I thought I'd interview the man's widow today. Or his associates. Or his priest, if need be. I figured I'd cover the funeral, too, while I was there. Those affairs can be quite enlightening. Boring, but lots to describe. Plus, one can tell a great deal about a person's character according to who shows up—and who doesn't.

"So, my friend and I," and here he reached back and patted the casket, "disembarked from the train, and I begged a ride with the hearse driver who came to pick him up. We got to Balonshere's funeral parlor—do you know it? No? Anyway, the hearse pulls up, and Mr. Balonshere comes out the back door, shaking his head.

"'What?' the driver says.

"'It's been refused,' Balonshere says."

"Refused?" Carrie asked, surprised.

"Refused."

Bemis, who smiled throughout the whole story, cracked a wider grin. "The wife refused the 'package'! Not only that, the Widow Evans was waiting on the front steps of the funeral home. She. Was. Enraged. She came storming around the back to where we parked, her dress aflutter and her hat practically flying off her head. She wasn't wearing widow's weeds, for sure. Just the usual attire, but a lot richer. She doesn't say a word to any of us, but stomped up to the wagon, rears back her head, and spits a gob on the casket!"

"Ugh!" Carrie shuddered.

"We had to turn around and bring Evans back to the train station, load him up, and cart him back here. Can you imagine?"

"Good lord. Why would she do that?" Carrie glanced back at the casket, expecting to see a streak of phlegm. Caskets containing embalmed cadavers were shipped regularly to be interred in family plots, or cemeteries in their hometowns, or any place of their choosing. *Lisbon & Shay* had shipped plenty of bodies, but had never had one rejected. The idea struck her as horrific, then funny, then scandalous.

Grinning wolfishly, Bemis went on. "Why, indeed! I had no time to pursue the interview with the widow. She took off without a word, and I needed to catch a ride back with the hearse driver. But boy, did he have an earful for me!

"Balonshere's has been the mortician of the upper class in and around Saugerties for a number of years, and while Mr. Balonshere—like all you undertakers—practices muteness like a virtue, his hearse driver had no such compunction, and my tip to him was equitably generous."

"Oh, Bill, you're impossible," Carrie tutted. The red-haired, heavily freckled reporter was a downright pest when it came to obtaining stories. "What did he have to say?"

Bemis grinned in a manner that stretched the freckles on his face and made his ears fan outward when hilarity overtook him. This was a look he couldn't stop when he had a lascivious story to tell.

"Well, it is widely known that Mister and Missus Martin Evans were at odds with each other. And by 'at odds,' the hearse driver intimated, Evans never went home. He stayed at his club, went to his office, or his job site, or a hotel. The house on Piedmont Street was her domain, as is often the case, and he left her to it. My verbose informant said that Evans married up, but the couple didn't care for each other, just the status and the wealth one brought to the other."

"Did your man say *why* she disliked him so much that she'd spit on his casket?"

"Not outright. But he did beat around the proverbial bush about the gossip he attained as a chauffeur for Evans' club. Apparently—my luck—the man hired out his hearse by day, and drove a cab by night."

"How enterprising. And why not? We don't do funerals at night," Carrie said with a reasonable shrug. Her profession didn't need to perpetuate any more spectral images. "No one wants to see a hearse in the streets after dark."

Bemis's freckled ears flared again. "And our hearse-driving cabbie was endowed with a prodigiously acute memory. He said Evans—in his cups, no doubt—groused about being denied his carnal due, if you catch my meaning. His usual destination after dinner and drinks was a series of brothels for which, my cabbie friend believes, Mr. Evans may have bestowed upon Mrs. Evans the unfortunate gift of 'a social disease.' You can understand the rage and the humiliation Mrs. Evans may have experienced as a result of seeking a cure—or not, as the case may be.

"So, with that information, I didn't need to interview the Missus, and it would not be likely that she'd grant me an audience. I felt it necessary to be present at this end." Bemis's freckled fingers sprang from his fist as he ticked off his relationship with Evans. "I was at the scene when the body was discovered, when it was embalmed, when it was shipped, and when it was rejected by the next of kin! Now I'm going to see what Worley does when he gets it back! The story's up here anyway. Evans died up here. It'll run in the *Duncan Herald,* and I can sell it to the downstate presses, as well."

"I can't believe Evans' wife refused the body. What are we supposed to do with him?"

"Balonshere handed papers to the driver, and the driver stapled them to the casket. I suppose Worley will open the envelope and get instructions."

Carrie shared Bemis's anticipation of Worley's reaction when they arrived at the undertaker's home. She also anticipated his jaded expression when she asked him to pry open the casket so she could snip a lock of Evan's hair. *At least there is no delay in getting a matching sample.*

Traffic slowed as they entered Main Street, given the volume of vehicles coming and going. Their wagon drew plenty of stares and raised eyebrows. She saw several people tap their companions and point to her. She wondered what she looked like. The implied lover of the incumbent sheriff, a widow not even dressed in half-mourning, legs dangling off the back of a cart bearing a casket, with burdocks in her hair, and seated next to yet another man who was not her relative.

The wagon stopped under a portico on one side of Worley's house, and the slender mortician greeted them at the side door. As soon as he recognized the casket, his gaunt face and lidded eyes looked even more disdainful than ever. The look didn't change when it was extended to Carrie and her tangled hair. The freight driver earned another coin by helping Worley and Bemis maneuver the casket onto Worley's coffin truck. They wheeled it into the formal parlor and parked it.

Worley hummed with disgust when he pulled the stapled envelope from the casket's polished wood. The metal spikes had left punctures. He pulled out a sheaf of paper and read to himself, then flicked his eyes upward at his audience. Bemis leaned forward expectantly.

Carrie spoke first. "Well?"

"I am first and foremost relieved that Mr. Evans is not to be considered abandoned property," Worley said dryly. "He is, however, my responsibility at this point. His next of kin has rejected the remains and all responsibility for its burial."

Bemis said. "Can she do that?"

Carrie and Worley nodded their heads in unison. "He's freight," Carrie said. "Anyone can reject freight."

Bemis shook his head, but his eyebrows rose and he asked with an impish grin, "Does Mrs. Evans have a first name? My gabby cabby didn't know it."

"She does," Worley said. "Annetta Evans." He spelled it for Bemis, ensuring her name and baseborn behavior made the papers. Carrie cleared her throat, but didn't catch Worley's eye. Bemis's source wouldn't be known, nor would she disclose Worley's retaliatory breach of a client's name. The spiteful woman dropped an unwanted corpse on him; he'd drop her name in the papers.

"She has, however, thrown me a small bone." Worley held the letter and a check between his elegant fingers. "This document indicates there is a family crypt in Bitter Hay. Her family. The Wilson crypt. We are to inter Mr. Evans there."

Carrie knew of the tiny crossroads hamlet, but had never been there. It was north of Hope Bridge, along the network of backroads Bale had mentioned earlier today. *Didn't he say something about Eddie passing through that little town?* In any case, every town and hamlet, even large farms, had cemeteries or family plots. It was curious that Evans had family up here and, that family owned a crypt, no less.

"I wonder if I might send you to inquire about the whereabouts of this tomb, Mrs. Lisbon?" Worley's question caught her by surprise. "I have an appointment to lay out Silas Preston at his home this afternoon. He passed away this morning."

Carrie hesitated. For some, crypts were revered places, but they weren't her preferred resting place. Generally made of stone, with heavy iron doors, a crypt spoke of wealth and preeminence, not comfort. A nice, clean grave, covered in grass or creeping thyme, was more to her liking than a dank and spidery tomb with its shelves of coffins. A trip alone on an unknown road, to an unknown hamlet in search of an obscure tomb, and then a return trip, possibly after dark, wasn't to her liking either.

But, an awkward house guest, the urgency of getting Mr. Evans to his final resting place, and keeping Worley on good terms swayed her.

"All right. I can," she said. "It's just past noon, isn't it? I may be able to get there and back before it's too dark. Can you go with me, Bill?"

Bemis shook his head. "Much as I believe in the chivalry of the proposition, Mrs. Lisbon, I need to file this *tout de suite* in order to get it into the papers tomorrow. This is too extraordinary a story."

Carrie shot him a frustrated look. His decline meant she had to chat with a hired driver the entire afternoon.

"Fine," she said, and turned to Worley. "I'll see to this. Can you arrange a carriage for me?"

Worley acknowledged her request with another hum. He took a ring of keys from his desk drawer. All skeleton keys of various lengths, widths, and ornamentation. "These are spares I've collected over the years. One of them might open the tomb. If you can find the minister of the church up there, he may have a key as well. The Widow Evans didn't send one."

Carrie took the keys and gave him a resolute look. "I can be ready to go in about an hour." She made an embarrassed motion at the mess of hair and burrs. She hadn't let go of the camera and its one glass plate. "I just need to drop off my things and fix my hair."

Chapter Seventeen

Carrie almost didn't recognize her own kitchen. The table was stacked with washed and dried bowls, plates, and silverware. Canisters of flour and sugar were arranged on a shelf next to the stove, where they were more readily accessible to the cook. The curtains on the windows fluffed out with rearranged folds.

Katrina handed her a fresh cup of coffee as soon as she came in, assessed the condition of her hair, and insisted Carrie sit so she could address the problem. Using her own brush and comb, Katrina went to work. Every once in a while, a single strand of hair was yanked out with a pinprick of pain, but the tresses were cleaned and smooth in no time.

Carrie had to admit, having someone run their fingers through her hair was surprisingly relaxing. Even as her conscience shrieked, '*She's your lover's wife!*' her shoulders relaxed, her eyes closed, and her scalp warmed. Katrina lifted the dark hair up over Carrie's head, wound it into a bun, and secured it with pins. Her touch was light and sure, and the resulting volume was flattering.

Of course, she can fix hair better than I can. The lazily drifting thought carried no malice. Just an acknowledgement of Katrina's competence as compared to hers.

A rich, gravied combination of potatoes, carrots, and marbled beef bubbled in a pot on the stove. Another example of Katrina's mastery of the domestic arts. Carrie huffed a laugh at herself when Katrina provided her with a bowl. She hadn't given a thought to making some sort of provisions for food, now that she had a house guest.

"I put that together when Del and I came back," Katrina said. "I cook when I'm nervous."

"I've noticed."

While she ate, she thought about the cause of Katrina's continued food production and house cleaning. She spooned the last morsel from her bowl, cleared her throat, and broached a delicate subject.

"Katrina, does Eddie have a girlfriend, or a sweetheart?" She implied, of course, that perhaps, Eddie and a young lady were holed up somewhere, in a love nest, or, maybe, they'd run off to be married. The boy *was* sixteen, competent, from a good family, tall and handsome. Old enough for all sorts of scenarios involving a girl. It may be that they needed to consider the possibility of Eddie and a young lady succumbing to desire before a marriage.

Katrina inhaled sharply and set down her bowl. "Oh, dear. I hadn't thought of that." Without Carrie's hair or another pot of stew to fix, her idle fingers began fluttering and clasping at each other. "I know he's visited a young lady in Duncan. Sarah Paine. She's a sweet girl. A *nice* girl. Eddie would never dream of doing anything untoward, nor would she."

The firm grip Katrina held on the niceties of youth was too naïve for Carrie. She had Bemis's story of Evans' infidelity fresh in her mind—*as well as her own!* — but if it gave this mother some peace about her missing son's character, then let her have it.

"Maybe you could call Sarah, or wire her. Ask her if Eddie has come by today or yesterday. We should at least ask about that."

They discussed how Katrina could use Sav's account at the post office to send a telegram. It wasn't ideal. Once Katrina's message was received at the telegrapher's office, it had to be hand-delivered by a courier carrying a handful of other messages destined for recipients in the general direction of the Paine's house. The courier would have to wait while the note was read by the Paines on their doorstep, then wait some more while they penned a reply. Running or riding a bicycle, the courier would deliver the rest of his messages, collect *those* responses, then hoof it back to the telegraph office with the assorted replies. They might have to wait all day for a response.

On the other hand, she could use Morgan's 'phone at Clevinger's. Although the network of drooping telephone wires was often unreliable, and the persistent static crackled painfully in one's ear, often obscuring the conversation, Katrina could get an answer from the Paines that would relieve her fears in an instant. She'd have to exchange the privacy of a telegram for the ears of numerous busybodies listening in. That's *if* the Paine's owned a telephone.

Katrina rose from the table and made her way toward the cooking pots. There was no more room in the kitchen for more food. Carrie made a decision.

"I have to run an errand this afternoon for Mr. Worley. He needs to know the condition of a crypt for an unexpected burial in Bitter Hay. I'd like you to ride up there with me. It will give you something to do while we wait. Let's try to 'phone the Paines, and if that doesn't work, we'll send a wire."

They had cleaned up the kitchen and prepared for the outing when the front bell tinkled on its curly wire. Carrie found Del Morgan on the stoop. Katrina's hands reached earnestly for her husband's, and he took them up.

Morgan shook his head in answer to his wife's unspoken question. Katrina pressed her fist to her mouth, suppressing a grimace.

Morgan looked at Carrie over Katrina's head. "If you don't mind, Mrs. Lisbon, I have young Ransom with me. I thought he might get a bite to eat and spend some time in Tom's shop this afternoon."

Ransom stepped into the hallway at Morgan's summons. Raggedly dressed, he greeted the women with a shy nod and shuffled his bare feet.

Still no shoes? Carrie thought angrily. She'd remedy that today, this minute before she left. *Damn, the carriage will be here soon. I won't have time.*

"Where are this young man's shoes?" Katrina asked, and ushered Ransom into the kitchen. Carrie and Morgan followed, watching her clattering about with bowls and stew and milk.

"I got 'em at my house, ma'am," Ransom offered, then hung his head. "They ain't likely to fit, though, come to think of it. Been a while since I wore 'em."

"Well, we'll take care of that," Katrina said briskly. "Del, Carrie needs to get to a crypt in Bitter Hay this afternoon and I was to go with her, but can you go instead? Ransom can stay with me. I'll get him decently shod for winter. I'm going to call Sarah Paine—Eddie's sweetheart. It was Carrie's idea. Maybe Sarah's heard from Eddie."

Ransom balked at the handout with a sullen look and started to cross his arms. Katrina countered with a shaken finger. "I believe Mr. Bale has put you to work? Then you'll work off the shoes we're going to buy this afternoon. I'll hear no more about it."

"Yes, ma'am," Ransom said, and turned his attention to the brimming bowl in front of him. He dove into the stew with a singular focus, wasting no time in finishing his portion. Katrina became a whirlwind in the small kitchen space, quickly whipping eggs, milk, and flour together and pouring perfect circles of batter onto a griddle. Carrie was stunned that golden pancakes were produced within three minutes. She would have taken half an hour to find the ingredients, and burned at least half of them, if she'd been inclined to make them at all.

Del accepted a bowl of stew from his wife. He ate standing. The kitchen was crowded. Carrie kept her distance, staking out a place in the doorway of her suite. Katrina chattered away; Morgan smiled and nodded. When Ransom finished the last bite of a substantial stack of pancakes, Katrina made plans for him to draw water for a bath.

"In the middle of the day?" Ransom protested.

Katrina handed him a bucket and prodded him out the back door toward the well pump in the yard. She followed. Before the door shut completely, they heard her respond, "…and a haircut…"

Morgan turned to Carrie. The scent of clean sweat and warm tobacco drifted off him in a puff. She kept her face neutral, although she wanted to lean forward and inhale deeply.

"Ransom and I walked downstream this morning, looking for his raft. The River Road runs fairly close to the water. We found it about two miles downstream. The creek gets narrow there. It got hung up on the rocks and ledges. Ransom carved his initials in the wood, otherwise it could have been anybody's. I wished I had your camera, Mrs. Lisbon. There was more there that I wanted to get a picture of."

"What more?"

"Blood. All over it. Some had washed off, where water sloshed on it, but for the most part, it looked like someone had slaughtered a pig."

Carrie stared at him, thinking about the railroad track, the blood, the nearby raft. "Ransom kept his raft down by the bridge. Evans was killed on the rail. Someone took the raft, poled it upstream, loaded him onto it, then dumped him at the bottom of the bridge."

"That's what I was thinking. Then the raft was floated downstream to get rid of it."

"Surely someone would have seen all that happening."

Morgan shook his head. "Butler was probably dead drunk. There was no moon. And it was Hallowe'en, remember? There were a lot of noisemakers. Carousing. Fireworks. People yelling all night. It was easy to slip by."

Carrie flushed and looked away, feeling intimate muscles tighten at the memory of their encounter that very night. *It* had *been easy to slip by!* She remembered being grateful for the deep darkness and the commotion from revelers that hid Morgan's entrance to her house. *He dares to bring it up? In broad daylight, and Katrina within earshot?*

The sound of the pump handle going up and down came to them from out in the yard. They heard Katrina say "…one more bucket…"

He didn't bring it up. I just connected the two events. It's the guilt. I won't make a fool of her!

"I also found a poster." Morgan went on. "One of mine. It was caught in some weeds, right next to the shore. About a mile or so up, close to the road. I fished it out. It flattened out again, but I could still see where it had been wadded up and thrown away."

Carrie waited. The plummeting sensation she'd felt at Mrs. Lamont's returned. She could see he was bothered about what he found. He was thinking about something dreadful—something about Eddie.

"Someone pulled it off a wall and threw it in the creek," she said. "Someone who doesn't want you to be sheriff."

He shook his head slightly. "There were no torn edges. There was no glue sticking it together. It wasn't torn off."

"Maybe he dropped one."

Again, Morgan shook his head. She couldn't help but think *he should be sharing this fear and grief with his wife.*

"Eddie kept them in a saddle bag, in a pasteboard folder, with a string around it."

"Okay, so maybe someone asked him for a poster, then wadded it up and threw it away."

"Sure," Morgan said. "That's possible. But I can't shake a really bad feeling about this."

"Do you still have it? Maybe it was misprinted?"

Morgan pulled a damp, folded paper from his back pocket. He opened it, smoothed it out. It wasn't misprinted.

"If there had been an error, Eddie would have fixed it and hung it anyway. He isn't wasteful."

"What's the bad feeling?"

"We haven't seen that man Wheeler since Halloween. The last time anyone saw Eddie was Halloween. I wonder why neither of them are around."

Carrie looked at him skeptically. "You're worried about him, Del," she said, risking his name in order to counter his fear. "You're thinking the worst. Didn't you say Wheeler associates with Evans, or Maxwell. He wouldn't have anything to do with your campaign." If there was a possibility that the shady character had caused Eddie any harm, she didn't want to say it out loud.

Morgan scrubbed a hand over his cheeks and chin. He nodded, and the smile he produced was more of a grimace. Katrina and Ransom stepped back into the kitchen, lugging water buckets and chattering like house wrens. Morgan took the buckets from his wife and set them by the stove. Ransom fetched the wash tub from its hook outside the kitchen door.

"Here's another thing we found," Morgan said, when Ransom returned. The boy beamed in anticipation. Morgan dipped into his vest pocket, pulled something out, and opened his hand. Everyone leaned in to see.

Carrie gaped. "Is that Evans' key? Where on earth did you find it?"

"Young Ransom, here, the little magpie, found it at the dump. On the riverbank."

"It was just lying in the gravel!" Ransom piped in, proudly.

"I don't know if this is Evans' key," Morgan said, "but—"

"—what a coincidence." Carrie finished his sentence.

She plucked the key from his hand and examined it closely. It was short, brass, and gray with a slightly green patina. Worn, old, only as long as her little finger, but stout and heavy. The shaft was hollow and embossed with two decorative rings. The oval handle was molded with willow branches that curved together, meeting in the center over the letter W. She hefted it and looked at Morgan with a humorous shake of her head.

"This is an *amazing* coincidence."

"If we only knew what it fits."

"I know what it fits," she said, and smiled widely. "It's a crypt key."

Chapter Eighteen

"Would you mind putting on your undertaker's jacket?" Morgan asked before they left. "It will look better if I'm escorting the undertaker, not you."

In her bedroom, Carrie saw that Katrina had made the bed and neatly folded all her clothes. The chamber pot was emptied, the bureau dustless. Tiny alterations that showed nervous energy extended to freshening her negligent host's quarters.

She changed into her work ensemble, an ivory blouse and a charcoal woolen skirt. Her sweater and knitted scarf were a soft dove gray. She pinned on a black felt hat, the same style as her well-worn straw boater, and checked her reflection in the mirror, noting Katrina had polished that, too. She considered her undertaker's bag. *May as well go for the full ruse.* She dropped Worley's keys into it, in case she was badly mistaken about the Wilson crypt key. She stepped into the hallway and witnessed the Morgans saying their good-byes, assuring each other that they'd hear from Eddie today. To counteract the lurch in her heart that stemmed from a sudden longing for her own husband, she concentrated on pulling on a pair of gloves that once belonged to Phee. They were too big, but tremendously warm.

When she and Morgan closed the door on Ransom and Katrina, the two had resumed planning their shopping trip, still jabbering like birds on a wire. The child was eager for his haircut after Katrina told him to go use Tom Bale's whetstone to sharpen the scissors while the bath water heated. The suspicious resentment he showed to Carrie and Morgan melted away with Katrina.

The young man who delivered the horse and trap to Carrie's door was more than happy to take a coin from Morgan and abdicate his job as driver. He'd use his unexpected free time to make money elsewhere. Carrie mounted the carriage and arranged her skirt over her knees on the upholstered seat. The noise on her street was relatively subdued, save for the clatter of a cider press a few doors down. Morgan got on from the other side, took up the reins, and they set off.

He had to sit in the center to manage the horse. Carrie kept her trade bag on her lap. Their proximity to each other was acceptable for two people in a light trap. They passed several wagons on the road, acknowledging each driver with a nod or a wave. Regardless, there would no doubt be talk of this excursion. Talk that would most likely make its way into Clowe's campaign.

Carrie and Sav lived on North Street, on the west end of town. Its terminus was one block south, where it met Main. It ran for several miles in the opposite direction, meandering through pastureland and scattered woodlots, eventually turning west, and intersecting the Shunpike at an oblique angle.

Back when the Turnpike used to charge travelers every few miles for maintenance, the Shunpike was created and named by those who wished to avoid the tolls. It traveled a more or less parallel route that was not nearly as well maintained. Navigable, yes, but as their horse and buggy bounced eastward over stones and ruts, Carrie thought there was no substitute for the comfort of a graded road.

Nearly an hour later, they were relieved of the bumpy ride when the narrow Shunpike intersected River Road. Morgan turned the horse north for a mile or more, then west again onto Tannin Road, another laneway that was surprisingly wide and level. They passed by more woodlots, stubble fields and depleted orchards, by several redolent barns with lowing cows and gangs of boys loading corn cribs. They pointed out election posters. Sometimes it was Clowe's image defaced with pointed teeth and screwy eyes, sometimes it was Morgan's.

The time passed with discussion. Carrie told Morgan about Maxwell's aborted telegram and her theory about its nature.

"You snooped through the postmaster's telegrams?"

"You know I snoop."

She described Butler washing away the blood from the rail with his shirt, and making her own getaway with the single photograph of the scene.

"I'll question him again as soon as I get back," Morgan said.

"Don't tell him it was me who saw him."

"I don't—and I never will—tell anyone anything about you."

She put her gloved hand over Morgans in a moment of appreciation, murmuring, "thank you." The gesture caused their eyes to lock. This was not a lover's moment, laden with hot desire. This was a heartfelt appreciation between companions, a mutual agreement acknowledged and kept.

She pulled back her hand and described what Bemis had told her about Evans' body being rejected by his bitter widow. Morgan shook his head and grimaced at the woman's refusal to take her husband's body back.

"How often does that happen?"

"I've been in this business a long time. I've heard of it, but it's rare." She told him about Bemis's encounter with the talebearing cabbie/hearse driver, and the contentious nature of the Evans' union.

Tannin Road cut through a glade of paper birches, bright white in the weak afternoon sun. The hamlet of Bitter Hay appeared on the other side. A row of clapboard houses lined the street, with multiple barns and outbuildings clustered behind them. A miller's waterwheel chugged somewhere off in the distance. Chickens chased each other across the road.

Morgan nodded to people as they passed, muttering that he really should stop and greet them properly, but he kept on, passing through the little town and maneuvering the horse and carriage into the graveyard farther on. The laneway into the cemetery had a strip of dry and colorless turf between each wheel track. Grass and weeds had been trimmed away from the stones. Remembrance flowers had been left to fade and wilt on top of grassy mounds.

The carriage moved almost soundlessly past immense cedars, dried hydrangeas, granite monuments, and carved stones. They passed the dump pile, heaped with clippings, spent flowers, and trimmed sticks. The careful groundskeeping fell away as the horse walked on two long divots in the ground, a ghostly remnant of the lane. They crept deeper into the old part, where the gravestones leaned, their inscriptions mere dimples, inscribed when the land was young. And here, they found the crypt, dug into the base of a hill. Morgan pulled to a stop, dropped an iron horse tether to the ground, and tied a lead rope to the horse's collar. They approached the tomb on foot.

Limestone blocks emerged from the slope, forming the sides and the front of the structure. Shaggy grass tumbled over the mounded roof. The stone lintel over the double doors was carved with a name. Wilson.

They exchanged glances. Morgan shrugged and took a step forward, then stopped abruptly. With an outstretched hand, he held Carrie back and pointed to a worn footpath that led to the crypt's door.

November's weeds were dried and tall, not yet flattened and mashed from winter's heavy snows. The entire neglected hillside was covered with unruly vegetation from the laneway to the top of the crypt. All around them, the tips of long-forgotten gravestones were subsumed by overgrowth. No one tended this back corner of the cemetery. No one came here. And yet, Morgan pointed to a worn path that led from the lane to the crypt door.

He bent down, studied the beaten track, straightened, looked all around. He went forward, walking slowly, scanning the ground. Carrie followed. The trail led directly to the limestone pad that served as a front step for the crypt. Brushing aside the thick screen of vegetation, they stopped at the double iron doors.

They were black, rusted around the edges, but sturdy and solid. Ghostly cobwebs flapped gently in the corners. Two blackened iron loops were fastened to the center of each door.

"Why would there be door knockers on a crypt," Morgan asked. "Who's going to answer?"

Carrie couldn't help but laugh. The heavy iron loops were used for pulling the panels open for an interment One simply pushed the doors shut. She saw that the dull surface of one of them bore a shiny patch. She tapped Morgan on the sleeve and raised a palm parallel to the door. The shiny patch was exactly where she intended to place her hand.

Some crypts were secured with a hasp and padlock. This one had a keyhole built into the right-hand door. The keyhole had the same, out- of- place, glossy patina around its perimeter. It had been recently—and frequently—used. Carrie pulled the key Ransom had found from her skirt pocket and cocked an eyebrow at Morgan.

"Go ahead," he said.

The key slipped in without any effort. Carrie paused, satisfied with that tiny success, then turned it slowly. The stout key rotated upward, and the lock came apart with a series of tiny clicks. She pulled the key out, tugged on an iron loop and the heavy door opened without a sound.

"Everything's rusted, but the hinges have been oiled?" Morgan murmured. He peered into the darkness from behind her shoulder.

With the door opened wide, the expected scents of damp stone and cold earth rose to meet them, but Carrie recognized other odors immediately. It was the tang of chemicals. Not embalming chemicals. Judging by the age and condition of the interior, the Wilson family hadn't put anyone in here since before embalming became standardized. And the solvents of that time, creosote and tannins, were easy to distinguish. This was another smell, and she regularly used those chemicals herself.

The waning daylight illuminated the vault and its contents. Carrie and Morgan shot each other the same disbelieving look. She stepped in. He turned away, found a rock, and propped open the door, testing its firmness before following her.

A wooden work table occupied the far wall. Its surface held three oblong glass pans, a wire mesh drying rack, a glass jar with a set of wooden tongs, a print- roller, and a frame. Rags in a small pile lay on the dried dirt floor underneath. Beside a trio of graduated brown jars with glass stoppers and paper labels was a lantern with a red chimney.

Three crypt shelves on the left were sealed with marble slabs bearing a plaque with the decedent's name and the dates of their birth and death. On the right, only the lowest shelf was sealed. The middle shelf held a cigar box and a heavy pasteboard container of six-inch square panes of glass. The upper shelf gaped open and empty, waiting for an occupant.

"What the hell is this?" Morgan said quietly.

"It's the perfect darkroom for developing pictures," Carrie said. "See? Here are the solutions for developing and fixing. Shellac for preserving the plate. And here's a box of blank cabinet cards."

"Why is there a red lantern?"

"The glass plate can't be exposed to any light while it's being developed. But the photographer can't operate in darkness, so we use a red lamp. We can see what we're doing, but the red light doesn't ruin the image on the plate."

"Are there…people in here?"

"Yes, it looks like four have been interred. Three on that side, one over here." She leaned over the darkroom table. The screws that sealed the marble slabs in place were intact. "They haven't been tampered with, thank goodness."

"How does it work?" Morgan asked, making an all-encompassing gesture at the production equipment.

"It's much simpler, now that we've got dry plates. It used to be that we had to prepare the glass on the spot, pour collodion on it, dry it, keep it dark, then expose it. Then, very quickly, develop and fix the image. It was all so cumbersome. You needed a lot of equipment, and a dark room, and an assistant. People drove around with portable dark rooms in special carts. It's much easier in a studio.

"With the dry plates, the glass is already prepared. We just have to mount it into the holder, slip it into the camera, pull the panel, and take off the lens cap. The best part is, once the shot is made, you don't need to develop the negative right away."

"So, you can take the plate somewhere to be made into a photograph?"

"Simply put, yes. The plates have to be prepared in three different baths. Then, they can be used to make a print. All the supplies are here."

She picked up an object that looked like an empty picture frame with hinges and brass wing nuts. "The paper is prepared—using this print frame and another chemical process—and the glass is laid on top. After a few minutes, the photograph appears. That's—"

"—a process. I understand," Morgan interrupted. "Why the hell is it being done in a crypt?"

When she took mortuary photos as one of *Lisbon & Shay's* services back in Nanuet, Carrie had used a closet adjacent to her parlor. In Hope Bridge, she used the cellar at Sav's house. When one of Worley's clients wanted a mortuary photograph, she was grateful for the convenience of the dry plates, so she could just walk home, develop the prints that night, and present them to the family the next day. But why here? One might keep company with the bodies in a crypt if one didn't want one's operation to be discovered. She raised an eyebrow to Morgan, indicating that was the crux of the matter.

They looked around, bumping into each other in the tight space. Carrie browsed the equipment. She lifted the pans and dropped the tongs back into their jar. "Whoever is working here is very well endowed. This is top -of -the -line stuff. The fixatives are expensive. Look at these trays. They're not old baking dishes. They're photographer's pans. Specifically made for this purpose. Not cheap."

"This is supposed to be Evans' wife's family crypt. Was he the one funding this operation? He's rich enough."

"Or has someone, somehow, gotten a key to this place and is just using it for their own purposes, unknown by Evans?"

Morgan shook his head, as if rejecting that theory. "Who has keys to these places?"

"The family, mostly. Sometimes, the church or the local undertaker keeps a key."

"Evans had his key in his shoe. But is he the person who has been up here, developing pictures? Doesn't it take a while to develop a print? And we just spent the better part of two hours getting here. I would think he wouldn't have the time to get away from the bridge to sneak up here to do this."

He edged over to the shelves, glanced at the name plaques, and tightened his lips with determination. He pulled the cigar box from the shelf, turned to the table, and set it down. He flipped open the lid and sucked in a startled breath.

Inside were printed photographs. Black and white, on stiff cabinet cards.

Instead of scenes of buildings, or cameos, or people holding babies in their Sunday best, the photographs showed naked men.

"Oh, Jesus," he muttered.

Carrie shoved in next to him. Her jaw dropped as well. She picked one out and examined it closely. A man stood next to a flouncy bed on which a young lady sprawled. She lay on her belly, naked to the waist, her bloomers cinched with ruffles. Her legs were bent at the knees, her feet in the air and crossed at the ankles, as if she were whimsically engaged with a journal entry. She wasn't engaged with a book.

Morgan snatched the picture away. "You shouldn't see that!"

"Why not?" Carrie snatched it back. "Del, the whole box is full of them!"

"Don't look!" He pulled the box away and turned his back to her.

She laughed, incredulous at his modesty. "I'm aware of what they are. I've even seen them before. They're naughty pictures. *That's* what's being developed here."

Morgan stepped out the open door and set the box on the ground. He crouched next to it, still with his back to her, shielding her from seeing any more. In the better light, he rifled through the photographs.

"Oh my god, I know that man," he murmured. "It's the manager at the Union Bank of Duncan. Holy shit, Carrie. The bedroom is the same." He turned a stricken face to her. "These men have been photographed with a… a girl—a woman—"

He turned back to the box and picked out one more shot. Then he went quite still. Carrie saw him stop breathing. As she took a step forward, she saw the picture in his hand begin to tremble. She crouched next to him.

"Del, what is it?"

He turned a ghostly pale face to her and whispered, "It's Eddie."

Chapter Nineteen

It wasn't just the picture that trembled. Morgan's whole body was rock hard and shivering under Carrie's hand. She tugged the photograph out of his death grip, closed the box, and guided him away from the tomb.

"Are you sure it's him," she asked quietly, studying the picture while Morgan's mouth gaped open and shut like a fish.

She really didn't need to ask. The boy in the picture was Eddie, all right. The photographer had caught him full in the face. He was in the same flouncy bedroom, standing at the foot of the same frilly bed, his shirt unbuttoned, exposing a hairless chest and belly. He clutched the tall bedpost with a look of unfocused surprise. The same girl who engaged with the banker bent over in front of him, her back to the camera, one hand on his naked hip and the other out of sight, presumably busy with another body part. Tears sprang to Carrie's eyes. She turned and saw the same in Morgan's.

"What do I—" he said, gasping for air. "I can't—"

Carrie jumped to his side and pressed his shoulders down so he bent at the waist. "Breathe, Del!"

With his hands on his knees, he took in a great whooping breath. Some color returned to his face. He stood and stumbled backward, panting. He clenched the back of his head.

"I'll destroy this picture for you," Carrie said quickly and made to tear it up. "No one will ever know."

"No!" he whispered hoarsely. "Not yet!" He swallowed, coughed, shook his head. "Not yet. This has to be some kind of blackmail scheme. I'll take it." He held out his hand. It still shook.

"If you have it in your possession, Katrina will find it. Let me destroy it, Del. What good will come from keeping it?"

"I have to find this photographer," Morgan said. His voice becoming tight with growing rage.

"Yes, of course. And his…studio, where these shots were taken. But you can do all that without Eddie's picture. I'll keep it."

When he didn't answer, she tucked the picture into her skirt pocket. Out of sight, certainly, but the image would never be out of mind. She knew Eddie Morgan to be a fine young man, raised by upstanding, law -abiding, productive parents. She thought of him as an independent boy, capable of self-discipline and fortitude. He worked to save up the money to buy his own horse, for chrissake! What was he doing with a prostitute? When was this picture taken? Was this his first time with that activity? *Good lord, what if it was his first time, and he was captured in a picture?* She sucked in a breath. *How awfully embarrassing this was going to be for him.*

Clearly Morgan was angered about the indignity done to his son, but he could just as easily be scandalized by his son's actions. He witnessed Eddie's loss of innocence, an uncomfortable event no parent wanted to actually know about. And, in that moment, someone had taken his picture.

Carrie flipped through the graphic images in the box, focusing on the girls. A second girl was featured at work in the bedroom. This one had dark hair, piled up in a messy bunch of ribbons. In her photograph, she sat on the end of the bed, leaning back on her arms, with her chest arched. Her eyes were closed, her mouth open. She wore a nightie that bunched up around her waist and gaped down to her navel. The man in the picture—a much older man, judging by the paunch and jowls—had been posed in profile.

"There are two girls. Do you recognize them?" she asked carefully, gauging Morgan's breathing. "Is it Sarah Paine?"

Morgan was startled. "Sarah? No! That's not her. Whoever gave you that idea—oh, Katrina must have told you Eddie was sweet on her. She wouldn't—she's not that—no. No, that's not her."

"How about this girl?"

Del winced, too, as he peered at the photograph in the dimming light. He shook his head.

"Do you recognize the room?" Carrie held up another photo, carefully placing her thumb over the lovers. Morgan studied it for a moment.

"No."

"I hate to say it, but we need to see if we recognize any more men in the rest of the pictures. I can try, without you, if you'd like."

Morgan looked around at the remaining daylight, at their carriage with its patient horse nearby. "We could, but I'd rather you took the horse and buggy back home. I'll stay here and see if this sonofabitch comes back tonight. He'll tell me who the girls are. And where these pictures were taken. That'll be faster than identifying and interviewing anyone we recognize." Morgan's teeth clenched along with his fists. "I'll make sure of it."

The photographer might not survive that interview, Carrie thought. "You're thinking of spending the night here? Where? In the crypt?"

"Above it. I can see and hear him when he comes. I'll wait until he's inside. Can you handle a horse?"

"No. I've never driven before. But…well, I suppose I can." She made feeble motions, more like shivers than assertive commands. "You snap the reins to make it go. You pull to make it stop."

"That's it," Morgan said brusquely. "You'll make it back to Hope Bridge after dark, Keep the horse in the center of the road. Take Tannin Road back to River. Turn south and go straight down to Main Street. Find Tom. Send him here. Tell him what's going on. I don't think Bitter Hay has a telegraph. I didn't see any phone lines either."

"All right. Take my scarf. It will be something to keep you from freezing. What do I tell Katrina?"

He squeezed his eyes shut. In pain, again. Then his expression slid into neutrality. "Tell her I've encountered a 'development' in the Evans murder up here. It was unexpected. I'll spend the night, interviewing people. I'll be home in the morning."

"She'll want to know if we've had any word from Eddie."

"Let her know we haven't. She'll be upset and want to come up here herself.

Tell her I want her to remain with you." Morgan's bland expression tightened. "Let's put the photographs back in the crypt and lock up. I need to hurry you out of here. If the photographer comes back, he'll likely do it at dusk. I want you long gone before then."

They placed the box back on the shelf and Carrie glanced around to see if they'd disturbed anything else before pushing shut the noiseless iron doors. The tomb closed with a soft gush of chilled air. She turned the key and stepped away. Morgan stood with his back to the tomb, and his face to the lowering sun. As she stepped to his side, he put out his hand for her to take. She was surprised to find it so cold.

She took him as a lover in May, had fought against a fierce desire for him all summer, until late in August, when they had been flung together by another murder, and their mutual feelings won out. Since then, she'd bedded him twice, once after arranging a trip to Oneida by train, on the pretense of visiting the National Casket factory, and again two nights ago, in a terribly risky caper that brought them to their knees with blind desire. At no time had Delphius Morgan's hands ever been ice cold.

*****

"Stay clear of Clowe," Morgan said, after handing her up. She took the reins and jiggled them timidly. The horse obliged her with a slow walk. As the carriage inched along the lane, she glanced back at Morgan. He stood with his head bowed, one hand gripping the back of his neck.

She successfully steered the horse through the darkening cemetery and back out onto the road toward Bitter Hay. She hoped to pass through the hamlet unnoticed. Someone might notice there was only one passenger in the trap on the return trip. She regretted leaving Morgan behind as much as she regretted wearing her mortician's clothing. It made her distinctive and memorable.

Thankfully, no one hailed her on the length of road through Bitter Hay. As the sun went down, evening chores kept sensible folk inside their houses and barns. Beyond the tiny hamlet, she saw the birch grove and clucked to the horse with more confidence. She just needed to follow Tannin Road a short distance to River Road, turn south, and keep going until she got back to Hope Bridge. Simple. She'd be home in an hour. No more than two.

The evening became colder, and she wished she had a lap robe. Or an umbrella, held vertically to deflect the breeze. No help for it; she'd survive. She thought of Morgan's icy hands and wondered how *he'd* survive the night, out in the open, with only his coat and her scarf.

What on earth have we found? With a self-directed horse and an open road to navigate, Carrie's thoughts turned to analysis. Expensive equipment in a secret dark room, glass plates and chemicals. A collection of photographs that went well beyond French *risqués*. Eddie mixed up in it.

Prominent men using a girl was not unheard of. But, caught on a voyeur's camera? It was inconceivable that any of them would consent to be photographed with a *femme de nuit*, so this was a trap, a scheme of extortion. The girls must be luring men to a bed chamber, where a hidden camera was set up, probably in an adjoining room with a concealed hole in the wall. The photographer was noiseless while the couple was engaged. The resulting photograph could be sent in an envelope indicating a price for silence, otherwise…

How did Eddie Morgan get caught up in this? Was he lured upstairs so someone could blackmail his father? The Morgans weren't well off like the banker. What other possible reason could a blackmailer have when the target had little money? To compel Morgan to drop out of his election race? Her mind automatically damned Howard Clowe. If this was his doing, she'd see to it personally that he was run out of town!

When was Eddie's picture taken? Weeks ago? Two days ago? She tried to remember what Bale had said about Eddie's travels. He was supposed to arrive in Hope Bridge from somewhere north on Hallowe'en night. Thomas found evidence of his having been in some place near Sussex Mill. She and Morgan hadn't passed that town on the way up here. *It must be farther north.*

Thomas had said he'd found Eddie's newly pasted posters on barns before the bridges over the Little Duncan, and the Something-something Creek. She and Morgan hadn't crossed any bridges on their excursion. Had she missed them, or was she on a different road? Evening was coming on fast. For a startled moment, she thought she may have missed a turn.

The sun was no more than a finger's breadth above the horizon. She had allowed her mind to wander instead of keeping an eye on where the horse was going. The landscape didn't look familiar. She should have looked backward on the journey here, so as to orient herself for the way home. Her shoulders and forearms ached from the unaccustomed task of holding heavy leather reins.

The horse seemed to be trotting with some urgency. *Does it need food and water?* She hadn't thought about it. Or was it just taking over from a lax driver? Once it got dark, would either one of them be able to stay on the road and not trot off into a ditch? With a jolt of alarm, she took a firmer grip on the leather straps and sat up straighter. She murmured to the horse and peered into the darkness for any road sign, or familiar landmark.

'*Take Tannin to River, then down to Hope Bridge,*' Morgan had said. She'd steer the carriage directly to the livery stable, give the horse a grateful pat on the nose, and walk home from there. They'd arrive well after dark, but at least she knew those streets.

And what would she tell Katrina when she got there? The thought made her suck in an involuntary breath.

'I left your husband in a graveyard. He was hoping to catch a photographer who took very naughty pictures of men. Well, yes, now that you mention it, I *did* see Eddie!'

She had a thought about Eddie earlier today—*Old enough for all sorts of scenarios involving a girl*—and suddenly, her salty humor shamed her. Lying to Katrina was not going to be easy. Bale or Ransom might be there to ease the tension, but there was no guarantee. She'd be trapped in her house, spewing lies to a sweet woman whose son was missing, and where would that lead? Would she trip up trying to answer Katrina's questions and incriminate herself and Morgan?

She felt a tremendous need to avoid going home. When she reached the intersection of River Road, she pulled the horse to a stop.

She sat still and listened to the evening. A subtle wind rustled the dry grass.

The horse breathed easily through its velvety nostrils and looked around. From far away, south of her, came the rhythmic pounding of the drill in Hope Bridge, like the monotonous tolling of a cracked bell. Then it stopped. She was lucky to have heard it. It gave her confirmation about where she was. A right-hand turn meant she was headed south toward home. But if she turned left, she'd be heading north.

I don't want to go home and face Katrina. The kind and capable woman would no doubt ply her with questions and easily discern that she was holding something back. Carrie would have to spend another restless and guilty night tossing and turning up there in her uncle's bedroom, agonizing over Katrina lying in the bed where she and Del had been just two days earlier.

Nor did she want to return to Hope Bridge and encounter Howard Clowe and his nasty, but right-on-the-money accusations. Or the righteous Mrs. Lamont, who, no matter how kindly she may have presented, was still judgmental. Or Bill Bemis. He'd get her to slip up somehow. Or the sidelong stares of townsfolk who nudged one another and pointed at her. *What if I turned north?*

Telegraph lines draped from pole to pole alongside the road, possibly leading to Sussex Mill. That was a good sign. Thomas had said he 'went up' to Willies Tavern (*and thank God I remembered* that *name*), but anything north of Hope Bridge was 'up.' If she turned north, she could perhaps find the telegraph office, find the inn Thomas had spoken of, get the horse taken care of, and not be too far from Morgan. She could put off facing Katrina, but still deliver Morgan's messages if she could send a wire. She'd contact Tom Bale, too. He would come to Morgan's aide.

The horse blew through its lips with impatience. It turned back to look at her with big brown eyes that questioned her choice.

She snapped the reins and pulled to the left. The horse trotted with determination, as if to let her know it would not be stopping again until it arrived at a proper stable. She watched its breath rhythmically, fogging the air until it grew too dark to see. When her hands in their woolen gloves ached with cold, and she'd begun to tremble with fatigue from handling the reins and worrying about going off the darkened road, she spotted the hamlet of Sussex Mill and what she hoped were the porch lights of a tavern.

134

Chapter Twenty

"Of course, we have a stable. And a carriage barn. We'll take care of your horse right away, Mrs....?" The tavern lady's gaze swept up and down Carrie's undertaker clothes.

"Lisbon," Carrie said, rubbing her icy hands together.

She was right about the two-story house being Willie's Tavern and was surprised at its polished appearance in such a remote hamlet. She knew enough to swirl one of the leather straps around the iron ring on the stone -hitching post before leaving the horse and carriage and ascending the porch steps. New paint on the clapboards and lantern lights blazed a welcome. Inside, the place smelled of beer and fried potatoes, roasting meat, and the bounty of apples cooked into everything this time of year. The dining room was bright with lamps and crowded with tables atop an enormous braided rug. Matching tablecloths and cheery curtains warmed the room.

"Oh, *you're* Mrs. Lisbon!" the tavern lady said with enthusiasm. In her middle years, she moved with bustling energy, and her smooth, round cheeks glowed with health. She wiped her hands down the apron that covered her gingham blouse, "We've read about you in the paper! You're not here to bury someone, are you?"

Carrie shook her head marginally and huffed a laugh. "No," she said, and nothing more.

"Well, are you looking for work?" A grinning man stepped up from behind the innkeeper. He was trim, compared to her plump, dressed in a white shirt, a pale gray vest, and faded trousers. He smelled like he had come from plowing. Dirt, leather, sweat, horse hide, and a hint of something else.

Carrie looked at him a moment longer than was necessary, at risk of offending him, then turned back to the tavern lady. The trim man went on, eager to reengage.

"We usually summon Ol' Worley when we need an undertaker," he said. "And me and Abe Zimmer dig the graves, mostly over the hill in the big cemetery. We didn't get word yet to start on a new one. What brings you to Sussex Mill?"

Before she could answer, the tavern lady elbowed him. "You don't have to go on so, Clyde. This is Mrs. Lisbon. She's the lady undertaker from Hope Bridge. She's always in the paper."

Clyde's eyebrows shot up appreciatively. "Oh, that's you! That Mrs. Barnstable says you really know your stuff. We'll git you in a room that's right nice! We aim to please!"

"She does go on," Carrie said, intending to politely dampen his star-struck interest in her. "And no, I'm not looking for work. Just a room for the night. I'm hoping you can bill me. I didn't anticipate needing a room. I didn't bring my purse."

"Oh, that's no trouble," the tavern lady said. "I've got all you need. Of course, we can give you credit. We know Mr. Worley's address. Clyde, take Mrs. Lisbon's bag to the front room upstairs."

The tavern lady turned out to be Mrs. Wilhelmina Ellis. Clyde was her husband. "Everyone calls me Willie," she said cheerfully. She led Carrie outside to the backhouse, it being Carrie's first order of business after several hours on the bumpy roads. The structure was a tall, narrow clapboard shed with a sign that read LADIES *Only*. The one-holer had ruffled curtains over the window and fashion magazines in a wooden rack nailed to the wall. There was a shiny spigot over a basin, and the faucet handles were marked H and C in the center of their porcelain inserts. Hand towels hung below a pine shelf that held a cake of soap in a blue dish. It was a luxurious and delightful set up. Quite fancy, Carrie thought again, for such a remote place.

Back inside, Willie produced a mug of hot cider, handed it to Carrie, and resumed bustling about. The tavern was named for her, she explained. "The place has been a tavern for about seventy years. My parents bought it just before I was born. They decided to name it after me. When they died, I inherited the whole shebang. Next nearest tavern is six miles farther up, in Mariet." Before she disappeared through the open door to the kitchen, she called over her shoulder, "Made a pork roast with cabbage and apples tonight!"

In front of a blazing fireplace in the dining room, Carrie gratefully shook off the chill from the road. She caught a glimpse of Clyde outside, driving her horse and carriage through the glow of the inn's porchlight. She'd need to send another telegram to the livery in Hope Bridge, explaining what happened to their rig. She downed the cider and found the doorway to the kitchen.

A black and silver cookstove dominated the room with Willie between it and a massive worktable piled with plates, mixing bowls, vegetables, and cutting boards. Off to one side, the pantry door was open, revealing well-stocked shelves; on the opposite side was another half-closed door showing the foot of a bed. The proprietor's bedroom. Carrie knocked on the door jamb and asked Willie for the location of the telegraph office.

Orchestrating the evening meal, Willie responded from a cloud of steam, "If the post office ain't open, just knock. Clarence lives there, so he keeps all hours. You'll see it, three doors down." She clapped the lid back onto the pot she'd been stirring, waved a hand in the general direction of town, and moved on to another task.

Carrie bundled up and stepped back outside into the cold. She walked along the main road in the dark, counting houses. Sussex Mill was even smaller than Bitter Hay, with no sidewalks. Within a few minutes, she arrived at a tall, narrow building with a window taking up most of its façade and a swinging Post Office sign. A single lantern glowed, indicating the postmaster was still in. She opened the door to the tinkling of a small bell and a breath of warm air. Brass bars in front of the transaction window secured the pigeon holes, the various shelves, and the telegraph set.

Clarence was an old man with a bald, spotted head and a broad smile that changed to delight when she introduced herself. Clarence knew Uncle Sav, a fellow 'brass pounder,' and he warmly reminisced about their membership in the National Telegrapher's League, and isn't it nice that Sav's turning his hand to setting up a library; why that'll be a monument to the coming age, now, won't it? He went on and on until Carrie inserted her need to send a telegram into the first available pause in his monologue, thinking *are all telegraphers so long-winded?* Clarence, like Sav, didn't seem bothered by the interruption. He picked up a pencil and note pad.

She crafted her message to Katrina first. NO EDDIE STOP HUSBAND FOUND SOMETHING STOP STAYING THE NIGHT AT WILLIES SUSSEX MILL STOP BACK IN THE MORNING

She deliberately left out the detail about *who* was staying at the Tavern, banking on Katrina's faith in her husband. Would it spark suspicion, given Howard Clowe's relentless suggestions? She hoped not. If she received such a message, she'd be suspicious as hell.

But she couldn't tell Katrina that her husband was staking out a crypt in the middle of the night either. That statement would lead to questions about Del's reason for being there. Carrie wasn't going to even hint about Eddie's involvement.

Her message to the livery in Hope Bridge was simple. She stated, misjudging the time, that she'd secured a place for the horse and trap at Willie's Tavern, and she intended to square up with them tomorrow for the extra time and stabling fees.

She addressed Bale's telegraph with more urgency, knowing he'd understand this was a summons for his duties as a deputy. NEEDED IMMEDIATLEY IN BITTER HAY TONIGHT STOP SHERIFF BUSINESS AT WILSON CRYPT

As she watched Clarence tap out the message, she was filled with misgivings. She had countermanded Morgan's instructions, turning north to avoid going home, running away like a criminal. How could she leave Katrina alone in her house without a friend to lean on for comfort while the search for her only son entered its third day? Would Thomas know where to find Morgan? He knew everyone and everything in Hope Bridge, but did that knowledge extend to Bitter Hay and its lonely cemetery? How could she leave Morgan out in a graveyard, alone, at night? He was already hesitant to be in the vicinity of the recent dead. How would his mind wander, sitting atop a whole tomb filled with bodies? She clasped her hands together below the service counter and squeezed.

You've done what you've done! Get ahold of yourself.

Katrina would have told Thomas about the casket being returned, she assured herself. Katrina would have told him about their mission to find the crypt. Katrina was not alone. She would still be busy feeding up Ransom, who was likely eating as much as a whole family of starvelings, and admiring his new shoes. Surely Thomas knew where Bitter Hay was, and its cemetery. He'd have to creep around in the dark to find the tomb, but if he got there after Morgan's quarry did, the sounds of Morgan's rage being loosed on the poor photographer would lead him to the very spot he needed to go.

She'd have to hope the conversation between Thomas and Katrina had taken place, that her telegram said enough, and that Bale would be able to safely navigate the roads at night.

Except, she worried, there would be no sounds of struggle at the tomb, because Morgan's quarry wasn't on his way to the crypt at dusk—

"Emmett Cross stays up late like I do," Clarence said, breaking into her thoughts. "He'll get these to the recipients tonight." Carrie thanked him, and started back to the tavern.

As she approached the glow of the night lamp on the porch, the nagging itch of unanswered questions made her stop and consider the Ellis' outbuildings. The horse barn was a dark hulk, looming against the darker night. No lamplight shone in the tiny windows to indicate Clyde was still tending the horses. The carriage barn was situated between the barn and the tavern. She stepped carefully across the trampled grass to where her rented trap was parked in one of three open bays, alongside two buckboards. All three vehicles faced outward. With only a rudimentary understanding of how to make a horse go forward, she had to admire Clyde's ability to make a horse go backward, with a carriage, into a narrow stall. *The trim man has many talents.*

She made her way carefully in the dark toward the horse barn. The scents of manure, fresh hay, chickens, and the warm hide of horses enveloped her when she pulled open a side door. She waited for her eyes to attain some better focus in the dark room. She walked past several stalls and found her borrowed horse. It seemed content, having been brushed down and given a manger of hay. Other horses scuffed and bumped quietly nearby.

A ladder at the end of the row of stalls reached up into the hay mow. Could a corner of the loft have been converted into another sleeping room? One with a frilly bed and a hidden chamber for a camera? She climbed until her head was above the floorboards and found nothing but an expanse of mounded hay. When she was back down on the main floor, she used the rails of the horse stalls to guide her to the back of the barn. A wheelbarrow filled with manure-laden straw awaited disposal. No hidden rooms there, either. All the horse tack and tools were hung from the walls and laid out on shelves. The barn was a simple affair, meant for the business of putting up horses.

Outside, after the relative warmth of the barn, she shivered without her scarf. She hoped Morgan's rage continued to fuel him, because this kind of cold led to illness. She went in through the tavern's front door and made straight for the fireplace.

Two gray-haired couples sat at separate tables in the dining room. Both men wore the tough, homespun clothing of farmers. Their wives had put on their Sunday best for traveling. They took in Carrie's work clothes and paused briefly, as everyone did in the sudden presence of an undertaker. Carrie nodded a greeting to each couple and seated herself. Hesitant pleasantries were exchanged until Willie brought her the promised pork with apples and cabbage, a generous portion of fried potatoes, and bread and butter. Served on matching plates, followed by excellent coffee and pumpkin pie, Carrie could easily see how Willie's Tavern made a profit.

But the guests were farmers and undertakers, and the place was far off the beaten path. Willie's expensive tablecloths, matching plates, and porcelain faucet knobs were costly. She wondered what kind of bill she'd get, but more so, she wondered if it was only Willie's cooking and accommodations bringing in the revenue.

"I put you in the front room. It's small, but it's quiet," Willie informed her as she cleared Carrie's plate. "I got some nightclothes and a robe for you, too. I'll get your hot water up to you, right now."

Carrie thanked her and made herself comfortable in the parlor, along with the other travelers. One farmer had gone to bed; the other dozed over a book. His wife chatted with the other farmer's wife. The clicking of their knitting needles punctuated the conversation about the winter forecast, and the new cheese factory, and what their respective Granges had to say about the price of wheat. Carrie was polite in return, but excused herself to leaf through last week's *Herald* and the summer edition of *The Ladies Home Journal.* But not even the articles about flowers and practical housekeeping could settle her restlessness as the evening wore on. Her foot had been bouncing for the last hour, and she wondered if it would be improper for her to ask Willie for a brandy. Instead, she stood, bade the ladies good night, and found her room upstairs.

Willie proved to be a thoughtful hostess. She provided a small lamp set on the bureau. There was a hot, wrapped soapstone on the bed, and a night dress, robe, and socks laid at the foot. A hairbrush and tooth powder were placed carefully next to a small stack of precisely folded towels and a pitcher with hot water on the bureau.

Carrie should have been tired from traveling, from the emotional blow she'd taken with Morgan after finding Eddie's picture. From the heavy meal she'd eaten, after long hours riding in the cold. Despite not carrying out Morgan's exact instructions, she'd done what she could to alert Thomas to come to Morgan's aid, and to inform Katrina about Morgan not returning home. She should lay down, try to get some sleep, relieve her aching muscles, and put it all to bed until morning.

Instead, she was upright, second -guessing her decision to come here, stiff with worry about Morgan out in the cold and damp November night, and unable to reconcile the familiar and curious scent coming off Clyde Ellis. She stopped pacing the rug, picked up the finger lamp from the bureau, and stepped out of her chilly bedroom.

Chapter Twenty-One

There were five rooms on the second floor of Willie's Tavern. Hers was at the far end, at the front of the building. It overlooked the street. Two more small rooms completed her side of the corridor, and two doors—presumably leading to larger rooms—were across the hallway. All the doorknobs matched; white porcelain on brass stems. More evidence that Willie's Tavern was prospering. The floor gleamed with polish. She walked slowly, close to the walls where the boards were less likely to creak.

She stopped in front of the room adjacent to hers and leaned toward it, listening carefully to catch any sounds from within. Silence. She lay her hand on the doorknob, testing it with a slow, careful pressure. It didn't budge. Locked.

Tiptoeing, she moved along the hallway and listened at the third door. Silence. She tried the doorknob. It, too, was locked.

And why wouldn't they be? she scolded herself. An innkeeper would clean and lock an empty room so that guests couldn't get in to spoil it, or help themselves to the accoutrements they found pleasing. So ill-behaved children couldn't jump on the carefully prepared beds. Willie's Tavern might do a brisk business at other times, but tonight, the vacant rooms were rightfully inaccessible. Carrie moved like a wraith across the floor to the other side of the hallway.

As she expected, the two larger rooms on the opposite side were occupied. The farmers and their wives had been given the bigger beds. A light snore from within one room meant one couple was already asleep. When she had come up to her room, she left the other farmwife and her dozing husband downstairs. Their door was unlocked. Carrie didn't enter.

With a faint sense of frustration, she went down the stairs without trying to hide. The fire in the parlor was burning down, and next to it, in a warm and comfortable chair, the farm wife snuffled awake. Carrie offered her an apologetic wave and headed for the kitchen. If asked why she was moving about the inn at night, she could say she used up all the water in the pitcher for washing, and she had come in search of a fresh drink.

The kitchen was dark. The scent of tonight's supper lingered over the work table. The massive cook stove still radiated warmth. Willie had washed and hung her cookpots to dry, stacked her dishes, and swept the floor. Tomorrow's bread rose, warm and yeasty, from cloth -covered bowls. Seeing the manner in which Willie kept her kitchen, Carrie had a moment of guilt and doubt about her purpose for being here. She was snooping. Again.

Willie was as hard -working as Betsy Woodruff or Thomas Bale. She was as conscientious as Carrie or Worley with the tools of her trade, and she kept her workspace properly clean, organized, and on schedule. She cooked a hearty meal, set a fine table, and lavished her guests with novelties like a ladies-only outhouse. Of course, people would want to stay at an inn that was clean and well -appointed. Plus, it was the only one for miles around. Why wouldn't it be successful? Why wouldn't the Ellises put their profits back into the business?

What am I thinking? That she'd find the hidden camera and developing solutions in the middle of the kitchen? Maybe she'd imagined the scent of ammonia on Clyde. Maybe he just came in from the barn. Lots of things in a barn smelled the same as developing solutions and fixatives. *Should I have sniffed him more thoroughly?* She scoffed at herself, turned to go, and remembered the pantry.

Like the other doors, this one was made of painted, six -paneled pine, with a white porcelain doorknob on a square black rim lock. Would Clyde keep his developing solutions in there? Without hesitation, she reached out and tested the doorknob. Locked.

A good innkeeper would also lock the pantry door to prevent thievery of her pies or coffee. Who knew the habits of travelers? Maybe someone had raided the larder years before, and Willie had learned from that experience. Maybe the door was locked to prevent snoopers like her. Thwarted, doubtful, and feeling foolish, Carrie dropped her hand.

Back in her own room, she shucked off her clothing, set aside her corset to air out, and hung her coat, jacket, blouse, and skirt on the wall hooks. While she washed up in water which had become tepid, she heard the second farmwife and husband arriving at their room. She pulled on the warm socks and tugged the borrowed nightdress over her head. It was cotton and full length, with ruffles at the wrists and ankles. Much too ornate for her, but beggars can't be choosers. She inspected the hairbrush for lice and, finding none, brushed out her hair. She started to bind it up for the night when she stopped short, catching her reflection in the mirror.

She hadn't tied the strings of the nightdress around her throat. They hung between her breasts. With her skin stiffened from the cold, she looked like the young girls in the naughty pictures. Her eyes narrowed.

Everyone was flush these days...

How *was* a remote place like Willie's Tavern benefitting from the same boon experienced by folks down in Hope Bridge, an hour south? No local workers would stay here. The daily travel to and from the worksite was too far, their needs too simple. They stayed in town, two or more boarders per rented room. Always within walking distance of the job site. The management stayed at the Chester Inn. Willie must have inherited a windfall from her parents, as well as the building and the business, in order to afford matching dinner plates, faucets in the outhouse, and new doorknobs.

Or...

She rummaged in her undertaker's bag for the set of keys Worley had given her. She curled her fist around the lot to silence their minute jangling sounds, and stepped back out into the hallway.

Creeping close to the wall, without the benefit of the finger lamp, she tapped silently until her hand touched the door next to her room. By feel, she selected a small key from Worley's ring and slowly eased it into the lock. It jammed. The tiny sound could have been mistaken for a mouse somewhere in the walls. She chose another. This time, the serrated bit was too big for the key hole. That one slipped from her fingers and made a distinct *ting*. She stopped breathing and waited. The snores from the first set of farmers were joined by snores from the second. The knitting wives and their husbands slept only a few feet away.

She selected another key. And another. There was no getting by the miniscule tumblers. There had to be twenty keys on the ring. Frustrated, she stopped again and waited until her impatience died away.

Why am I bothering? It's locked to keep out pilfering guests. She stood still for a moment, considering the proximity of Willie's Tavern to the crypt in Bitter Hay and the incongruous mixture of scents that came from Clyde, even the fancy nightgown she was wearing. She could be wrong about this.

Or...

She tugged a hairpin from her hair, and dabbed a kiss for Phee on it. She inserted it into the hole. Spun it slowly with her fingertips, felt it advance, twisted one prong, wiggled the other. The tumbler inside the lock disengaged.

Slowly, she turned the knob and pushed slightly on the door. It wouldn't do to have made all that effort breaking in, only to have the hinges squeal like a steam whistle. But, like the crypt, the door hinges were well-oiled and made no sound. She stepped inside.

The Ellises hung a lantern from the sign out front, so that anyone seeking lodging late at night would know to come here. Its ambient glow provided just enough light in the bedroom for Carrie to see the bureau, the rim of a chamber pot in the dark recess below the bed, the hooks on the wall like those in her room, and a closet.

Well, well, she thought. Closets were unusual in old homes and taverns. Nailed together with leftover lumber, split-wood lathe, and horsehair plaster, a closet was an afterthought, or an addition years after the original construction. This one had been built against the inside corner of the room, requiring even less leftover lumber to make it. The door was made of thin, vertical bead board, but painted and secured with a latch and hasp from which dangled a small brass padlock. Another unusual feature. Who needs a lock on a closet door?

Carrie gave the Ellises one last benefit of the doubt. *It's probably filled with bedding and summer clothing. Willie locks it to stop theft.* She could still be wrong about this.

Or...

Her hairpin easily disengaged the mechanism, and the shackle popped free. Carrie moved in slow motion, dreading every tiny sound she made. She lay the lock on the rug, stood, and sniffed the door hinges. The scent of fresh grease dispelled any doubt she had about the Ellises. All the door hinges in this place, as well as the crypt doors back in Bitter Hay were lubricated to the extreme. It might be that the host wanted her guests to go undisturbed by the annoyance of squealing hinges, but a closet door? A crypt? That was going too far to ensure silence.

Gingerly, she pulled open the door. Inside was a tiny, empty space. The walls had been papered in here as well. *Interesting.* An effort to keep the damp and dust off the clothing, or a means to keep other activity from being detected? There was no pole across the space for hanging clothes, no hooks, no trunks. No bedding and no summer clothes. Carrie shut the door behind herself and looked around, trying to spot any pinpoints of light coming through. But there was no bright light in the bedroom, only the weak glow from the lamp outside. She couldn't see a thing.

She tapped on the rear wall. It was solid at the corners, but in the center, her tapping produced a hollow sound. She swept her hands around and found a cloth tab. She tugged gently, and most of the back wall came toward her. The wallpaper was being used as a hinge. Without a sound, she pulled it back all the way, ducked her head, and stepped through.

She was in another space, in complete darkness. She reached out sideways, touching a plastered wall on her left, wallpaper under her fingertips. The solid wall on her right felt like the original bedroom wall. This closet was a mirror image of the one behind her. It wasn't quite empty; no clothing muffled the sound of her breathing, but within a few inches of her body, her fingers brushed a wooden object.

It felt like a railing, extended downward at a diagonal, then upward to connect to the base of a camera. *Ah!* She felt the supple leather bellows and worked her fingers quickly along the body to the lens. She moved her hand forward through the empty space and connected to the wall on the left. There, she found and swept aside a loose circle of wallpaper.

The disc, no bigger than the bottom of a shot glass, held in place by a tack, revealed the lighter dark of the bedroom beyond. The lantern light outside barely reached the room. She squinted through the peep hole, waited until her eyes adjusted, breathing through her mouth. A familiar four -poster bed materialized as a ghostly shape in front of her. The bureau, the chamber pot. All that was missing were the occupants.

Chapter Twenty-Two

Filled with revulsion, she couldn't get the nightdress off fast enough. As soon as she was back in her own room, she yanked it over her head and threw it down like it was on fire. As she put her own clothes back on, her mind raced.

A photographer used the room next door to enter the closet of the third room to take the pictures of the men who went upstairs with the girls. Willie wasn't one of the young women in the photographs, but she must be in on the scheme.

Had she and Clyde installed the closets? Or, had they simply modified them? Who were the girls? Was Clyde the cameraman? When was Eddie's picture taken?

She wrapped one of the blankets around her head and neck as a makeshift scarf, pulled on her coat, and carried her mittens. She debated taking her undertaker's bag for a moment, then decided it was too heavy. She needed to be quick.

It was not late, but everyone seemed to be asleep in their rooms. She used the advantage of the inn's noiseless bedroom door, crept down the hall, and stepped onto the edges of the stair treads to eliminate their creaking. At the bottom, she eyed the kitchen to the left and crept past it to the main door. That opened, ironically, with a slight squeal from the hinges. She slipped out, and hurried off into the cold night.

She had no choice but to walk back to Morgan, to tell him what she'd found. She didn't know how to hitch a horse to a carriage. She didn't know how to saddle a horse, much less ride one and steer it back to the Wilson crypt in the middle of the night. But she had to try. She had to tell Morgan that his quarry wasn't coming to the crypt; his man was here at Willie's Tavern.

In the dark, the houses of Sussex Mill blurred into the shadows. Main Street was wide and empty. She trotted down the road, hoping no one looked out a window and saw her bundled form jogging past. Thank goodness her work clothes were black. Thank goodness it was still moonless. If she were seen, she could always say she had an urgent telegram to send. She half walked, half ran toward the intersection of River Road and Tannin—*good lord! How far away is that?* —and then she was away from the village, alone and running through the dark of night.

If nothing else, she escaped from the tavern where illicit photographs were being taken, where prominent men were caught on glass, engaged with girls, for the purpose of extortion. It was how the Ellises could afford the good food and plush amenities. Now that she knew, now that she was a witness to the crime, fear spurred her flight as well. How far would these people go to protect their racket? To save themselves from prison? To keep raking in their profits?

There were no houses on this stretch of road. No cowbells rang, no dogs barked. She was alone with no human resources in sight. The only sound came from her shoes chuffing on the cold earth and from her ragged breathing. She was winded, with a painful stitch in her ribs. She couldn't keep up the pace. She slowed, gasping and pinching her side.

When she was riding in the carriage, the distance hadn't seemed so far. A horse traveled much more swiftly. She tried to remember how long it took her to get from the crypt, back through Bitter Hay, then to the intersection of River Road. How long had she sat at the crossroads making her decision to turn north or south? What time was it now? How far had she come?

Her eyes adjusted to the dimness. Stars covered the sky as thick as mist. Pale forms of corn shocks, woodpiles, and water wells stood out against the darker landscape. She hadn't noticed them on the way to Sussex Mill; she'd been too busy concentrating on her aching arms, on the indecision of turning north, finding the Tavern. *Good lord! Did I miss the turn!*

She'd never walked this far when she lived in Nanuet. Hoofing it a few blocks wasn't out of the ordinary, before a cab could be hailed. Even a funeral procession wasn't a miles -long trek. And there were always legitimate sidewalks, not these cart tracks and unlit dirt roads. Outside the city, nights were profoundly dark. She might easily get lost, and end up north of her destination, blundering around, and freezing before anyone found her. This pell-mell run, down unfamiliar roads, alone in the dark, after sneaking out of the inn, now seemed scatterbrained.

A cold breeze kicked up. Trees creaked and moaned. *What if Clyde heard the door squeak? Was not greasing the front door hinges a purposeful omission? What if he was on his way in pursuit?*

What lay ahead? Just up the road, there could be evil men. Or bears. Or wild pigs. What did she know about bears or wild pigs? She wished Marta was with her, or Thomas. Having lived in the country, they'd at least have answers to her wild animal questions. At most, they would know the way, and at best, they'd have more sense than she did, running through the dark. An owl hooted across the field, a warning that creatures were on the prowl.

Just as she recognized the upright masts of telegraph poles marching past the intersection of Tannin Road, her sigh of relief changed to the frozen stance of fear. Something was moving up ahead.

She listened intently. She couldn't see a thing, even peering hard into the dark. The sound was definitely coming from the same road she was on. She opened her mouth wide, noiselessly pushing her breath in and out. Her ears strained.

The muffled tread of horses. A faint creak of saddle leather.

A man's voice, speaking a few words.

That was all she needed to hear. She bolted to the side of the road and dove into the weeds. She crouched down, pulling the strands of tall grass back into place. She knew the darkness hid her. She knew the man couldn't hear her pounding heart, and the night hid the vapor clouds of her breath. She was safe, as long as she was still. As long as the rider didn't have a dog to sniff her out. *My God, did Clyde have a dog?*

The man's voice came again; a protest. "…an outrage…you have to understand…"

Another voice responded with a deep resonance she knew well.

"I can shut that mouth for you, if I hear another word," Thomas Bale said.

Carrie stood up, parted her weedy sanctuary, and stepped into the road.

Her sudden appearance spooked Bale's horse. It jerked its head up, balked, and snorted. Bale reined in, drew a pistol from his side, and pointed it stiffly at her.

Carrie threw her hands up across her face and shouted, "Thomas, it's me!"

Bale hesitated, holstered his gun, slid off the horse, and closed the space between them in a few strides.

"Miss Carrie! What in God's name are you doing out here?" He reached out, and she grasped his hands tightly, immensely relieved. *Here, he was family*.

"I stayed at the tavern in Sussex Mill. You got my telegram?"

"No," Bale said, puzzled. "I was following this character in the middle of the night. He led me up here." He swung his chin at his companions.

Morgan approached out of the dark. Carrie looked him over, searching for signs of frostbite or injury. His face registered surprise and worry and inquiry all in one deep frown. He held the reins of another saddled horse in one hand and a man's arm in the other. Carrie stared at Morgan's captive.

It was Warren Maxwell.

Chapter Twenty-Three

"What are you doing here, Mr. Maxwell?" Carrie blurted.

"I'm being held against my will for one thing," he snapped. He tried to yank his arm from Morgan's grip, but Morgan clamped down. Maxwell winced and stood still.

Carrie clamped down on herself as well. She slowed her breathing, repositioned her blanket scarf, and made a show of regaining her dignity while she checked her impulse to ask Morgan if he was all right.

"I'm sorry to find you in such circumstances," she said with deliberate formality. "I'm sure Mr. Morgan and Mr. Bale are within their rightful duty to detain you."

"You would say that!" Maxwell spat. He turned to Morgan. "Please! You're not only detaining me; you're keeping me from important business!"

Bale growled at him. "I will tie your hands and gag your mouth, Maxwell. Last warning."

Morgan loosened his grip, and Maxwell shook himself free, glowering. Morgan spoke formally to Carrie. "Can you explain *your* being here, Mrs. Lisbon?"

"I came to find you. Why is Mr. Maxwell your prisoner?"

"He tried to break into the crypt," Morgan said.

"You?" Carrie sputtered. "You're the one—"

"As I said," Maxwell said angrily, "I have important business there!"

Carrie stared at him, unable to form words. In the darkness, everyone was bleached of color, but Maxwell's presence was such a shock that Carrie looked him up and down. He was disheveled, his hair uncombed, his vest rumpled, his pants sagging and wrinkled. His mouth hung open, as though exhausted. He seemed thinner and more desperate than the last time she'd seen him—*earlier today?* —at the post office. He said something just now that plucked her memory. His telegram had also contained the word 'please.' His demeanor wasn't that of an apprehended criminal. It was that of a desperate man.

She turned to Morgan. "What about the—are all the materials we found earlier still there?"

"No," Morgan said. "I have them with me."

"What were you after, Mr. Maxwell?" she asked. He turned his face away from her and said nothing.

"You didn't find the key to the Wilson crypt, did you? So you tried to break in. How did you know to look there?"

Maxwell's chin lifted. "I found out Evans' wife sent his body back. The whole town was talking about it! She wants nothing to do with him, especially dead. That undertaker—Worley? —said he had instructions to put him in the old family crypt. It's her family's, not his. Worley told me where to find it."

"What the hell are you looking for, Maxwell?" Morgan asked. "It's time you told us."

Maxwell looked away, his face changing from desperate anger to a stubborn scowl.

Bale swore. "Now you can say whatever you want, and you clam up?"

Carrie added to the pressure. "I don't think you can be in much more trouble, Mr. Maxwell. Graverobbing is a very serious crime."

"So is blackmail!" Maxwell shouted at her. The word rendered them speechless for a moment.

"What do you know about it?" Morgan asked evenly.

"I know enough!"

"Are you married, Mr. Maxwell?" Carrie asked.

Maxwell's eyes flew wide. "Yes. Why?"

"Most people who are blackmailed are married," Carrie continued, keeping her voice carefully low and deliberate. "They lead respectable lives. They would do anything—or pay anything—to not have their indiscretions known." She paused. Maxwell didn't take his eyes off her.

"They might break into a crypt to steal or destroy evidence of their poor conduct. They may try to neutralize their blackmailer."

To her surprise, Maxwell muttered 'oh, God,' at the same time his knees buckled. His stubborn streak collapsed. He covered his mouth and paced a wobbly circle. Morgan and Bale let him go. When he faced Carrie again, he made no attempt to hide his despair.

"You don't understand!" his voice cracked.

Carrie watched the man crumbling under pressure. He had hidden his agenda from them for days. His pleading telegram, his search of Evans' rooms and clothing, his snappish rebukes to Morgan's questions, and his quest for Evans' missing key had brought him to the clandestine photography lab.

"Not if I don't have the information," she said quietly. "Tell us, Mr. Maxwell."

Morgan and Bale drew closer to Carrie. The horses shifted quietly. An icy breeze stirred around them.

"I need some photographs," Maxwell said dully.

"What kind of photographs," Carrie asked. If the collection of naughty shots contained pictures of Maxwell, she could imagine his shame, hence, his stubborn silence.

"Dirty pictures. Of men. With women."

"Used for blackmailing the men?" Carrie asked. Maxwell started, taken aback at her direct question, then nodded.

"Pictures of you?" Morgan asked.

"No!" Maxwell snorted, then shook his head, and repeated quietly. "No."

"Pictures of Evans?" Morgan asked. "Did he want you to retrieve pictures of him and a woman. Was he being blackmailed?"

"No."

Bale blew up. "What the hell, then! Spit it out!"

Maxwell's anger and desperation resurfaced. He took an aggressive step toward Bale, stood toe to toe with him, and shouted, "Evans takes the pictures! There! Are you satisfied?"

Bale stared down Maxwell. "You're not making this any better," he menaced. "You need to back off."

"Mr. Maxwell, explain yourself," Morgan said. "All of it. Now."

Maxwell stood down, shook his head. The standoff was his last effort at bravado. "Martin Evans had a stable of women. Back in Saugerties. And in Albany. You know what I mean. When one takes a customer, the other takes the photograph. Of him. With her." He paused, flicking his eyes up at them in embarrassment. "You know what I mean."

They stared back at him, silently. *More will come.*

"I found this out when I became his secretary. He'd say, 'I have business with Mister So and So. Find me his address.' He has a man—or had a man—Carver. He'd bring cash to Mr. Evans. I thought nothing of it. Evans had clients from all over the city. They all bring something. They all leave with something.

"But Carver didn't make appointments. Didn't stop at my desk so I could announce him. He snubbed me and walked by. Usually, at the end of the day. He'd just walk into Evans' office and close the door. He wasn't there long. He'd leave, and that was that.

"He was a mean bastard. And he carried a knife and a pistol, and he walked like he was going into a cockfight. He had those shifty eyes and a nasty smile. I never stopped him or questioned him after the first time.

"*That* day, he came in and walked right past my desk, straight for Evans' door. When I protested, when I tried to stop him, he put his hand on my shoulder and pushed me into my chair. He leaned over me—he smelled like a bar—and all he said was, 'Your pretty wife and kids take a stroll in the park every day, don't they?'"

Maxwell covered his face with clawed fingers and stopped talking. They could hear his sobs, hollow and loud behind his palms. He drew his hands down, revealing a face as tortured and despondent as the damned. "I thought my heart stopped. I reported him to Evans, but he brushed me off. Said Carver was an old friend. Old friends didn't need appointments."

Maxwell's face changed into a twisted mask. He shook a righteous finger.

"But Evans was obsessed with time keeping and schedules. He hated it when people showed up unannounced. He was livid when people were late for appointments. He had to have his goddamned cake from Duncan *every other Tuesday!* I found it hard to believe that he'd be friends with a man who just walked in, unannounced. Especially an ugly brute like Carver!

"I saw Carver take a fat envelope out of his coat, once, before the door closed. I heard Evans say something to him. He didn't sound happy. I *knew* he didn't like it when Carver just barged in! Carver came out, folding up bills and stuffing them in his pocket, like he was showing off his wad of cash.

"So, one night after Evans left, I went into his office and went through his drawers. I found a file with Carver's name on it. I think Evans bailed him out of jail in 'ninety-six. There were pictures in envelopes in the file. Like the ones I'm after."

Maxwell shook his head as if to clear his mind of what he had seen. Carrie remembered Morgan shaking his head with the same disbelief outside the crypt.

"On the back of each picture were two dates, about two weeks apart. And a dollar amount in between. He makes two prints. One goes in his file, and the other goes to the man. I guessed that Carver was collecting the money from the man in the picture. That's all I saw. I closed the drawer and left the office. I walked home thinking Carver was following me the whole time. I kept looking over my shoulder to see if he was there. I was so afraid that somehow, *he knew* that I'd found out."

"Is Carver here in Hope Bridge? Is he still threatening your family?" Morgan asked.

"No, Carver's dead. Before we came up here, he was stabbed to death in a fight."

"So, Wheeler is Evans' new man?" Morgan asked.

"No," Maxwell groaned. "Wheeler is Clowe's man."

In the dim light, on the cold road, Carrie watched Morgan's eyes narrow. She felt the same expression on her face.

"What do you mean?" Morgan asked quietly.

"*Wheeler is Clowe's man,*" Maxwell said again. "Evans took Clowe's picture.

Clowe sent Wheeler to get the picture from Evans. But when he was killed, Wheeler told *me* to find the pictures. If I don't find them, he's going to hurt my family!"

Maxwell's news was met with silence for a moment. Then, Morgan said, "Bullshit."

"Agreed," Bale said.

"It's true!" Maxwell shouted. "All of it!"

Bale and Morgan shook their heads. "No. You're the one in the photographs," Morgan said ruthlessly. "You got the blackmail envelope. What are those dates on the back? The date of the whoring and the date you're expected to pay up? How much did Evans demand for silence, Maxwell? What was the dollar amount on *your* picture?"

"Oh my God, that's not it at all!" the desperate man cried. "Clowe's the man in the picture! *Wheeler has my family.* I find the picture. I give it to Wheeler. He frees my family! You don't understand!"

"No," Morgan said, grabbed Maxwell's arm again and started walking. "We don't."

"Wait a minute," Carrie said.

Maxwell's story may be true. It explained his desperate searching. It explained the word 'please' in the telegram. It explained his fainting when he saw Evans' body. With Evans dead, Maxwell had no chance of getting the key or finding the lock it opened. No chance of retrieving the pictures. No chance of saving his threatened family. It was fortuitous for Maxwell that Evans' wife had refused the body. He took a chance that Evans hid the pictures in the crypt. A desperate man, intent on saving his family, rides a horse into the dark of night searching for a deserted crypt.

"Why should we believe your story of Carver and Wheeler and your family, Mr. Maxwell," she asked slowly.

Maxwell spun toward her and jammed his hand into his trouser pocket. He yanked something out and thrust it toward her. A child's braid lay across his palm. One end was tied with a dirty piece of string. The other end with a thin ribbon, its color pale and indeterminate in the dark.

"I was warned not to involve anyone! The day Evans was found—when you still had him at the undertaker's—this came in the morning mail. It's my daughter's hair. He cut off one of my daughter's braids and sent it to me." Maxwell choked on the explanation. "The note said it's unfortunate that my son doesn't have long hair. If I don't find the picture, it…it will be something else he cuts off my son!"

Carrie took the little girl's plait from Maxwell and examined the length of dark hair in her palm. Soft. Wispy. The kind that everyone loves to brush and braid and tie up in a bow. By the length of it, she guessed the little girl was no more than three years old. She handed it to Morgan. He challenged Maxwell.

"This could be the braid of any child, Mr. Maxwell," he said. I'll need the envelope and the letter you received. It must have been postmarked. The handwriting has to be identified as Wheeler's."

Maxwell stuffed a hand inside his breast pocket and pulled out a ragged envelope. He handed it to Carrie and said, "It's my wife's handwriting. He forced my wife to write the note."

Carrie turned to Morgan. "I'll tell you why I believe Mr. Maxwell's story. But, we need to get to Sussex Mill. Can you ride on ahead with Mr. Maxwell, Thomas? Go to Willie's Tavern. Wake the innkeepers; keep them in sight. I'll walk back with Mr. Morgan."

Carrie added a final instruction. "Don't say a word about my being here tonight, Thomas. They think I'm asleep upstairs."

Bale nodded, turned, and mounted his horse with one quick, smooth motion. Maxwell hopped while his horse danced a circle around him. When he was up, he murmured "hurry" to Carrie and Morgan, then turned his attention to staying astride. They had ridden only a few yards away before the darkness swallowed them up.

Chapter Twenty-Four

She wanted badly to throw her arms around him. To hold his living body and know he was well; to feel a reciprocating embrace that meant she was no longer alone.

To her surprise, Morgan turned on her and said fiercely, "You're lucky we found you, Carrie. There's a foot path that runs straight from Bitter Hay to Sussex Mill. We didn't use it, because of the horses. If we did, we'd have missed you by a mile. You could be back at that crypt, freezing to death before anyone knew you were gone."

The rebuke stung. She jerked her head back and said, "Give me some credit, Morgan. I'd have knocked on someone's door well before that."

They walked in stiff silence for a few yards. The exchange felt like a spat between spouses. She had admonished her late husband for making her worry. Her sudden appearance on the dark road must have caused Morgan to feel the same. When he'd last seen her, she was supposed to be headed for Hope Bridge.

"Sorry," they said at the same time. She reached for his hand and at the instant of contact he smothered her in a bear hug. It lasted a full minute.

"Good lord, I was worried about you!" she said.

"What are you *doing* here?"

"I found the bedroom."

Morgan stepped back. "What?"

"I found where the pictures are being taken. It's Willie's Tavern. And no, Evans isn't actually behind the camera. There are two different girls in the photos. Maxwell was right. One operates the camera through the closet, while the other engages the men."

"Closet? Tell me everything." Morgan said, and Carrie spent the next mile catching him up, from her decision to go north, to getting a room at Willie and Clyde's, to sending telegrams as a means of carrying out Morgan's instructions despite her not returning to Hope Bridge. How she arrived with no baggage, and how the kindly tavern lady provided night clothing and tooth powder, and how that night dress looked just like the one worn by Evans' young whores.

She told him how she picked the locks and found the panel between the closets, the camera, and the wallpaper flap that gave access to the action.

"Jesus, you pick locks, too?" Morgan asked.

"It comes in handy when a casket shuts inadvertently. Believe it or not, Phee and I were inexperienced undertakers at one time. We got good at picking locks."

Morgan shook his head, but his voice was appreciative. "I'll keep it in mind."

"We'll have to ask Clyde how he's delivering the photographs to the men," she said, thinking ahead.

"Why Clyde?"

"He's the one developing the pictures at the crypt. He's probably taking that foot path you mentioned, back and forth."

In a few more strides he said, "Maxwell said Evans has run this fraud before. With that man Carver. He comes here to build the bridge and sees the same opportunity. He finds a good place. He gets himself another thug— this Clyde fellow—to collect the money. He catches the banker. He catches Howard Clowe. But I'm not sure he wanted to threaten Howard's election. There would be no gain for Evans if he did that. He's only after money."

"These pictures are motive, don't you think?"

Morgan nodded. "No doubt."

"Del," she said kindly. *I have to say this out loud.* "Motive for Eddie?"

Morgan didn't say anything. His face was inscrutable in the dark. His silence loud and clear. She knew what he was thinking. When was Eddie's picture taken? A few days ago? Weeks ago? When did some wickedly grinning brute hand him an envelope? Had he intercepted the picture when he got the family mail? Did he come into Hope Bridge on Hallowe'en night, confront Evans? Kill him? Load his body onto a child's raft, dump it, then flee?

Morgan shook his head. "How would Eddie have known it was Evans behind the blackmail. Another man was collecting the money, not Evans."

"That's what I thought, too. And another thing. Eddie may not know his picture was taken. None of them did, until they got the envelope."

"What if we get an envelope with a photograph in it, Carrie? What if Katrina opens that mail."

She could hear the thinness of his voice. "We don't know when the pictures are presented to the men, Del. We don't know if *they* know it's Eddie with the girls. And if Eddie was photographed after Evans was killed, he's safe. The whole scheme falls apart. Evans wouldn't have seen the picture. He wouldn't have known who Eddie was. Besides, Eddie's a young man. There's no gain in blackmailing him." But as soon as she said it, she knew that wasn't right either.

"Not Eddie. Me." Morgan said.

They walked in silence for a while. Then Morgan said quietly, "Eddie's the best thing that ever happened to me. I'm—we're—so proud of him. You've met him. You know. He's grown to be such a fine young man."

"That's because of you, Del."

"I know, but, it's not just upbringing. There's a certain quality to him. A kindness, an understanding about things. He thinks ahead, like Katrina; he's level-headed. He's not naïve. I can't imagine why he went with those girls."

Carrie said nothing. If she and Morgan were any example, *he* was being naïve.

"We need to get into the light" Carrie said. "We need to see the dates on those photographs."

"I'm going to kill every one of them," Morgan said.

"Not tonight, though," Carrie said. "You need to look at Willie and Clyde at the Tavern. They would remember Eddie. They'll be able to tell us when he was there. We're closer to finding him."

"I'm not going to say anything about Eddie to these people. They can never know he's my son."

"Unless they do already," Carrie said gently. She pitied Del's position. The proprietors of Willie's Tavern would know when Eddie stayed there. They may be responsible for him getting involved with the girls. But it wasn't as simple as checking the tavern registration. There was no register; the remote village inn didn't keep that kind of record. It would be foolish to have their marks sign in, providing written proof that they were there. Only by asking could that question be answered. And that wasn't going to happen.

* * *

The walk back took the better part of an hour. Midnight had come and gone. They entered the tavern to find lanterns lit, a renewed fire blazing and Maxwell pacing. Willie sat on a hard settee in her nightgown and robe, bleary-eyed from being prodded awake. Barefoot, Clyde sat rigidly next to his wife, looking anxious in his red union suit. Bale stood behind them with his arms crossed. That's all it took to keep them in their place. Their sleepiness turned to alarm when Carrie came in.

"We're used to all sorts!" Clyde said with a forced laugh. "Lodgers come and go at all hours." His smile faded when the comment was met with stony silence.

"Show me the closets, please, Mrs. Lisbon," Morgan said, looking hard at Clyde who wrung his hands under Bale's watchful eye. Willie sat still, frowning at them all.

Carrie took a lamp and led him upstairs. The farmers and their wives still snored. She brought Morgan to the middle bedroom. She hadn't locked the closet door. They entered with the light, pulled open the wallpaper panel and ducked into the second closet. Morgan reached beyond the tripod and camera, pushed aside the peep hole flap, and peered through. When the lock on the second closet door resisted, he leaned back and bashed his foot against the door jamb, smashing it to pieces. They stumbled out into the whore's bedroom.

Morgan reached into his coat pocket and pulled out the box of photographs. He set it on the bureau, pushing aside the pitcher and wash bowl. The china clinked against a vase stuffed with dried weeds and twigs. He set down the lamp and turned up the wick. He took out the top photo—the one of the banker—and held it up. He took out another, and another. They all matched the room. Carrie stood close beside him, noting the single date on the backs of each picture. They were all dated sometime this fall. There wasn't a second picture of Eddie.

Morgan squeezed his eyes shut. "It's in the mail," he groaned.

"We don't know that," Carrie whispered back.

They found the picture of Howard Clowe.

Fully clothed, his white hair unmistakable, Clowe was posed with a look of concentration, his big hands holding on tightly. Morgan made a sound of disgust, deep in his chest.

"We're lucky," Carrie said, stepping away from him.

The comment meant a lot of things. They were lucky to have found the photo. Maxwell could save his family. Morgan had evidence of a scandal that would ruin Clowe's election. They were lucky not to have been caught on glass like Clowe. *That* photograph would destroy them all. Katrina, Eddie, Morgan's election, his future, Carrie's hard won, but fragile standing in the community. They were lucky to have gotten away with their own affair thus far. They were pushing their luck.

"Give this to Bill Bemis," Carrie said. "He'll do the rest."

Morgan let out a short explosive breath. "In good conscience, Carrie? I want to win this election. I know I'm the better man. I like this job. I like the power of it. I like keeping order. I love this county. I *know* this county."

His face was stiff; his fist a knot against his chest. The hard angles of his cheekbones and the shadows thrown by the lamplight turned him into an aged man.

"But I can't burn Clowe to the ground when I'm living in the same house."

With her own face feeling like a tight mask, Carrie countered. "The hell you can't," she whispered harshly. "*This* man is holding Maxwell's family hostage. Or his hired rough is! *This* man has *used* a young woman. What we've done is not the same. And you know it."

She paused, breathing hard. "You take this picture to Albany. You trade it for Maxwell's family and then you show the public back here what kind of filthy bum they want to elect."

He didn't say anything, but the tenseness in his face remained. "Let me see Eddie's picture."

"No," Carrie growled. A glimpse of his son in such a devastating pose would crush him. Even the few hours after seeing it for the first time had not blunted the impact on her. She wasn't about to hit him again with the image. "I'll look at it."

She stepped away from him and pulled the photograph from her pocket. Like the others, it was taken in the same room, printed on the same stiff cabinet card paper. It had gotten bent, but the image was not compromised. She turned it over. There was nothing written on the back. No dates, no dollar amount. She breathed a sigh of relief and told Morgan.

"I'm still going to kill them," Morgan muttered. "Keep that with you. I'm going to have Tom come up here and take a look at this. I'll explain what's happening. Even about Eddie. I need you to go sit with Willie. I'm arresting her and her goddamn husband tonight."

Chapter Twenty-Five

"If I *could* vote, he wouldn't get mine!" Willie grumbled viciously.

Seated next to Clyde on the settee in the dining room, she scowled at Carrie with crossed arms and a belligerent chin. In the wee hours of the morning, Bale and Morgan had kept the couple awake with questions. Willie refused to answer anything. She encouraged her husband's silence with jabs of her elbow.

Carrie could hear Morgan and Bale, walking the rooms upstairs, waking up the farmers, exploring the closets and the attic. Maxwell sat in another chair, dozing off, jerking awake, and firing resentful glances at Carrie. An erstwhile guard for Morgan's female prisoner, she kept awake by adding a stick to the fire every once in a while, but even that effort was becoming inadequate. The weight of sleepiness was inexorable, especially after being out all day in the cold, up all night, and now idle, in front of a warm fire. When the Ellises fell into a half-slumber, Carrie stood, waved her arms around to get her blood flowing, and walked the room.

She pulled a lamp close and took Eddie's picture from her pocket. She pored over the details, keen for anything that might tell her something about his disappearance. There was not much to go by. There was no baggage visible. Eddie wore most of his clothing. The girl wore the same frilly nightie she wore in all the photos. The room contained the same bed, bureau, and a chair by the door. There were no pictures on the wall or baskets for dirty clothing. The chamber pot was presumably in its usual place, under the bed.

She brought the picture closer, wishing for a magnifying glass. Like the equipment in the crypt, the camera in the closet was top quality, and the focus was sharp. Clyde had taken care with the developing. The printed image was crisp. There was detail in the wicker on the seat of the chair, eyelets in the frilly nightgown. Behind the girl's body, was the dried bouquet on the bureau. It wasn't tastefully arranged, just the haphazard result of someone's meandering on a fall day, collecting pretty things to bring inside.

That's something. She put the photo back in her pocket, shook Maxwell awake, and told him to stand up, so he could guard the Ellises. Ignoring his grumbling, she ran up the stairs to the third bedroom.

She found Morgan there, with his head bowed and his hand clenching the back of his neck. The vase was still where he'd left it, wedged up against the wash bowl. She examined the handful of wheat stalks and dried milkweed pods, along with a twig of beech leaves. She knew the species. Autumn beech was one of her favorite floral design elements. The color of pale- brown leather, they were commonly used for accenting taxidermy scenes of birds and wildcats. She collected them annually and used them for pressed flower arrangements. She had to get them into the press that same day, otherwise, they dried and curled, becoming unusable. The beech leaves on the bureau were not pressed and no longer supple. She touched one. As brittle as a cracker, it dropped to the floor.

"Eddie was here on Friday, Del. Three days ago."

His shoulders slumped with fatigue, but at the mention of his boy, his eyes grew sharp. "How do you know that?"

"The leaves in this picture are fresh. See? They're flat, and they stand upright on the stem. Now they're all curled and dried. I'd say they were picked and arranged about three days ago. When this picture was taken."

Morgan's hand slid to the nape of his neck. "So, where the hell is he now?" he whispered.

"And where are the girls?"

When morning broke, the tavern was thoroughly sacked. Morgan and Bale had gone through the cellar, the outhouses, the horse barn, the carriage barn, the Ellises rooms, and the attic. The other guests had yanked opened their doors, startled by the disturbance, then retreated under Bale's curt instructions. There was no sign of the girls. There were no more pictures, no more altered closets, no more camera equipment.

Carrie made herself useful in the kitchen, just as a rooster started crowing in the barnyard. Bale and Morgan had left the pantry door open after their search. The narrow room was bright, with a tall window at one end, and high shelves stacked with dry goods, dishes, spices, platters, tins, and jars. She spotted two thin, wooden boxes labeled "Seed's Dry Plates" on the middle shelf. The same brand as the box in the crypt.

She also found the coffee sack. The label painted on the tightly woven burlap was from an expensive brand. Not sold in Hope Bridge. She'd seen this label at the grocers in Duncan, the county's largest village where the most affluent lived. She scooped up a generous portion of beans, ground them in Willie's Imperial coffee mill, and ladled them into a pot to perk. While the coffee was brewing, she washed up right there in the kitchen. The fresh water issuing from new taps over the heavy sink served to clear the cobwebs of her sleep-deprived brain.

She brought a tray of matching cups, a carafe, creamer, and a sugar bowl into the dining room. The prisoners still leaned on each other on the couch, still obstinately silent. Morgan and Bale were at Willie's desk, paging through her account ledgers. Morgan twisted a stout key with a W at one end between his fingers. Carrie started to set the tray on a table near the Ellises, but Bale shook his head. She brought the tray to him. He prepared a cup for himself, and sniffed deeply, making a hum of appreciation.

"I take mine with a good bit of cream, don't you, Mrs. Lisbon?" he asked in a theatric manner. Carrie nodded. After such a long night, she couldn't wait for that first sip.

"I know some folks like it with sugar," Bale continued. "My papa drank it black. I think Mr. Morgan takes his black, too. Is that right, Sheriff?"

Carrie caught the twinkle in his eye and understood. Morgan glanced at them both, toasted her with his cup, murmured appreciatively, and resumed browsing the books. She poured cream into her own cup, took a sip, and smiled. *We play the game well together,* Carrie thought.

Willie, whose mouth was set in stubborn lines, followed Bale's cup as he brought it to his mouth again.

"Mmm…" He closed his eyes. "That's fine. Nothing starts my day like a good cup of coffee. And this is really good coffee. You made it just right, Mrs. Lisbon."

"Thank you, Mr. Bale. I sometimes have trouble with it. Depends on how old the beans are. But these are an excellent variety." She took another sip. "I'll make some more for the other guests. If Mr. and Mrs. Ellis are going to be detained, I can start the breakfast. You think toast will be adequate?"

Willie grunted, indignant. "Don't you touch my pantry," she said and rose to her feet. "I'll make breakfast. They're my guests!"

Without looking up, Morgan said quietly, "Sit down, please, Mrs. Ellis. We haven't finished our business." Willie gave Carrie a malevolent glare. Defiantly, she reached for a cup of coffee. Bale stepped between her and the table.

"If you wouldn't mind taking this tray back in with you, Mrs. Lisbon?" he asked sweetly. He stood in front of the Ellises, smiled, and took another sip. "Now, where were we? Tell us, please, where are the girls?"

Willie plopped back down, scowling at them. Carrie clattered the plates together and 'tinged' the forks, knives, and spoons as she prepared the place settings for the other guests. She saw Willie wince at the irritating sounds and caught her worried look at the rough treatment of her matching dishes. When the two farm couples came down and took up seats in the dining room, Carrie greeted them, apologized for the disturbance last night, explained that *she* was making do this morning, and asked them to ignore the scene that was taking place right in front of them. She brought out two plates of toast, butter, and jam, and the whole coffee pot, pouring for them right at their tables. Clyde leaned toward the smell.

"I can attempt to fry some eggs," Carrie told the farmers cheerily. "I don't think they're *too* old." Both couples simultaneously declined. While they hastily ate their toast and downed the coffee, Carrie found the money box in a drawer in the kitchen and gave them a refund for their troubles. Willie gasped with fury. The farmers beat a hasty exit after their meager breakfast, muttering darkly about having to hitch up their own wagons.

Carrie did produce a plate of eggs (which were perfectly fresh), potatoes (for once, expertly fried to a delicate crisp), toast (miraculously unburnt), and butter and jam for the lawmen. Maxwell, who slept in a hop picker's cot for an hour or so, stumbled in, looking marginally better. He showed his resentment at this waste of time with a wordless, puckered expression as he ate. The Ellises were excluded from the meal. Carrie made a show of relishing her second cup.

"Ooh! All this coffee. I need to use the ladies again," she said, wincing at Willie, who'd begun to fidget badly over the last half hour. They all stared rudely when her stomach rumbled. Bale rose and prodded Clyde, who was beginning to fade.

"Which one of us should stay until the girls get back?" Bale asked Morgan over his shoulder.

"Which one of us should find the deed to this place and bring it to probate?" Morgan responded. "Where do you think their stash is, Mrs. Lisbon?" He used a conversational tone, but Carrie understood the implication of their questions. Each and every one of those proposals would bring ruin to a tavern. She played along.

"I'm not so concerned about the money they were paid. I am curious about the process." She turned to Clyde. "How did you find the time to get away to the crypt, Mr. Ellis? Developing photographs takes an hour or so, and with the travel to and from the crypt, that would take you away from your duties here at the tavern. Did you use the footpath between here and Bitter Hay?"

Clyde's eyes went wide. Willie groaned. It sounded like a warning growl.

"I take mortuary photos, Mr. Ellis, and I develop them myself," Carrie explained. She inclined her head toward Morgan and Bale. "I don't have to worry about *my* subjects moving."

She turned back to Clyde. "I smelled the developer and fixatives on your clothes. Tell me, how did the girls get their targets to stay still for the thirty seconds it took to expose the glass? I mean... given their activity at the time."

Clyde's mouth and shoulders softened as all the breath went out of him. Carrie paused to let the effect of her statement sink in. "I think I know," she went on. "They took turns behind the camera. The one with the man knew when he was in the right position. She told him to hold still, while she, I don't know, *adjusted* something? Pretended to need a moment to enjoy the *situation?*"

Clyde's face turned beet red. Carrie turned to Morgan with an arched brow and said brightly, "If the spoils of war are still to be enjoyed, Sheriff, I'll take the camera and tripod that's upstairs. I could use the upgrade."

Morgan smiled, looking down at the floor. A rarity in any circumstance, here it showed his appreciation for her intuitive barb. "That's evidence for the trial, I'm afraid."

"What trial?" Clyde squeaked.

"The trial for the murder of Martin Evans," Morgan said, looking at him with the intensity of a lion over its meal. "Mr. Evans funded your little enterprise. The girls. The photography equipment. The remodeling of the rooms." He raised his cup. "The good coffee."

In the silence, Willie's stomach growled again. Morgan went on. "He approached you over the summer? Said there would be money to be made? Said there was no risk? He provided the girls and all the equipment. You came up with the crypt. How did you come by the key?"

Clyde gripped his mouth and chin hard. He shot a quick glance at Willie, who glared up at Morgan.

"Let me guess," Carrie said. "You've been helping out the sexton in Bitter Hay, digging graves at that cemetery. What did you say his name was? Abe something? But you got ahold of his keys, and took off the one with the W on it. Am I right?"

Morgan picked up the thread. "Except now, Evans is dead. The girls are gone. We have the photos that were taken in this very inn, and you're the only ones in custody. I think that means you wanted more than Evans paid you every month. He wouldn't agree, so you killed him and kept up the scheme. Now the girl's customers pay you. Correct?"

Carrie knew this was pure conjecture. Maxwell said Evans had been doing this for years in Albany, well before bringing his scheme to Duncan County. And she couldn't picture Clyde, slim and cowed by his beefy wife's evil eye, collecting blackmail money. But Morgan's bluff paid off.

Clyde was shrill. "We didn't kill him! We just let the girls do their business here!"

"Shut up!" Willie cried out, elbowing her husband sharply. Clyde grunted but continued to protest.

"We just let the girls do their business!" he shouted again. He stood up. "It's not our fault who they invited up there! Evans paid three times what those rooms are worth!"

"Oh my god," Willie muttered and slumped back, cradling her head in her hand.

"How did you learn to develop pictures, Mr. Ellis," Carrie asked.

Clyde swallowed. His face was eager. He aimed to please. "A correspondence course. Out of Rochester. Mr. Evans paid for it. I got a certificate and everything." The room fell silent, except for the clock ticking on the mantle.

"Where did the girls go, Willie?" Morgan asked.

Willie pursed her lips like she'd tasted something sour. She rubbed her forehead for a moment, then dragged her hand down over her face. The pressure of Morgan's silence was enormous. Haggard and defeated, Willie sighed and answered.

"Some tall kid took them back to Albany three days ago."

Chapter Twenty-Six

Morgan swore at the same time Maxwell jumped to his feet. "That's where I live!"

"Where in Albany?" Bale asked.

Willie waved her hand dismissively. "I dunno."

"Did they say anything before they left?"

Willie frowned. "Not a damn word! They heard that Evans turned up dead, and they packed up and lit out."

"When was the tall boy here?" Carrie asked.

"Hallowe'en night. No, it was almost the next morning. He rode in on a real nice horse and took a room. He was mightily vexed about something. Didn't say much. I went back to bed."

"What time did they leave?" Bale asked.

"About half past nine that morning," Clyde said. "They walked out together. He mighta gone for a buggy over to the livery."

Carrie glanced at Morgan and Bale. Within the space of a few seconds, she could see the same calculation and conclusion in both their faces. It matched her thoughts. She was no longer thinking about the photographs. She was thinking about the missing son.

Eddie came to Sussex Mill and got a room in Willie's Tavern in the early hours of November first. He slept with one girl, was photographed by the other, then he'd left with both girls for Albany the next morning. Word of Evans' death had traveled very fast. Someone must have telegraphed Sussex Mill, and that news made it all over the hamlet within the hour. The girls, presumably in Evan's employ, knew their current livelihood was over and got out of town as quickly as possible. If Eddie was traveling with them by carriage, with his own horse tethered behind, he'd have made it to Albany late the same day. He would have delivered the girls to their destination, and hopefully, that place wasn't the sort where he'd be waylaid. But his horse would have been done in. He'd have found a place to stay for the night and started for home the next day. If it had gone without a hitch, he should have been back yesterday. Why wasn't he?

"Enough about the kid," Morgan said, flatly. Carrie could see his half-lidded eyes kept his emotions about Eddie in check. "You made two pictures. One went to the victim, and you kept the other. When Evans was paid, you were supposed to destroy the second photo. I see that you didn't." He patted the box inside his coat pocket. "This is also evidence, Mr. Ellis."

Clyde's throat made a dry click when he swallowed. Willie looked around sullenly, her eyes glistening with tears.

You're going to lose your tavern today, no matter how much you love it, Carrie thought. She didn't feel an inkling of pity for the woman.

"How did the pictures get delivered to the man?" Morgan asked.

"He must have mailed them," Clyde said. "I kept the second one here. That's all I know. I date the back of both and send one to him."

"Why didn't you destroy them?"

Clyde's eyes couldn't get any wider.

"You piece of shit," Morgan said. "You thought you'd get some money from these men later on, when the bridge is finished and Evans is gone. Or did you keep them for your own pleasure?"

Willie shot her husband another dirty look. "You stupid idiot," she sneered. "I told you!"

"Did you always make two copies?" Carrie asked Clyde. If there was only one picture of Eddie, the Morgans were safe from the blackmail. She had Eddie's picture in her pocket. Katrina would never receive a horrifying picture of her son in the mail.

"No, only if a man looked like he could afford it," Clyde said eagerly, as if his disclosure would redeem him. "They took a picture of the tall kid, but he ain't worth anything. The girls were just having some fun with him."

Morgan dropped his head to his chin and turned away. He paced around the room, clenching his fists, not saying a word. Carrie saw the tremble in his hands. Was it relief or rage? She expected him to either get himself under control, or race across the room and break Clyde's neck.

"You don't leave this place until I tell you to do so," he said finally. He swept up his hat and turned to Maxwell. "Please come with me, Mr. Maxwell. We have business to do. Mrs. Lisbon, would you please accompany me as well?"

Bale slipped out the door. Carrie knew he was going to the livery to confirm the rental of a carriage, and to Clarence the postmaster *cum* telegrapher to confirm receipt of the news about Evans' death last Friday. She also knew he was now aware of who the tall kid was.

Carrie looked back at the Ellises. Clyde stood stunned. Slowly, Willie sat back down, put her head in her hands, and wept. Morgan found a grease pencil and put up a closed sign on Willie's Tavern himself.

* * *

Sussex Mill had no jail. Clyde and Willie were taken to the post office to wait under the sharp eye of Clarence, who stood proudly while Mogan deputized him. Morgan wired Leo Lamont to come for the Ellises and escort them back to the jailhouse in Duncan.

"And you're the one who collected, aren't you, Mrs. Ellis?" Morgan said. "The dates in your ledger indicate you went into Duncan for supplies every two weeks. Tell me about that."

Willie sat down heavily on a bench, all the bluff and bluster gone.

"Clyde made two copies," she said without any more rancor. "Evans put on the dollar amount and the payment date, and sent that one to the man. I went every other Tuesday to Duncan to collect. Dropped it off to Evans on my way back here. Brought him his goddamn lemon cake from Stockwell's. The money was in the cake box."

She turned to her husband, her face crumbling with anguish. "You were supposed to burn them, Clyde!"

They turned away from the Ellises. Bale came in and reported Eddie hadn't rented a carriage. If he'd taken the girls to Albany, it wasn't likely they traveled by horseback. Three people didn't ride one horse. Even if Eddie walked beside them, delivered the girls to whatever hovel they wanted to get to, then rode back, which was something a young man was capable of doing, he should have been back late yesterday.

Their voices rose in frustration. Walking to Albany wasn't likely. No one did that. Was Willie telling the truth about where the girls had gone? Why would Eddie agree to escort the girls anywhere? They more likely took the train from the depot in Mariet, only an hour north. Eddie should have put them on the train and rode back home. But he didn't. Was he so enamored with the girls that he followed them to the city? During the debate, Maxwell lost his temper.

"Quit wasting time on some dumb kid!" he demanded. "Gimme that picture and let me get the hell home!"

Morgan squeezed his temples. Bale took in a deep breath. "And once you get there? What do you plan to do, Mr. Maxwell?"

"Give him the picture. Save my family!"

"You show up with the only thing keeping your family alive, and Wheeler may kill you all, so nobody identifies him or Clowe."

Maxwell pulled his hair with both hands, growling in exasperation. "Then help me!"

Morgan held up a hand, led them outside, and convened a small council of war. Maxwell was to send a telegram to his home, with another plea for mercy, letting Wheeler know he was coming today with the picture. He, Morgan, and Bale would travel fast, north to Mariet, then take the train into Albany. Once they overpowered Wheeler, and Maxwell's family was safe, Morgan was free to find his boy.

"I've got an idea for you, in regards to Wheeler," Carrie said. She went back inside and returned with Clarence's notepad. "Here's the name of an undertaker in Albany. He's an associate that my father and I dealt with often. I just sent him a message. He'll help you. Just give him my note," Carrie said. "If I'm right, this should get Wheeler's attention. The rest is up to you."

Chapter Twenty-Seven

It was still early morning, and still very cold. Bale hitched up Carrie's patient horse, helped her up, and swung her trade bag into the box at her feet. She took up the reins and felt her muscles protest.

"You know how to get back," Morgan said with his hand on the sideboard. "You know what to do." They both kept their faces neutral.

She was to return directly to Hope Bridge. She was to steer clear of Howard Clowe. She was to keep a vigil with Katrina until her son's return. It was a simple set of directives.

But so much could go wrong for Morgan. The plan for Albany depended on the good will of a colleague she hadn't spoken to in years, the sleight of hand Bale had to employ, and the fortitude of Warren Maxwell, who was an emotional wreck. She tried to suppress the fear that came along with the thought of Morgan, Thomas, and Maxwell confronting Wheeler, a kidnapper and a possible killer.

Maxwell described him as a dangerous man who casually mentioned knowing what his vulnerable wife did every day. The man held a woman and her children captive for days. He had chopped off the little girl's braid. Was he in contact with Clowe all this time? Would Clowe pressure him to send parts of Maxwell's children to the poor man, as incentive to keep looking? *Had he killed Evans?* What would happen when the two lawmen came to the door?

After that, neither Morgan, nor Bale had the slightest clue where to look for Eddie.

"I'll be fine," Carrie assured him. She gestured to the horse. "I'm just along for the ride. I'll tell Katrina what's happened with Maxwell and the Ellises. Nothing more."

Morgan nodded, a bare twitch of his head. "Tell her I'll bring Eddie home today."

Bale approached from across the carriage yard, holding the reins of two horses, saddled and prancing. Maxwell was already astride another.

"Keep everyone safe, Thomas," she said. He lifted a hand in return. She snapped the reins over the horse's back and got underway.

Tannin Road came up faster than she expected, and she fumbled with the reins, pulling too harshly. The horse tossed its head in protest, but came to a halt at the intersection. Carrie settled back, her hands in her lap, thinking. She was supposed to have made a simple trip back to Hope Bridge last night, from this very spot. But she made a different turn, and that decision had yielded tremendous results. She sat here again in a quandary. Going one way, and sticking to the plan, would bring her home. The other brought her to Bitter Hay and the Wilson crypt.

South was Hope Bridge, where she would dutifully, and not dishonestly, tell Katrina that Eddie had taken up the cause of two young ladies who needed an escort to Albany. Just as they thought, he was, in fact, helping someone.

"Why hasn't he sent a message?" would be Katrina's first question.

And how will I answer that?

As Morgan's emissary, she was instructed to tell Katrina everything. The blackmail scheme, including Clowe's involvement. Katrina would be aghast, but she'd keep the story to herself. Carrie was to tell her about the Tavern, the closets, the darkroom in the crypt, the arrest of Willie and Clyde, and the rescue of the Maxwells that was underway. No matter what, she wasn't to say a word about Eddie's photograph.

On the other hand, she wore the scarf that she'd given to Morgan last night. It smelled of him. Warm tobacco and the scent of his unique sweat. She breathed it in while she made up her mind. She and Morgan hadn't thought of destroying the glass plate negatives. True, they were locked behind the iron doors of crypt—a place no one would think to look—but a sharp rock and a heavy blow would open the doors and everyone's secret would be out, including Eddie's.

West was Bitter Hay. Morgan was counting on Carrie to deliver news to his wife. But there was not a definitive time for her arrival, was there?

This won't take long. She tugged on one side of the horse's reins, and once the turn was made, she snapped them with assertion on its back.

* * *

At mid-day, the horse trotted smoothly, south on River Road. The dirt lane was empty of other travelers and fairly well maintained. Despite that, she was on high alert to keep the carriage in the center of the road, alert to any deviation that might put them in the ditch. Her hands and shoulders cramped up badly.

River Road took a long, curving arc to the west with a wide view of Duncan Creek on the left, and an orderly farm enclosed with stone walls on the right. Cattle lowed in the barnyard, and in the rolling fields beyond, men and boys hefted shocks of corn onto a wagon. As she approached, she spotted half of a VOTE for MORGAN poster flapping on the corner of the barn. She slowed the horse—gently this time—stopped, and hopped down.

She found the other half on the ground among the weeds. She picked it up just as a courtesy to the tidy farm, and spotted a thin pile of Morgan posters strewn in the tall grass. Frost covered the topmost poster. The rest of the pile was soggy. They'd been here a while. She picked those up, too, much more slowly.

Bale said Eddie had been by here, pasting up campaign posters on barns and bridges, and that Clowe's people hadn't bothered to put up posters in this area. Had the farmer who owned the barn torn these off? Bale said Eddie had to ask permission before he put up the bill. If the farmer chose to back Howard Clowe, then permission wouldn't have been granted.

It didn't explain the dumping of the rest of the posters. Why would Eddie have dropped these and not picked them up?

He was mightily vexed about something, Willie had said.

Eddie had been here three days ago, on Hallowe'en. Something—the lure of the girls at Willie's Tavern? —had kept him from coming to Hope Bridge to rendezvous with his father that night. But he was closer to Hope Bridge than to Sussex Mill, as evidenced by these posters. She could clearly hear the clanging of the construction equipment from here. She had no more than thirty minutes on the road before she reached home. It made no sense that he went back to the Tavern instead of coming into town to spend the night at Clevinger's.

She collected the discarded bills and remounted the carriage. It rocked badly, and she remembered she hadn't set the brake. The horse muttered an admonishment as it braced itself until she was settled. She didn't have to snap the reins. The horse just carried on.

Entering Hope Bridge, the horse's singular purpose was to get back to its stable. But Main Street's chaotic throng interfered with the animal's training. Carrie's slack hand contributed to its confusion among bad-tempered draft horses, teamsters shouting profanity, and the crashing rumble of the steam crane's engine. The horse balked and tossed its head. It worried the bit and jerked the carriage forward, only to stop abruptly after the next step. Carrie pulled the reins and brought the animal to a halt so they could both regain their wits. She didn't dare go any further in the surly traffic.

Ransom Butler was dodging through the crowd on the nearby sidewalk. At her call, he skirted around a pair of ladies carrying market baskets and stopped at the side of her carriage, eyes wide, face flushed. Katrina had truly cleaned him up. His hair was cut to a respectable length. His 'new' shoes were worn but serviceable. Suspenders held up clean trousers that pooled around his shoes, but his shirt had all its buttons and he wore a rough brown jacket open, cooling himself as he ran his errands.

He agreed to run to the stable and get the man to rescue Carrie and the flustered horse, but only after he delivered Mrs. Wilson's scissors. He brandished a gleaming pair, just sharpened, and darted off into the throng. Exhausted and impatient, Carrie sat on the carriage bench, watching the teeming streets, regretting all the coffee she'd consumed to taunt Willie, and needing the backhouse and her bed in that order.

When Howard Clowe ran his fingers through his thick white hair before he and his hangers-on stepped off the steps of the Chester and approached her, she closed her eyes in despair, but she didn't cut off a disheartened groan. *Stay clear of Clowe.*

"Our fair sheriff and his intrepid lady undertaker leave the village yesterday and she returns without him today. My, doesn't she look flush with satisfaction, boys?" Clowe spoke loud enough so those outside his circle would hear. It worked. People turned from their business and stared at her. She couldn't help her jaw from dropping in simple, disgusted surprise.

"How dare you, Mr. Clowe," she said quietly as he sauntered toward her. The image of his hands on the young woman in the picture flashed up. She ground her teeth. "Your slander shows a remarkable lack of respect for my station and my profession. You can see I'm on an undertaker's business." She held up her trade bag as evidence of her mission without taking her eyes off his gloating face.

"Oh, I'll beg your pardon, then," Clowe mocked. "I should have known that our fair sheriff is supposed to accompany the undertaker on *her* business." He turned to his followers, "I'll keep that in mind when I'm sheriff!"

That garnered a nasty round of snickers, during which Carrie became quite cold and still. She looked down at her hands.

If Del Morgan were here, he would have summoned his own scathing riposte. If Thomas Bale were here, Clowe might suffer a broken nose from the former boxer. If her Uncle Sav were here, he'd have pointed out a perfectly logical explanation for not only Del's legitimacy in accompanying Carrie, but, no doubt, he'd quote an obscure legal precedent that would embarrass Clowe for accosting Carrie in public. In addition, Sav would have left Clowe ashamed of his incompetence for not knowing the very laws he was trying to get elected to uphold. If Bill Bemis were here, well, he'd be writing everything down.

But all the men in her life, whom she counted on as friends and protectors, were not here. She looked up and straight ahead, feeling the grim face smoothing out her features. The bustle of Hope Bridge slowed. Of course, folks stopped to watch. Clowe had featured her in the paper, questioned her character, and hinted at indecent goings-on. With Morgan absent, she was just as good a target as he.

She remembered Morgan's anguish at finding Eddie's picture, Katrina's steady façade slipping from the strain of worry. She saw the blood on the rail, and the mud in Martin Evans' mouth. She remembered Mrs. Lamont gently beseeching her to come to church. *This has got to stop.*

A curiously tranquil feeling overtook her rage and exhaustion, as if all the stress she'd endured had squeezed her into some flattened, unresponsive form. As if there were no more room for fear. As if she were made of something else now. And it was liberating. As the man from the stable arrived and took hold of the horse's reins, she held up a hand.

"Just a moment, please," she said to him and swung down from the seat. Clowe's smile stiffened as she approached. She was tall enough to look him in the eye.

"Pfft," she scoffed, very quietly in his face. Only he would hear her words. "You must know a sheriff deals with the dead alongside an undertaker in many cases? Perhaps you don't. And you think my association with Mr. Morgan is sexual? Even though you have absolutely no evidence to support that juvenile supposition? Even though his wife is a guest in my house?"

She stepped closer and angled her mouth toward his ear, whispering, "Even though, you, yourself, could be involved in that very. Same. Act?"

She stepped back and watched his smile fade. Aloud, staging her own show, she said, "Thank you, Mr. Clowe. You've just reminded me of something."

Clowe's smile was brittle as he attempted a response. "And what would that be?"

"That you're an ass." She turned her back on him, stepped up into the carriage, and beckoned the stableman to lead the horse away.

Chapter Twenty-Eight

She walked from the stable, lugging her bag, tripping and catching herself on the uneven flagstones, and cursing Howard Clowe. Clara darted out of Worley's front door as she stumbled past, calling for her to come inside. Carrie groaned. Beyond everything else, she had been sent to Bitter Hay at Worley's request. She hadn't thought to send *him* a telegram last night. She gave him her report about the Wilson-Evans crypt, and its use as an illicit dark room, and hence, full of evidence of a crime. Worley actually rolled his eyes.

Katrina plied her with questions as soon as she walked in. With hopeful news of her boy so close at hand, her resolve to wait patiently for answers failed. It took her no more than a minute to punch holes in Carrie's story.

"Where in Albany would he go? How does Del know where to find him? What's become of him? Why hasn't he sent a telegram?"

Carrie had no answers. Her evasions sounded suspicious, even to herself.

"What does Del intend to do?" Katrina didn't let up. "He can't search all of Albany for him? We're still no better off!" She rose abruptly from the table, placed a hand on her hip, and turned away from Carrie to stare out the back door.

The picture of Eddie was still crammed in her pocket. Carrie touched it nervously to ensure it didn't stick out. She stroked it with her thumb, trying to extract herself from Katrina's rampant emotions. *Maybe I can erase Eddie's likeness. Maybe I can destroy it, regardless of Del's objections. Maybe I can distract her.*

Carrie tried to soothe. "We found a possible reason for Mr. Evans' murder as well, Katrina. Mr. Morgan remained in Bitter Hay last night in order to uncover the whole nasty plot. There's a great deal more. Come and sit with me. Mr. Morgan wanted me to tell you everything."

The recounting of the blackmail scheme had Katrina frowning and tutting in disgust. She wore the moue of a sensible woman offended by the nefarious actions of others. It was Katrina who concluded "Del will put an end to this," before rising to busy herself with another cooking task.

Carrie intended to collapse into a deep slumber the minute she got home, and the dust-up with Clowe, and countering Katrina's fears increased her exhaustion. She was about to head up to Sav's roomy bed and quilts when Bill Bemis appeared at the back door. He knocked quickly and walked in without waiting for either woman to answer.

"What did you say to Howard Clowe, Carrie?" he asked, smelling of frosty air. His freckled ears were red from the cold.

"Everyone is talking about his challenge to you when you came into town. They say that you walked right up to him and whispered something in his ear. He hasn't been seen since. Tomorrow's Election Day. And where the hell is Morgan?"

"One thing at a time, Bill," Carrie said, massaging her forehead. She grasped the back of the chair to keep from swaying and waved a hand at Katrina. "You've met Katrina Morgan, I presume? Sheriff Morgan's wife. It would be more appropriate for you to ask *her* for her husband's whereabouts. I'm only an associate, as you know. And don't say anything, Katrina. My friend, Mr. Bemis, will write every word in his paper."

"That's not fair, Carrie!" Bemis countered testily. "I've met Mrs. Morgan—in your absence, I might add—and I'd treat her 'every word' with the same respect I treat yours. You know me better than that. But Election Day is tomorrow, and Clowe's been stumping all over Hope Bridge, declaring Morgan a coward who couldn't solve Evans' murder and so has run off with his 'Negro deputy' in shame."

Katrina gasped. Carrie scowled. "Neither one of those statements are true. Has anyone countered them?"

"Morgan has plenty of supporters here and since this is where the action has been for the last few days, Clowe's supporters and Del's have been arguing in the streets about it. It's reportable, but not as good as the incumbent's statement would be. Where is he, Car—uh—Mrs. Morgan?"

Katrina drew herself up. "I'm going to follow Mrs. Lisbon's advice, Mr. Bemis. I've made my statement in the paper. My position is inviolate. That's all I'm going to say. Would you like some supper?"

"Bravo, Katrina," Carrie said. Fatigue bloomed from her belly to her head. She fought to keep her mind clear.

"Okay, okay." Bemis waved his hands as if to wipe clean a slate. He turned to Carrie, focusing a sharp reporter's eye. "Did you find the place where Martin Evans is to be buried?"

"Yes."

"Where is it?"

"A little hamlet called Bitter Hay, north of here, on Tannin Road, off the Shun Pike."

Bemis looked confused. "That's it? A simple answer? What's wrong, Carrie? Why aren't you prevaricating, like usual?"

"I'm tired. Next question."

"Uh," Bemis frowned, at an unusual loss for words. "Are there burial arrangements?"

"I don't know what Mr. Worley has planned."

"Why did Morgan go with you?"

She put up her guard. It was a legitimate question. She had been tasked with evaluating the burial site for a man whose death Morgan was investigating. It was Katrina who suggested Del ride with Carrie *before* the crypt key was identified. Bemis knew nothing about the raft or the bloody gore on Butler's hidden piece of railroad track. He didn't know about Evans' blackmail scheme, or the Ellises, or the photograph of Howard Clowe. But if he did, what would he do? Would he spike Clowe's election in tomorrow's paper? She was tired, too tired to think. She shook her head. *Now,* she'd prevaricate.

"He was catching a ride north. He didn't say."

"Oh, come on! Don't hold out on me now."

"I believe he was following a notion he had about Mr. Evans' business dealings." She offered that tidbit, at least.

"And why did you spend the night?"

Bemis was clearly attempting to take advantage of her fatigue. Caught off guard, would she answer a question far more important than the funeral arrangements of a stranger?

She was not caught unawares. She raised tired eyes to her friend's face. Her eyebrows rose a fraction. "What part of Howard Clowe's rumor -mongering will you contribute to, Bill?" she asked quietly. "One that exonerates Mr. Morgan, or one that defiles your friends?"

Bemis's freckled complexion went ruddy with frustration. "I've waited on Del Morgan for three days, Carrie. He won't talk to me. I'm trying to support him! Do you know how hard it's been to counter Clowe's libel? Election Day is tomorrow, and the man we are backing is nowhere to be found. He's off with you! Is he looking into a suspicious death? He won't answer a single question about anything. The *Daily Times* is selling a lot of papers because their man is getting all kinds of quotes and answers from Clowe. I'm twiddling my thumbs, waiting on a single word from an absent incumbent. Doesn't he care? He'll lose this election if he doesn't show up *today!*"

Carrie rubbed her face with both hands. Even her bones felt weary. "I can't speak for Del Morgan, Bill," she said. "I'm so tired. I can hardly explain myself."

"You've goaded Howard Clowe into silence, Carrie. You found out something up there in Bitter Hay, didn't you?"

She shook her head, gripped the chair harder.

Bemis pulled the latest *Duncan Herald* from a coat pocket and laid it gently on the table next to her. It was opened to the 'Talk of the Town' section. A letter to the editor was circled in heavy pencil. Carrie skimmed down to the identity of the writer. She kept her face neutral, but inside, her bowels threatened to come loose as she read.

To the General Public of Duncan County,

It is with great pride that I present to you, as candidate for Sheriff, my husband, Delphius Morgan. He has served this county since January, 1899, having been appointed by our former sheriff, Mr. Nate Edwards, who found him worthy, entrusted him with our safety, and positioned him to uphold the laws of the land.

Since his appointment, Mr. Morgan has proved to be worthy of our trust and thus, our votes. You may think that, as his spouse, I am biased, and that is certainly true. But more so, my position, if you know me, is unique as an endorsement.

I have been a witness to Mr. Morgan's virtuous character for the last eighteen years. He is known by all in the county to possess a fair mind, and to be judicious in all of his dealings, even as a young man, and especially as your Sheriff.

I have read with Christian dismay the lowliness to which our fellow man, a rival for the position, has stooped in order to besmirch the reputation of my husband, and that of a woman in our midst who is herself above reproach in her character.

I will personally vouch for my husband's unblemished faithfulness, and I would ask that the public, who knows my husband well, cast their vote for his continued tenure as our County Sheriff.
Mrs. Delphius Morgan.

Carrie stifled a groan. Her hands felt icy; she would never be warm again. *This has to stop!*

"That's a rousing endorsement," she managed to murmur. Her lips felt thick. "Katrina is a loyal wife and a dear friend."

Did my voice shake? Why is my vision dimming?

"Carrie!" Bemis shouted, grabbing her shoulder as she wobbled toward the floor.

Chapter Twenty-Nine

She woke abruptly, disoriented. She was in her own bedroom, fully clothed, tucked under her own covers. Warm, rested, but wary. *Why?* She spilled out of bed and stumbled to the doorway of her bedroom. *What time is it? How long have I slept? What's happened?*

Katrina occupied a chair at the kitchen table. Ransom sat opposite her with his finger pointing word by word as he read aloud from a book. Outside, the blanket of clouds that covered the sky for days had torn apart, leaving raspberry-stained shreds glowing in the setting sun. The room smelled of molasses, beans, and corn bread.

Katrina put down the apple she'd been paring and wiped her hands on her apron. "I decided you were better off just getting some rest. A good supper and some tea with sugar will help. Here, sit. I'll fix you a cup."

As Carrie slid into a kitchen chair, Bemis came in from the front parlor, tucking a newspaper under his arm. He inquired about her health, noting better color in her cheeks, and stood expectantly in the doorway.

This is why I'm on guard. He's still looking for answers. She stopped herself from slapping her pocket, covering the gesture by itching her leg through her skirt. *Thank God, it's still there!*

"Do not question Carrie right now, Mr. Bemis," Katrina warned conversationally. "I shooed you from this room once, and I'll do so again, if need be." She smiled and turned to stir an aromatic skillet of something sweet and savory.

Bemis frowned, but his appreciation for good cooking resolved the standoff. Carrie made room for him at the table. She took a sip of the sweetened tea and rested her chin in her hand. Her voice was gravelly with sleep.

"Good lord, Bill. You've camped out in my parlor? Waiting for me to wake up to give you a statement? You're a pest."

Bemis snorted in grudging agreement and sat down. Katrina slid a bowl of rich pork and beans in front of him. She served Carrie and Ransom before seating herself. Ransom waited a mere second after the blessing before diving into his bowl. While the bread was sliced and buttered, and the pitcher of cider passed, while Ransom gobbled beans without taking a breath, and Katrina and Bemis laughed at him, Carrie watched them with a sudden tenderness.

For some reason, they had become her people. Ransom, the little magpie, a thieving waif from the dump, with the new haircut and a respectable job. Bill Bemis, a friend and colleague from her old life. And Katrina, a woman who thought of nothing but caring for those within her reach, a dear wife and mother, who took care of Carrie without a moment's hesitation. They'd all found a place in her home and in her heart. They'd come here for shelter, for respite, for the support of friendship during a difficult time. They were comfortable here, and protected.

How did that happen? She certainly wasn't cooking up a storm, clucking over their need for clothing, thinking ahead, and providing a sandwich. She hadn't thought to shop for their meals, hadn't considered what they needed for lodging.

She had done the opposite. She'd been selfish, thinking only of herself and what she had to hide. She had ditched them yesterday; rode off with Katrina's husband—and with Katrina's full trust and blessing! She chose to avoid spending another night in her own house, leaving Katrina alone with her worries. She evaded Bill's questions like a slick politician, obstructing and holding back. She felt pity for Ransom's poverty, but Tom Bale had rescued him, not her. Her spoon felt heavy. She had no appetite.

"Eat something, Carrie," Katrina said gently.

Ransom piped in. "Can I have yours, if you're not gonna eat it?"

"There's plenty more, son," Bemis said. "Thank goodness, because I'm up for seconds, too."

Carrie wiped a hand over her suddenly moist eyes, pretending to clear the sleep from them. She brought a spoonful to her mouth and blew on it. *I still have so much to hide.* But she had gained some clarity from her impromptu rest. She was beginning to see how to untangle some of her knots.

"Don't tell me you've been waiting idly for me to wake up, Bill, or for Morgan to return and make a statement," she said. "I know you better than that. What have you dug up?"

"Well, my astute friend," Bemis said brightly. "I've been looking into Mr. Clowe's background. I have a chum who knows another newsman in another one of the small towns near here—a place much like Hope Bridge—who has had more than a passing acquaintance with Howard Clowe over the years. This fellow considered Clowe, as we do, to be a man of, shall we say, dubious character. We dislike him because he's a downstater, an outsider, who's come to town and crapped on our man—beg pardon, Mrs. Morgan. My friend's friend told me that Clowe's reputation as an intimidator is only surpassed by Clowe's reputation as a man who employs a mirror too much. Which is to say that he's a swellhead."

This garnered a smile from Carrie. She took a second bite of her meal.

"So, I dug some more," Bemis smirked. "And my friends dug. Pests we are, Mrs. Lisbon! We found Mr. Clowe has had a career in law enforcement for many years. Mostly downstate as we know, but also, mostly, as a paper pusher, a toady for one mayor or another. He manages to get himself assigned as the man who stands at some muckety-muck's right hand for all the pictures, not the man who gets his hands dirty in order to have the victory photo taken. It is rumored that he has a man for that."

Wheeler! Carrie blew on her spoonful to cover her sudden shock.

"He's easy to find, too. He leaves that mop of white hair uncovered so all can see its glory. And he moves around. He's like a big fish who outgrows his little pond. With his penchant for being seen, we find him in lots of little towns like ours. Do you know that he and Del Morgan were previously acquainted?"

"What?" Carrie and Katrina said together.

Bemis grinned widely at their reaction and laced his fingers proudly on his belly. "Mmm," he groaned. "I wish everyone cooked like you, Mrs. Morgan."

"Spill it, Bill," Carrie barked.

"I believe the reason Clowe wants to be the sheriff of our little podu— excuse me—our *enlightened* county stems back to a time when both men were players at a baseball game in Albany in 1882. The game was underway, in an unnamed park, between two league-less, hoodlum teams, the Depot Dogs and Cherry Street Blue Socks. A ruffian's match, to be sure. The outcome was a complete sizzle due to the performance of one young buck named Delphius Morgan, who played for the Dogs. He smashed the ball every time he was up, resulting in three home runs, and a spectacular catch that eliminated the last hopes of the opposing team."

"Del played baseball?" Carrie asked.

"In his youth," Katrina said. "He gave it up when we married."

Bemis continued. "And so, as with all such battles involving young men wishing to demonstrate their contempt for their vanquished foe, the post-victory revelry involved a singular act of humiliation upon the losers."

"Oh, dear," Katrina murmured. "I haven't heard this part of the story before."

"It was reported in the Albany paper that the wagon carrying the defeated team back to their side of town was subjected to a bombardment of inconsiderate huzzahs, *and* a rain of horse dung. The Depot Dogs then retreated to a nearby bar to continue their victory dance."

"Wait a minute," Carrie said. "Was Howard Clowe on the losing team?"

"My friend of a friend reports that the batter, known as 'Whitey Clowe' hit a massive ball with bases loaded. It would have won the game for the Blue Socks if not for the outfield phenom known as 'D. Morgan.'"

Carrie sat back, folding her arms, and drawled, "Howard Clowe is running for sheriff of Duncan County to get back at Del Morgan for losing a baseball game?"

"Oh, no, dear woman," Bemis wagged a freckled finger at her before reaching for an enormous piece of corn bread. He bit into it and kept them waiting while he chewed appreciatively. "As with all vanquished foes, their humiliation required a like response. The paper had a tastefully worded article describing the retribution. The horse-manured wagon returned to the park, equipped with dog waste. Buckets of it. While the winners were celebrating at the local pub, *their* conveyance was filled with *that* fecal material."

"Good lord," Carrie muttered, laughter tickling her lips. Bill made the disgusting exchange sound comic.

"Upon being alerted to the crime, not only was the hero of the Dogs a superior batter, and was carried off the field in triumph after his game-winning catch, he was also quite fast. It was reported that, although having imbibed more than a few pints, he managed to catch one of the fleeing Socks and stuff his head into one of the dog shit buckets."

Ransom brayed and dropped his spoon. Even Katrina burst out laughing. She hid her mouth with her hands and giggled. "That's terrible!"

"Oh, it was," Bemis said when he'd recovered from his own laughter and swallowed another mouthful of corn bread. "The exchange of animal dung on a rival's mode of transportation is one thing. The personalization of it was quite another. I believe it's the thing that drives Del's opponent at this time."

"Howard Clowe got the bucket?" Carrie asked. Bemis nodded solemnly.

"My friend tells me Clowe spent the intervening years as a law man of various degrees in several counties. It's likely he sees an opportunity here to defeat Morgan and return the humiliation."

"Does Del know it was Mr. Clowe's head he stuffed into the bucket?" Katrina asked.

Bemis gave her a withering look. "If he were around, I'd ask him."

Chapter Thirty

Oscar the macaw set up a screeching protest in his room on the second floor. He was considerably indignant when neglected. Carrie made a poor substitute for her uncle in the beady eyes of the big bird, but Sav wasn't due back from Albany until tomorrow. She hoped the peace offering she brought, in the form of Katrina's apple peelings, would prevent a nip on her fingers. She needed his cooperation.

As it was, Oscar flapped at her in annoyance and bobbed angrily up and down. She held out the slippery peels to the bird from a cutting board, putting the wooden panel between her fingers and the bird's powerful beak. Oscar snatched away a peel, glaring at her. She murmured endearments and watched him demolish the juicy skin. Bending slowly, she kept her eye on him as she turned to the bucket that contained his bird seed. He was known for launching himself at anyone who interfered with his can of seeds and nuts. Oscar paused, fixed her with a beady eye, as if deciding his level of tolerance. She paused, too, having had to fend him off before. He blinked first, fisted a length of peel in a gray, leathery foot, and resumed munching.

The scent of wheat and corn kernels, dried pumpkin rinds, and raisins rose up with the lid. She gingerly scooped a generous portion into Oscar's ceramic dish. Thomas had cleverly wired the bowl to a crotch of branches among the evolving jungle of ropes and sticks that kept the bird occupied for hours. Oscar murmured a parrot noise and waddled over to eat. He selected a piece of corn cob with his beak, transferred it to one foot, and cracked a kernel as if the rock-hard grain was made of clay.

Carrie caressed the bird's nape with her finger. Oscar hummed with pleasure. The act of petting the soft feathers helped to soothe her as well.

I've got several nuts to crack myself. Since waking up this afternoon, her brain had organized her multiple dilemmas into clearly drawn lines of logic. She now saw pathways to disentangling herself from the web of lies and intrigue she'd spun. So much became clear. Blood on a rail. Amos Butler being more flush than usual. Indecent pictures of men who ought to know better in intercourse with flouncy girls. There were common threads, and to her rested mind, they were no longer snarled.

Nor was her course of action. She just had to weave the threads into place.

She couldn't wait for her usual allies to return. She would use the people she had. Election Day was tomorrow. She could get Morgan elected *tonight* while he was in Albany, rescuing Maxwell's family. She thought it might be possible to unveil Martin Evans' killer, if one final piece fell into place. She'd lay to rest Clowe's rumor -mongering about herself and Del Morgan.

She stood motionless, staring at the bucket of dried bird food, considering its potential. She had the picture in her pocket. It had become creased, but the image was sharp and undeniable. She eased herself away from Oscar and bent slowly toward the can. Oscar paused and spread his wings. Birds of prey hunch themselves in a threatening posture over their kills. It was a prelude to attack in the macaw's case. Carrie stared him down.

After a moment, Oscar relaxed, muttered a clearly enunciated obscenity, and returned his attention to the corn cob. Carrie slid the photograph deep into the seed, twisting and shoving until it was buried. She put the lid on the can and straightened, murmuring words of comfort to the bird as much as to herself.

* * *

"Where's Ransom?" Carrie asked, when she came back down. The dinner dishes were cleared, and the boy had slipped away.

"He's in the barn," Katrina said. "He's been using Mr. Bale's sharpening stone like a mad man and running all over town, making money with it."

"Has he gone back to his father?"

Katrina's mouth turned down at the mention of Amos Butler. "I believe he's given his father a wide berth the last few days. And I'll be the first to say I'm pleased."

Carrie found the boy in the carriage barn, sweeping the floor. There was no sawdust. Bale hadn't been sawing, or sanding, or building anything in the last few days. The boy was fussing over his new responsibility. A lamp glowed, turning the shop into a snug cavern, cluttered with burnished tools and odd clamps. Ransom jumped to attention when Carrie came in. She held up a quieting hand.

"Hello, Ransom. Mr. Bale must appreciate you taking such good care of his shop."

Ransom dipped his head. "I work here now," he said with pride. "I mean to keep it nice."

Carrie sat on a stool. Ransom stopped sweeping. He wore his coat, unbuttoned, with a flannel muffler around his neck. One of Bale's. He twisted the broom handle in front of his belly, anxious. His hands were rough for a child, chapped and raw on the knuckles.

Already the hands of a working man. Carrie addressed him like an adult, the first of her allies.

"Ransom, Mr. Bale said that you could go home anytime you wanted. Your father is your family. But he invited you to stay and work here, because he knows a young man needs a job and a decent place—a safe place—to live. That hasn't changed, Ransom. You're not in any trouble."

Carrie hadn't mothered him like Katrina, but she would level with him like Morgan. She went on.

"That night, when we walked away from your house, your father yelled for you to keep your mouth shut. Do you remember him saying that?"

Ransom's chin bobbed up and down, his eyes never leaving her face. Bale had said if the boy remembered a bird flying overhead on the morning, he found Evans' body, that detail justified Bale's taking him from his abusive father. Carrie posed her question to elicit not just a tiny detail, but something much more.

"Keep your mouth shut about what?"

The boy went still, the instinctive pause of an exposed mouse. His knuckles whitened on the broom handle. He swallowed and looked back and forth in the middle space between them. She waited.

Ransom twisted his hands around the broom handle before speaking. "I can still stay here? If I tell?"

Her eyes closed involuntarily. Her chest ached with sudden compassion. *The enterprising little magpie is bargaining his safety for information.* "Of course," she whispered. "We wouldn't have it otherwise."

The broom twisting resumed, but Ransom pursed his lips to screw up his courage. Finally, he said, "I lied to Mr. Bale. About my raft."

Carrie waited. *More will come.*

"I told him someone stole it Hallowe'en night. But I think my pa sold it. I think I saw." The twisting sped up.

"Mr. Bale won't be angry, Ransom. He's a kind man. It sounds like you were scared of everyone. It's all right. What happened?"

Ransom swallowed hard before stuttering, "I—I was hanging around the boneyard at the church. I was hiding, 'cause I didn't want nobody to see me. All the big kids was jumping out from behind the gravestones and yelling 'boo.' They made everybody scream, and they laughed like it was the funniest thing. They all got run off. That sexton is mean!

"I went to the Chester 'cause sometimes the men will give you a penny if you help them home. There wasn't nobody there who was so bad drunk they couldn't walk, so I went home, but I didn't go to bed right away 'cause Pa wasn't there, and I thought to drink the beer he keeps for the morning. I ain't supposed to drink it, but I was hungry, and Pa always says it's the best breakfast. I only drank a little."

Ransom's confession ran like a flood. Carrie listened to the child's account, keeping her hands slack instead of curling into angry fists. It was a miracle he'd survived, living in a dump, scrounging whatever opportunities presented themselves for food and cash.

"I went to go pee—I mean—I'm sorry!" At Ransom's horrified look, Carrie smiled and waved her hand in a 'no bother' gesture.

"Beer makes you have to go!" he said. "When I went out, I saw Pa coming up from the creek. I could tell he was real drunk. He had a hard time walking straight. Well, me too, cause beer makes you all fuzzy. He was trying to count money—real greenbacks! —but he couldn't walk and count at the same time. Then he fell down, and I could kinda see the creek. I thought I saw somebody poling my raft away. I heard it, you know. It was real dark, but you can see the ripples in the water, and I know what it sounds like when the raft is getting poled away!

"Anyway, Pa saw me. He yelled at me to help him up and I did, but the whole time I was hearin' my raft going down the creek!" Tears sprang into Ransom's eyes.

"That was my raft," he finished plaintively. He struggled for a moment, then continued. "I could hear it. I said, 'Pa, my raft!' But he just grabbed me and pushed me into the house. He said for me to keep my mouth shut. I fell asleep after that 'cause it was real late, and I wanted to make sure I got up to go to the bridge and look around, next morning."

Ransom looked down and swished the broom back and forth listlessly. "I didn't mean to lie to Mr. Bale. I was real scairt, you know, about finding that dead man. I just forgot about seeing my raft for a little while. Now that I'm established here, I gotta make it right with Mr. Bale. And the sheriff. He took me to go look for it."

"Did you tell Mr. Morgan about what you saw that night?"

Ransom shook his head, his eyes focused on his new shoes. "I—I didn't think to do it. I didn't know how to not lie about it. I ain't never helped out the sheriff before. I thought he liked me. Joe Allen can't say he helped out the sheriff!"

"I'm sure he likes you, too, Ransom. We all do." Her assurance came out as rote. She was thinking about the movement of a raft up and down the creek, how a child couldn't pole it against the current. But a man could. A man might be able to maneuver it upriver in the dark, if he were desperate enough. A man could drag a dead body onto the raft. The dead man might lose a shoe in the dragging, and the exposed sock might become covered with mud. The shoe might have had a key hidden in the footbed. That key might have fallen out and lay there, unnoticed, while the man retrieved the shoe, and wedged it back on the dead man's foot.

"Do you think I'm a deputy now?"

"I'll ask Mr. Morgan about your status," Carrie said. "You saw the ripples, Ransom. What else did you see? Did you see the man on the raft? Could you make out anything about him?"

"No. It was dark." Ransom's feet shuffled with the broom. "I didn't see him, 'cept for his hat. He mighta had on a funny hat, like a cowboy hat. But it was real dark. And Pa dragged me into the house."

"I saw your father yesterday, Ransom. He keeps some things aside to sell later. You know about those things?"

The boy looked sideways. Nodded once.

"Who else knows about those things?"

"Nobody, I suppose. Pa don't let nobody go back there. 'Cept somebody who might want to buy stuff."

"Do you know where your father is now, Ransom?"

"He's most likely at home. It's Monday, getting on toward nighttime. He's usually slack on a Monday."

Carrie stood. "I'm going to go visit your father, Ransom. But I need you to do something for me." She gave Ransom the instructions—his role to play—and he listened carefully. "Good. Let's go see what Mrs. Morgan wants to do with you next."

"She already gave me a bath and cut my hair this week. I can't be cleaned up no more."

Carrie smiled and beckoned the child out the door. Night had descended. The air was cold enough to snow.

"Oh, you'd be surprised."

She heard Bill and Katrina as they approached the back door. She and Ransom stepped into the thick of it. Bemis's impatience had flared again, despite his good meal and the levity of his story. He flapped his bowler hat along his pantleg while trading debate points with Katrina.

"You've already taken a stand, Mrs. Morgan, with your letter to the editor. You may as well continue to campaign on your husband's behalf."

To which Katrina replied testily, "Your source will not be me, Mr. Bemis, and I don't appreciate the word 'hindrance.'"

"But how can you just…*keep cooking,* while your husband and your son are gone on the eve of election day? Surely, a statement from you will sway votes! Assure the populace that your husband has things well in hand."

"Assuring the populace is not my place."

"But you are the man's wife! Presumably, you know what he's up to. You can win this election for him!"

"Mr. Bemis," Katrina began, and her voice held rebuke. "I won't—"

"I have a statement for you, Bill," Carrie interrupted, stepping into their midst and regarding them both.

"Finally!"

"But first, I need your assistance with something."

* * *

Carrie watched Del's wife clap her hat onto her head, and tie it under her chin with swift, vehement jerks, before stomping out of the house and into the night. Dry leaves swept into the hallway before the door shut. Sharp anxiety swept into Carrie's stomach.

She always worried there would be some niggling doubt in Katrina's mind that would tip the scales in favor of Clowe's lies; Katrina would succumb to the gossip; would find the seed of truth in his ugly suggestions. Then what would Katrina do? She could only bank on Katrina's perpetual good will, and her rock-solid belief in her husband's fidelity. The veil was too thin.

She and Morgan had been so very careful. Their public encounters, so very staid and proper. They were so very sure they were unseen; that their trysts were ironclad in their secrecy.

But we took such a risk on Hallowe'en.

Carrie inhaled slowly, reasoning with her conscience. *We're taking another risk now.* And this time, it would be to the good. Or so she fervently hoped.

She closed the door, ignored the leaves, and turned to address Bill Bemis. The freckled man stood in the hallway, pulling on his coat, and thrumming with excitement.

"She'll be fine. It's time for us to go. I'll explain on the way," she said, wrapping a scarf around her neck. "I know we should be waiting for Mr. Morgan and Thomas to get back, but I have no idea when that will be. And I learned something from Ransom just now."

They hurried through the evening chill. The golden light from Main Street's gas lamps, and the lanterns in the windows made waypoints through the night. The streets were empty of teamsters, farm wives, and errand boys. There were no horses, carts, wagons, or carriages tied to posts; all were tucked in for the night. All the bridge workers had shuffled to their various rentals in weary groups, smelling of rock dust, oil, and smoke. The pounding drill was silenced.

Keeping her promise, Carrie disclosed the details of Martin Evans' death. She told him about the head wound, the raft, and the hollowed-out shoe. She told him about finding the bloody railroad track, with its sprout of human hair, the day Bemis returned with Evans' spittle-stained casket. She told him about taking a picture of the rail, moments before Butler wiped it clean with the shirt from his back.

"What happened to the photograph of the railroad track?" Bemis asked.

"I developed it the other night. It's at the house. I'll give it to Mr. Morgan for evidence."

She told him how Morgan found the raft and how Ransom found the Wilson crypt key. She told him about Willie's Tavern and the blackmail scheme, and the current rescue mission of Warren Maxwell's family. Bemis walked the mismatched sidewalks without looking down, focused instead on his furious note -taking.

He muttered a rueful explicative. "And I hounded Katrina…"

"Ransom said on the night of Evans' murder, he saw somebody take his raft. He thinks his father sold it. Ransom couldn't see if there was anything on the raft, but he thinks the person poling it away wore a cowboy hat. I'm hoping Mr. Butler will tell us—if he remembers—who took the raft."

They crossed Main, went South on Elm, past Ina Barnstable's house. The parlor light was on; Ina, no doubt, pecking away on a Sears Roebuck typewriter, filling her gossip column with the embellished events of the week. The plank sidewalk ended, and the house lights faded behind them. Navigating slowly in the dark, they took the spur to the end, where it paralleled the creek and led to the Banks, the forlorn end of town where the garbage was dumped. Their discussion was halted as the glow of a bonfire bloomed in the distance. By the time they had run to the top of the bank, Butler's cabin was a writhing cone of flames, crackling and snapping and sending sparks high into the air.

They clutched each other for a moment before Bemis pelted off into the darkness. He would alert the nearest neighbor, who would, in turn, relay the alarm to the fire brigade. Carrie watched the flames consuming the shack, hoping Butler wasn't in there. Hoping, that if he was, he'd mercifully drank himself dead before the fire consumed him.

Alone on the road, with the roaring fire hot on her face, Carrie paced, took a step forward, retreated. In the distance, the fire alarm began to clang.

She'd come here to question old man Butler. She came in the hopes that he'd either be so drunk, he'd spill his guts about the night of the raft, or that he'd be both drunk and impressed about having a big city reporter quoting him for the newspaper. She'd even brought some cash to ensure his loose tongue. Either way, he was supposed to blab like a lonely housewife.

Evans didn't hit his head falling off the bridge. On no account would he be up there, especially alone and in the dark. There was nothing more disorienting than that. She had found and photographed the place where he died, right here in this dump. And Butler didn't kill him. Amos Butler, a man generally unsteady at best, would have had to overpower a presumably sober and more nimble man in order to bash his head in on the end of the railroad track. And why would Evans be here in the first place? He wasn't buying junk to build his bridge.

Butler had sobered immediately upon seeing the carnage left over from Evans' dying. When he swore 'damn you,' he wasn't talking about himself. She had watched him clean up the scene, and he'd looked around to see if anyone saw him do it. He may be complicit in hiding Evans' body, but he was genuinely surprised to find the killing had taken place right there.

Where was Wheeler on Hallowe'en night? A man who chopped off a toddler's braid had a mean streak a mile wide. He was surely capable of murder. Clowe employed him to do his dirty work. Did that include disguising himself with a cowboy hat, rafting a body downstream, and dumping it below the bridge?

What if Butler demanded an exorbitant price to keep *his* mouth shut? Was this someone's response to his pathetic attempt at extortion? Was this fire a drunken accident with the lamp, or something more?

Oh, Ransom! This is really going to hurt you. She should stop the plans she'd put in motion tonight. Stop Ransom. Find him, break the news, comfort him. But then she'd have to stop Katrina, and Bill.

If she were right about her course of action tonight, she was playing with fire herself. She had chosen to provoke Howard Clowe with her "very same act" comment earlier today. She was supposed to stay clear. What had she set in motion with her impetuous words?

She backed away from the light.

Chapter Thirty-One

The Chester Inn may have been the finest hotel in Hope Bridge and was certainly the pride of the village with its gleaming white façade, but the backside of the hotel was where all the business took place. The yard was an obstacle course of barrels, boxes, wagons, laundry lines, and rubbish that hotel guests never saw.

Carrie and Bill picked their way through the yard and went up the steps into the kitchen sculleries, where people were still miserably busy, preparing pies and bread dough for tomorrow's meals. A stout woman with a kerchief over her hair and a flour -covered apron glanced up at their arrival, rolled her eyes, and resumed her rhythmic kneading. Several boys stood at another table washing and drying dishes from soapy buckets. The lamps were turned down. Voices and laughter came from the billiards room far beyond the kitchen.

They used one of the swinging servant doors to enter an unseen corner of the dining room. Bemis had set up a small table behind a heavy damask curtain to cover the election in its final days. He paid the Chester their usual bill for a room, a daily sandwich, all the coffee he could drink, and their staff's discretion for the right to leave his bag and workspace unmolested in this hidden corner. He'd be long gone by the time the Chester discovered the tiny holes he'd snipped in the fabric that hung between him and the dining room. From this vantage, they took turns peering out on the dining room's sole occupants.

The fire place had burned down to embers. Only a finger lamp lit the faces of the two people seated on opposite sides of a small table. Carrie knew them. She clamped shut her eyes, opened them, hoped the vision would change.

It didn't.

The crystal-clear vision of horror prevailed. In the lamp's glow, Katrina Morgan dabbed her eyes with an embroidered handkerchief and murmured low and fast. Howard Clowe leaned in, impeccably dressed in gray trousers, with a matching vest, and a pristine shirt. He clasped his hands on the table. But as Carrie watched, he started rubbing them slowly together, as if in anticipation of a good meal, or riches beyond measure.

Excitement suffused the concentration on his face. There was no sympathy in his smile of encouragement, just the gleam in a wolfish eye. Carrie slid a shaking hand across her mouth, stifling the unbidden intake of breath.

"If I'd known…" Katrina's voice trembled. "My letter in the paper…such a fool…"

Carrie would never have guessed Katrina could deviate from her stalwart path like *this*. Tears and lamentations didn't coincide with her surety. She must be letting go of all the troubled emotions she'd dammed up over the last four days, worrying about Eddie, having to accept her husband's absences, putting up with Bill's pressure. Seeing Carrie take *her* place as confidante to Del. With no more strength to hold it at bay and license to set it free, she gushed to Howard Clowe with a devastating purpose.

"They spent the night in Sussex Mill," Katrina whimpered. "That's when I knew. It must be true. I cannot support my husband after this." Her voice rose to a tearful soprano and cut off abruptly. She buried her face in the dainty cloth.

Carrie's stomach flipped. With Katrina's bombshell, the cat was very much out of the bag. And it would run squalling to the newspapers, yowling all sorts of damning stories for days on end. Stories of Del's infidelity. Stories of her, no better than the whores she'd discovered up in Bitter Hay. Stories of a God-fearing wife made a fool. Katrina was spiking Del's election, and destroying Carrie's career and reputation in her despair. No fury like a woman scorned? And no limits either.

The thought of all the repercussions she tried to avoid made her hands tingle; within a moment, the shaking extended to her limbs. Her heart pounding in terror, Carrie clamped her mouth shut, struggling to stay still and silent. She hadn't expected to feel such dread when the affair was finally discovered. She thought she'd have some semblance of dignity, that there might be some way to retain her composure and make a stately exit. But her legs turned weak. For a moment, she thought she might collapse again.

Bill Bemis looked away from the peep hole to stare at her. She shook her head and waved a hand in front of her burning face, and, turning, caught sight of the servant's door, which had noiselessly cracked open behind them.

Ransom stood there, dirt- smudged and tear- stained, his eyes reddened and wild. The clothing and shoes he wore with such pride this afternoon, were now caked with mud and ashes. He smelled of heavy smoke. And burnt flesh.

Carrie clapped a finger to her mouth and beckoned him forward. She needed him silent. He couldn't give them away. His face twisted with the effort, his mouth dropped open, but he came toward her, his eyes spilling more tears. He looked through the hole in the curtain, frowned, and wiped his face with a dirty hand. Peered again. Squinted. And nodded.

Bemis put a red-freckled hand on the boy's shoulder and pulled them both away. They moved quickly through the servant door and back into the kitchen, where the soft hubbub of activity drowned out the child's sobs. Bemis squeezed Carrie's shoulder and left them.

Whispering comforts, Carrie steered Ransom deeper into the warren of work tables. The baker started to protest the invasion. Carrie spun around with a scowl that would have stopped a cavalry charge. Savagely, she dug into her pocket and pressed some of the money she brought for Butler into the woman's hand. Left alone with Ransom, she found a barrel in one of the pantries, and a blanket from the linens room. She bundled him onto the makeshift seat and held him while he bawled into her belly, his arms strapped around her waist. Carrie held him tightly, as grief overcame him. Her own tears fell, her emotions spilling over with his.

Ransom had been unbelievably brave. He just learned his house—such as it was—had burned to the ground. He'd just confirmed what she feared: that his father had perished within the flames. He was in the same place she'd been a year ago, thrown over the edge and flailing about in a space with no foundation. Such instability was overwhelming. Coupled with profound grief, the child was helpless to do anything but cling to something, anything, that represented solid ground. By all rights, he should have abandoned his role at the sight of his burning shack. But he'd managed to keep his head. Somehow, he'd left the efforts of the fire brigade, and the smoking remains of his father to come back to the Chester Inn to take a look at Howard Clowe in the dark. He played his part for her even as his heart broke.

Ransom's harsh sobs took away all her feelings of triumph. The first hurdle had been cleared, but at what cost? Now, it was up to Bill Bemis to begin his part.

The freckled newsman was to circumnavigate the hotel, trek back through the kitchen, out of sight of the dining room, past the abandoned night clerk's desk, around the staircase to which Howard Clowe had his back turned, through a maze of side halls, and into the servant's entrance to the gaming room. There he was to engage with the bartender, and scribble in his notepad until Howard Clowe appeared, beckoning him with barely contained excitement.

Standing in the dark pantry, holding Ransom, Carrie could picture the scene. She envisioned Clowe's smirk as he enjoyed the moment. He had a statement for Bill Bemis now. The opportunity to humiliate the big-city reporter who supported Del Morgan was too good to pass up. He'd beckon Bemis to follow him into the dining room, from which the tearful Mrs. Morgan had just exited.

Bemis would hold up a hand. "Not here," he would say. "Walk with me to the bridge." Once there, Clowe would reveal the scandalous story with unbridled enmity.

"Ransom," she whispered. "Go to our house. Mrs. Morgan is there. She'll take care of you. We'll sort things out in the morning. We love you, Ransom. We won't let anything happen to you. I need you to be brave just a bit more, honey. Can you do that for me?"

Ransom sniffled and nodded, and let go of her.

"I have to get to Mr. Bemis now. But you're all done, sweetheart, you can go home—to our house. I'll see you in the morning." She pulled and tucked the blanket around his shoulders so he could wear it into the freezing night. Katrina Morgan's heart would break as soon as she saw him, bereft and smoky, on the doorstep. Carrie watched him slip away into the dark.

If she were honest, she'd like to do the same. Slip off into the night, pack her bags, wake the livery man, and hire that dear horse again. She could be in Duncan by dawn, in time for the six o'clock train. She could be back in Nanuet by sundown. Alone, but far away from the devilment that was about to come. The enticement was overwhelming.

But she hadn't played her role yet. She'd get Morgan elected. She'd wipe the superiority from the face of Howard Clowe. She'd bring justice to orphaned Ransom Butler. She'd hold her head high for those reasons alone.

With the frailty of pride shoring her up, she stepped from the pantry and walked with the last of her dignity away from the Chester.

Chapter Thirty-Two

The Duncan Creek, twenty feet below and invisible in the dark, clattered over its rocks and pebbles. Carrie positioned herself carefully on the edge of the girders, waiting for Bemis and Clowe. She shook with cold. The November wind bit into her skin. She patted the photograph in her pocket. A talisman, touched for luck before a battle.

Two men approached from out of the glow of Main Street's gas lamps. Howard Clowe's voice dripped with sarcasm.

"And so, in her distress, she felt there was no choice but to retract her letter to the editor, and to tell the people of Duncan County the truth."

Bemis scribbled in his notepad with the speed of a sewing machine.

"Mrs. Morgan's statement is clear to me," Clowe said with finality. He stopped at the edge of the bridge, just a few yards from Carrie. He jerked down the lapels of his great coat and ran a hand through his hair.

"I'll hold a meeting in the morning, here at the hotel," Clowe said. "You'll send your story out tonight to Duncan? They'll make an announcement in the morning paper. That'll do it for Morgan's campaign."

"By all means, Mr. Clowe." Bemis dipped his head, a movement just shy of deferential. "This is the story of the year. I'll make sure Mrs. Morgan is portrayed in the gentlest manner possible. She's a victim here, I should think."

"Of course." Clowe's tone was dismissive; Katrina's misfortune was nothing to him. She provided him with a means to humiliate his rival. He had no more use for her. He turned away, speaking to Bemis over his shoulder. "You make sure that gets in the morning paper. I need to prepare for tomorrow."

"There are, actually, just a few more questions for *you*, Mr. Clowe." Bemis interrupted the man's departure.

Carrie held her breath.

"Can you tell me anything about the dump fire tonight?" Bemis asked loudly, his hand poised over his notebook.

"What?"

"Mr. Butler's cabin at the dump. Out on the Banks. You know it. You bought a raft from him Hallowe'en night, remember?"

Clowe stiffened, his face stone-carved and shocked. Then his brows came together, and he scowled. "I don't know any man at the dump. I didn't buy anyone's raft."

Bemis dropped his bomb. "But you were seen."

Clowe paused, then shook his head slowly. "No one saw me. I wasn't there."

Bemis went on. "There's a witness. You dragged Martin Evans' body onto the raft. You dumped it under the bridge."

"Go to hell," Clowe spat and turned again.

"He would never come up here, afraid of heights as he was, especially at night. Didn't you know that about him? I'd like to get your statement for the papers about that."

Clowe turned back. Carrie could see his chest rising and falling rapidly. He barked at Bemis. "I brought you in to get the wife's story tonight, not to question me!"

"No matter. I can get your statement tomorrow. From your jail cell." Bemis said. "I'll have lots of questions then."

"But I have only one," Carrie said, emerging from the shadow of the iron pillar. She stood on the precipice of the emerging deck where the wind scraped past her ankles and tossed her hair across her face.

"You!" Clowe sneered. "What're you doing here?"

"I summoned Mr. Bemis because I know about the blackmail. About the photographs. You're involved, and that points to a clear motive for his murder. But more than that, I have a question for you."

Clowe didn't respond. His nasty grin wavered, and his eyes grew hard. *Stay clear of Clowe!* Carrie pushed on.

"I examined the fatal wound in the mortuary, and I found the place where Mr. Evans hit his head on the railroad track at Butler's dump. I have pictures of both. The wound matches the track, and the track had the remains of Mr. Evans' head stuck to it."

"Bullshit," Clowe spat.

"Not bullshit," Carrie said and took a step forward. "Evans took your picture and sent you a letter. You came to Hope Bridge not to campaign, but to confront him about it. You met him at the dump. Why? To offer payment in exchange for the picture? Did you fight? Did you and Wheeler bash his head against that rail? You got the raft from the crossing, poled it upstream—no child could have done that—and loaded Evans on it. Butler saw you. You paid him. Did you set fire to his cabin tonight? That poor man had *a child!*"

"That drunkard thought he could cash in with a cockamamie story about me and Evans. I simply bought the man a bottle for his troubled mind and sent him off to that shithole of his. It's not my fault he drank it all and fell over his own lantern. And as far as bullshit, Mrs. Lisbon, you have absolutely nothing—*nothing!* —to base this idiocy on."

Carrie pulled the photograph from her pocket. Held it up. Waved it back and forth, taunting.

Clowe drew himself up and advanced. He leaned forward and sneered. "The Morgan woman says you've been having an affair with her husband! You're the one who should be arrested, you whore!"

As if stricken by his hand, Carrie gasped and stumbled backward. Bemis lunged and grabbed Clowe's arm. Shaking, Carrie rallied, her voice trembling with rage.

"We found Evans' studio. You've been there! The bedroom at Willie's Tavern. One girl in the closet took your picture while you were involved with the other. Clyde made two pictures in none other than Martin Evans' crypt. One picture was sent to you. Pay the dollar amount, or else be exposed. Clyde was supposed to destroy the second picture after Willie took payment.

But he didn't. He never got payment, because you met Martin Evans and killed him first."

Clowe hissed through stiffened lips, said nothing. He shook off Bemis's hand.

"How did you know it was Evans behind the pictures, Mr. Clowe?" Carrie forced the question out.

Bemis stepped closer to her. "My man in Albany knows. Believe it or not, Mr. Clowe has been the victim of this act before. My buddy reported on certain members of the police force in that city being reprimanded for indulging in the carnal favors of certain young ladies. Young constable Clowe was one of them. His chief had the photograph. He knew who took them. A young bridge builder. That information was passed along to the constables, and Mr. Evans relocated to the city of Saugerties, presumably encouraged by a policeman's baton. Constable 'Whitey' Clowe wanted vengeance for his humiliating experience."

"Like the dog shit after a baseball game?" Carrie goaded.

There was a moment when no one said anything. Clowe, stiff with rage. Bemis, frozen at her profanity. Carrie gave it a moment to sink in.

"So, here's my question, Mr. Clowe," she hissed. She held the picture over the abyss. "Will you agree to a small bargain?"

Clowe looked from her face to the picture she held out. His eyes narrowed, his chin pugnacious. "I'm right about you and Morgan, aren't I?"

"No, you're not." Carrie lied as easily as Katrina produced pancakes. "But I'm right about you and Evans. So, here's the deal. Nothing Katrina Morgan said goes in the paper." Carrie bit off each word. "And the evidence of your whoring, for which you've been blackmailed and for which you murdered Martin Evans, goes into the water." She pushed her arm out over the edge of the bridge, holding the photograph by her fingertips.

"Oh, Carrie," she heard Bemis mutter. She hadn't given him all the details of her plan.

"Make up your mind, Mr. Clowe!" she shouted.

Her role was the riskiest. Without the picture, there was no motive for Clowe to murder Evans after luring him to the dump with the promise of payment.

Without Amos Butler, there was no witness to Clowe buying the raft to discard the body, only a drunken, thieving child peering into the dark and thinking he saw a man with a cowboy hat.

Without Katrina's vengeful statement, Morgan had a better chance of winning the election.

Without any of it, Bemis had no story.

And, most importantly, with no reversal of opinion from Morgan's wife, Carrie and Del's adultery would remain buried.

Carrie bet Clowe would be easy to hoodwink, given his conceit. She bet she could ask Katrina to pretend to believe Clowe's insinuations and seek him out to offer him a disgraced wife's story. She bet Bemis would play his part. The multiple stories he could pen were sensational. And, she bet poor young Ransom had seen a mop of white hair, not a pale cowboy hat.

"You sure you want to do this?" Clowe sneered. "This won't get any better."

When Maxwell told them Wheeler kidnapped his family, Thomas Bale had muttered the same thing on that dark road.

She, the harlot, had used her friends to keep her secret. She used Katrina's rock-solid faith in her husband's and Carrie's virtue. She used Bill's zeal to lure Clowe here so she could make her bargain with him. She'd even roped *a child* into her deception.

But here was the opportunity to keep the Morgans safe from scandal, to keep Eddie's indiscretion under wraps, to retain Katrina's belief in her marriage, and to ensure Morgan's election was back in the hands of the people of Duncan County, not Howard Clowe's.

She had come to Hope Bridge only six months ago to recover from Phee's death, to buck her hated widowhood, to collect the remains of her life. But since her arrival, she'd become a lock-picker, a liar, and a slut. Snooping was the least of her transgressions. She was a backstabber, a fraud, using her friends to cover her misdeeds. She remembered what she'd said to Maxwell. *People will do anything to not have their indiscretions known.*

"I don't make things better," Carrie growled back.

She bet it all on Clowe's ego at this moment. Would he choose to save his own skin, or would he pursue his desire for humiliating his enemy?

The wind kicked up a swirl of sharp dust that hissed across the space between them.

Clowe nodded his head once, decisively. He nodded as Bemis's hold on his notebook turned slack and fell away. He stepped back and grinned, a smirk that shone as white as his hair. A grin that widened when Carrie opened her hand and let the picture fall.

Chapter Thirty-Three

Carrie sat alone in front of the fire in the vacant dining room of the Chester Inn. Even the gaming room had grown quiet.

In the darkness, the weight of her deception lay on her shoulders, like a sack of grain. Her hands lay in her lap, too heavy for animation. She stared into the feeble blaze, seeing the conflagration that was Butler's shack, imagining the agony he must have experienced when the thing collapsed on him. Seeing Katrina's lively face as she agreed to deceive Howard Clowe as part of Carrie's plan to bait the man into giving Bemis a story. She saw Bemis nodding excitedly, eager to play along so he could have 'the story of the year.' She saw Ransom's face looking up at her with shining trust.

She pressed her cold fingers to her eyes so hard she saw red spots. She couldn't stand the thought of her actions tonight. Katrina was as pure of heart as any woman could get. Ransom was as innocent as any child in his circumstances could be. She betrayed Bemis, her oldest friend, who had always been sincere with her.

But her adultery was still hidden.

She heard the cooks returning to the Chester's kitchen. Morning was coming on. The bread needed to be baked. She smelled coffee. She realized dully that she wasn't tired. Just filled with an emptiness that she could not, and did not, want to name.

When Thomas Bale came in shortly before sunrise, he looked just as bad as she felt. Bags under his eyes, dark unshaven bristles; his shoulders slumped with fatigue. With his badge pinned to his coat, and a dark, warning look at the desk clerk, he walked into the dining room. He sat down beside Carrie, his exhaustion changing to a wary concern.

"What's happened?" he asked, looking at her face. "I went home, and Katrina said you were still here."

She had no voice for a moment. *Where to begin? Should I tell him what a charlatan I am? Should I unburden myself on this kind and capable man? Why not? I've trashed every other relationship.*

Instead, she asked, "What happened in Albany?"

Bale sat forward with his elbows on his knees and clasped his hands.

"We did what you told us. We went straight to the funeral parlor and you were right, Mr. Lourde didn't mind helping us out at all. He knew you and your papa, like you said, and he was happy to let us borrow his cart and horse, and one of his caskets. He even gave me one of those old-fashioned undertaker hats. Creepy. But it did the trick.

"Just like you said, I drove the wagon right up into the alley behind Maxwell's house, right up to the back door, and made a lot of noise doing it. When Wheeler answered the door, I waved a couple of sheets of paper in his face. They all flapped around. 'You gotta sign!' I said, 'you gotta sign.' I stepped right up onto the back porch, and kept waving and saying 'you gotta sign.' We argued about the address. I pretended I was hard of hearing. Del and Maxwell went in the front door.

"I held the papers between his face and mine so he wouldn't see the punch coming. Got him right in the nose. But he was tough. Maybe he'd been in the ring, too. I hit him a few more times in the belly, and he went down. Del came out, and we trussed him up like a hog, feet to wrists. I tried to stop him, but Maxwell got in one good kick that maybe resulted in some loose teeth. We left him out there in the cold.

"Maxwell's family was all right. They were scared, but Wheeler didn't hurt them. The little girl's pigtail was the only casualty, although Mrs. Maxwell had a bruise like he'd hit her at some point.

"I spent some time with Mr. Wheeler out in the back yard while Del found a constable. Wheeler said Clowe hadn't meant to kill Evans. He lost his temper and jumped on Evans. Evans went down. Wheeler got the raft and they loaded Evans onto it, then Wheeler had orders to go find Maxwell's family in Albany. He took off; Clowe dumped Evans. When the constable came, we went to find Eddie and those girls."

Bale glanced up at her, looked down again. He didn't go on.

"What happened to Eddie?" Carrie asked. They were speaking quietly. Still, her question came out in a whisper. *I think I know.*

"He did take the girls up to Mariet. He stabled his horse and took the train with them into Albany. The stableman made a joke, not knowing what was up, saying he almost hoped Eddie didn't return so he could keep that fine horse for his own. I stepped in front of Del, just in case he maybe wanted to kill that man, too. I pushed him out of there.

"After we took care of Maxwell's family, the constable pointed us in the general direction. Del knew a little about Albany. He'd been there as a young man. At school, I think. We weren't in terribly rough neighborhoods, but places respectable families wouldn't frequent. It took a while, but we found Eddie in one of the sporting houses. In a front parlor. He wasn't drunk, but he'd been drinking. We recognized one of the girls with him from the pictures."

Bale paused. Carrie didn't look up at him. She remained still, looking at the fire. Bale went on even more softly, as if reluctant to recall the rest.

"Eddie took one look at Del and jumped up. Del just stood there for a minute, and then he asked Eddie to come on outside. Politely, like he was talking to a man, not his kid."

Bale cleared his throat a little. "Eddie said he didn't think he'd ever speak to him again and walked out past Del, down the steps, out into the street. Del and I followed him, and Eddie turned around and hit his father right in the face. I gave that boy a few jabbing lessons. He used them."

Bale stopped again. He didn't look at her. And Carrie knew what he was about to say.

She knew because Eddie would not have gone back up to Sussex Mill when he was so close to Hope Bridge, on a dark night, unless he was overwhelmingly compelled to do so. What would make a young man, who was so excited by his father's bid for sheriff, turn around and abandon the campaign? What would make him disappear? Make his mother worry so?

What was that overwhelmingly compelling reason?

She knew because nobody tore campaign posters off the sides of barns and bridges. Nobody crumpled them up and tossed them into the Duncan. Campaign posters were best defaced. Lewd, scrawled remarks, blacked -out teeth, and crossed eyes were common. But Del's posters had been ripped off, and Eddie's stack of remaining posters flung into the dirt. That was the gesture of someone in a rage.

We took such a risk that night.

And they had been seen.

Bale still didn't look at her, but he plowed on. His warm and deep voice, now a monotone, a dissertation of facts. Words that needed to be said, but didn't need emotions clinging to them. "Eddie started screaming at Del, calling him all kinds of names. Calling you all kinds of names.

"I got between them and took them away from the house. Del tried to explain, but Eddie wouldn't hear any of it. He said he came into Hope Bridge late Hallowe'en night. He came down North Street from the Shunpike, like I thought." Bale stopped, and Carrie hung her head.

"He said he wasn't sure it was his father coming out of your back door. He said he didn't want to believe it. He followed Del to Main Street and saw his face in the lamp light. Then he got back on his horse and rode out of town. He ended up in Sussex Mill before dawn. Came across the tavern. Got invited upstairs."

"Why did Eddie go with the girls?"

"If I had to guess, I'd say he was most likely feeling a lot of anger and a lot of…" Bale sighed. "I don't know, revenge? A whole lot of 'I don't care' and 'why the hell not?' Mostly, I'd guess, he was feeling what all young men feel at that age when a girl offers herself in that way. Helpless."

In the silence, Carrie stared at the space between her lap and the table in front of her. A space where nothing happened. A space in which there was no future and no past. A space that couldn't last. After a while, she spoke.

"Where is Eddie now, Thomas?"

"He's on his way back to Duncan with Katrina."

"Where's Del?"

"He went to his room at Clevinger's.

"And Ransom?"

"At my place. He'll stay with me for a while."

"Uncle Sav is due back today. He'll be in Duncan later this morning. Then he's getting a ride back here to vote," Carrie said absently. The location of people she loved seemed the only orderly thing her mind could manage.

"If there's anything I can do for you, Miss Car—"

"You'd better distance yourself from me, Thomas," she said quietly. Her elaborate plan, in which she'd betrayed almost everyone she loved, hadn't worked after all. "Eddie and Katrina won't stand for this. Del will need you as a friend."

"Katrina doesn't know," Bale said softly.

Carrie looked up, into Thomas Bale's eyes. She saw only concern.

He shook his head, a small movement that spoke of great sadness. "Eddie threatened to tell his mother about you and Del. But Del told his boy he had a picture of Eddie and those girls, and that would kill his mother, too."

She couldn't stop the groan of pain, couldn't clamp her eyes shut hard enough. Her face dropped into her hands. She had ruined a sacred relationship. Father and son, at a bitter, unforgivable standoff. *I don't make things better.*

Eventually, Bale's voice came through her roaring ears. "Miss Carrie, I am not one to talk about love that shouldn't be. You know this. You've kept my love for Marta in your confidence, and I will surely do the same.

"But I am one to know about hard things and bad people. And I don't see any bad people here. I see only good people here. Good. People. This is too much right now. Too much for all of you. I don't have any answers for Del and his boy. Or for you and Del. Or for Del and Katrina. But I know answers will come. With time. You'll find the answers to this with time."

He stood and laid a hand on her shoulder. She reached up and covered it with hers. It might be the last friendly gesture she would ever know. When he had gone, she looked into the fire, finding the answers there.

Chapter Thirty-Four

Election Day in Duncan County arrived under a cold drizzle that chilled to the bone. By the time the sun had risen with any kind of authority, a stiff wind had picked up, blowing the rain beneath ladies' bonnets, and under collars and mufflers. Men grumbled on their way to the ballot boxes, their arguments made sharper by their discomfort with the weather.

"Don't know why I'm a-voting for either one! Ain't neither of 'em around now, are they?"

"Ya can't vote for that numbskull Morgan! He's skated by this past year. Ya want a man with integrity!"

"Ya want a man from the county!"

Other men gathered inside Bookhoudt's or Clevinger's and spat into the ash bucket next to the wood stove. "Never liked that Clowe fella."

"Where the hell is he, anyway?"

"He musta gone back to Duncan. All the big action's there."

"Don't know why I'd vote for either one of 'em!"

Five inflexible women linked arms and stood under the porch at the Town Hall, wearing sashes with "Votes for Women" sewn in bold white letters across their coats. They endured jeers from some, and curt nods of solidarity from others as the voting commenced. Inside, penciled checkmarks and Xs written decisively on paper ballots indicated the voter's choice. The tickets were wedged into the slot at the top of a padlocked wooden box.

"Didja hear about Butler? His shack burnt to the ground!"

"I heard the new bridge man came in yesterday. Ornery cuss, too, some said."

Art Worley acted as scrutineer during the voting, thereby eliminating all prospects of anyone posing as a deceased person in order to cast a bogus vote. When the voting was done tonight, Emmett Cross would glue a piece of paper over the slot and sign his name across the top. A deputy, always Leo Lamont in Hope Bridge, a position to which Thomas Bale acquiesced with grace, would lock the Town Hall precisely at six o'clock in the evening and turn his back to it, so that he could observe the counting of the ballots. The seal was broken, and two members from the opposing majority parties would carefully scrutinize the Xs, checkmarks, and signatures, and when the votes were balanced against the signatures in the polling book, the tally would be telegraphed to the post office in Duncan. Dozens of telegrams came in from townships all over the county. The winner of each race was announced in the morning paper once the reporters were made privy to the news.

Carrie Lisbon was unaware of the flurry of activity taking place, or of the fervor in which men argued about the candidates. While they carried out their civic duty with pride, she waded through the early morning with limbs as heavy as lead, packing and writing letters.

Her letter to Sav explained how, while she wished she could have welcomed him home, 'and I do want to see your library charter as soon as I can,' she'd been given a sudden opportunity to travel to Savannah for a month and upon her return, she'd book herself into a boarding house in Nanuet. There she'd stay, visiting old friends, until the undertaker's convention in February. She reminded him that they'd already discussed her plans to attend the conference. Of course, he could expect weekly correspondence from her.

She kept her tears from falling on this letter. She loved Sav and his buoyant innocence. He'd taken her in. She got back on her feet with his guidance and love. Her homely, rawboned uncle would surely understand her sudden waywardness, and he'd accept her abrupt departure with his full support.

Her self-loathing grew.

Worley's letter was of a similar nature, except she entreated him to take Thomas Bale into his occasional employ as a carpenter of well-crafted caskets, and young Ransom Butler, now a respectable young man with a whetstone. For pennies, he could keep Worley's tools sharp. She could easily envision Worley's withering expression as he read her request. She deserved it.

Why not include Ina Barnstable in my elaborate charade? The society columnist would report the travels of Mrs. Carrie Lisbon and her attendance at the conference ('And why not? Do not lady undertakers have just as much education and certifiable knowledge as our Mrs. Lisbon?'). Ina would be a frequent caller at Sav's, hoping to get a tidbit of information from Carrie's weekly letters.

She penned a note to Bill Bemis, explaining the dropped picture. She imagined him huffing in exasperation, doubting her integrity, but hustling to find Morgan, his reporter's zeal as unstoppable as a runaway horse. The story was explosive. He could write all he wanted about Howard 'Whitey' Clowe's impending arrest for murder and arson.

Another letter to Marta, apologizing for her abrupt departure and promising to keep in touch, completed the stack she tucked into her reticule.

She fed and petted Oscar while the bird cussed at her in return. In the parlor, she took Phee's picture from the mantle and slid it into her valise. She touched the smooth oak legs of her tripod. Ransom must have fetched it back for her at some point, another loose end Katrina had thoughtfully tied up. She'd send for her camera equipment later.

She swept the porch, locked the house, posted her letters, paid another boy to run to the Chester with Bemis's letter, and carried her undertaker's bag and valise to the creamery. She caught a ride to Sussex Mill on the hard wooden seat of a dairyman's wagon. She took her punishment, lurching uncomfortably over Duncan's rutted roads, enduring the ill-behaved children, the taciturn farmer, the incessantly talkative wife. Everyone reeked of sour milk. Of course, she paid them well for their accommodation.

She hired a young man at the Sussex Mill livery to drive her up to the train depot in Mariet. She only glanced at the darkened windows of Willie's Tavern as they passed.

Her journey would be complex. It would take several days. That was good.

She wanted to be alone and far, far away. From this rain-dreary countryside, the train would take her to Albany, then to Nanuet, then to New York City. From there to Savannah. She really did have an acquaintance who ran a funeral parlor down there. She'd make herself useful.

There were no other passengers at the tiny station. She paced the wooden floors. She watched an orchardist loading his barrels of Ben Davis apples, the hard and tart 'mortgage saver.' The doors to the freight cars rolled shut on rough wooden boxes stamped with the words 'Duncan County Cheese.'

Apples and cheese, she thought dully. *So simple. Maybe that should be my new chant.* The porters walked away to take their lunch, and she paced some more. She smelled the tang of cheese, horse manure, burnt coal, and suddenly warm tobacco. She spun around.

He hadn't slept in two days, had walked through the dark, from a crypt in Bitter Hay all the way to Sussex Mill, rode hard, and boarded a train to and from Albany to rescue a family he didn't even know. He'd endured a cataclysmic breach with his son, and his bid for election was uncertain.

Then he rode up here. His pebble-colored hair was either flattened or bent forward. His left eye was purple and swollen. His clothes sagged as if he'd lost ten pounds in the last three days.

They'd developed a telepathy since they'd met in the spring. They understood what the other was thinking, how the other was feeling. They'd completed each other's sentences. She recognized his reluctance to touch a dead body; he had championed her talents and resources. She enjoyed his candor; he called her his keen observer. They had engaged in the ultimate act of trust, and then relied on each other to keep that secret. She didn't need to hear him say how her leaving hurt. It was her ache as well.

The train whistle blew.

"Why are you here?"

"Bemis found me. Said you had a picture of Howard Clowe with the girls. *And* that you destroyed it," Morgan said angrily.

All of her letters hadn't been written. She intended to write him, using the hours on the train. She'd post it from the nearest station as soon as it was finished. Explaining it to his face was going to be excruciating.

"I needed that picture, Carrie," he went on. "Where did you get it? Clowe destroyed his. Maxwell burned the one we took to Albany. Now, there's nothing for motive, nothing to prove Clowe killed Evans. What did you do!"

Morgan would never have suspected she'd dupe him as well. The same despair she'd felt when Phee died bloomed in her chest. Her eyes closed in pain. After only a moment of that thin comfort, she looked up and addressed him quietly.

"I went to the crypt in Bitter Hay on my way back from Willie's yesterday. I destroyed the glass plate with Eddie's picture on it. I made another print of Howard Clowe."

"But Bemis said you made a deal with Clowe—"

"I dropped Eddie's picture into the creek, Del, not Clowe's."

"Jesus, Carrie."

The stationmaster sang out the 'all aboard.' She turned to go, but he stepped in front of her. He didn't touch her. It was a public place.

She huffed, agreeing with his sentiment, and picked up her chin. "I asked Katrina to pretend she found us out. She went to Clowe with her story, so he'd meet with Bill. So I could confront him. She was good; she scared the hell out of me. Ransom saw Clowe poling away with the raft that night. He'll say he saw a man wearing a light-colored cowboy hat, but it was Clowe's white hair. He never wears a hat. He's too vain. I think he set fire to Butler's cabin because Butler tried to get paid for his silence. Bill knows the story. Art Worley has the pictures of the rail and the gash on Evans' head. Willie and Clyde will testify to Evans' scheme to reduce their sentences. Clowe's picture is upstairs in Oscar's grain bin. Be careful. He bites. You can arrest Howard Clowe before the votes are counted tonight. I have to get on the train."

"Carrie—"

"I won't make a fool of us!" she said viciously. "Or Katrina! I'm so sorry about Eddie—" and here, her voice broke. "I can't endanger you or your family any more than I already have." She struggled to continue. Tears slid from her eyes. She dashed them away with a gloved knuckle.

"I don't know who I am anymore. But I sure don't like the person I've become. A liar. An adulterer. *I used my friends!"*

The conductor sang out again from the train steps. "'Board!"

Morgan glared at the uniformed man. Turned back to her. "You've become a dear friend to me, Carrie. And a confidante, and a woman I admire." His voice was thin.

She sagged. Morgan caught her elbow. The train's brakes let go, and steam whooshed around the pistons. She put on her grim face.

"I know," she said. "And I'm sorry."

She picked up her valise and turned her back on Morgan. She stepped up past the conductor, just as the car began to move.

She dropped into a worn upholstery seat by the window. She had watched her late husband disappear in the distance as her train left the Nanuet station a year and a half ago. She thought she'd see him again in just a few days' time. She never did. The receding figure of Del Morgan blended into her memory of Phee Lisbon. Phee had raised his hand in farewell. Morgan did not. His clenched fist was the only thing not obscured by the cloud of steam as the train chuffed away.

A Note from the Author

Hope Bridge, Duncan County, and all the hamlets and villages in this story are fictitious. Carrie's world is a combination of rural counties, landscapes, creeks, rivers, and small villages that make up a corner of New York State south of the Mohawk River and west of the Hudson.

Nanuet is a real place in Rockland County, New York. In 1900 it was not the bustling city Carrie hails from. It was a small town, with dirt roads, much like Hope Bridge. But I came across the name while reading the 1945 and 1946 diaries of a beloved member of my hometown. She had family in Nanuet, and I simply loved the name. When I crafted Carrie's life, I wanted her to come from an urban background, so I took the extraordinary liberty of applying the name Nanuet to the city of Nyack, an actual city, also in Rockland County, on the Hudson River. Apologies to the citizens and history of both places.

Women throughout time have prepared the bodies of the dead, but not necessarily as a profession. Their tasks included washing and dressing the body, arranging the house, applying herbs and ointments to mask odors, cooking the repass meal, creating the floral tributes, comforting the bereaved, caring for the children. When embalming as a standardized practice began in earnest in the United States during the Civil War, and grew in acceptance from that time forward as a way of preserving, sanitizing, and presenting the dead, women naturally had a hand in the business, under their husband's or father's administration. I've crafted Carrie Lisbon to be as knowledgeable and as practiced as any male counterpart in her time, and made her an expert in mortuary photography, cosmetics, floral arrangements and embalming.

In 1900, there were clubs, societies, organizations, and associations for everything, both professional and avocational. Carrie may have belonged to the Women's Licensed Embalmers Association, a real organization that promoted the professional interests specific to women in the undertaking trade. However, the National Telegrapher's League and the Association of American Funeral Directors (the "Double AFD," as well as its *Index),* are fictitious.

Identifying, photographing, and studying the dead, both grossly and toxicologically, as a means to assist law enforcement investigations and prosecution, isn't new. I was very pleased to come across *Principles of Forensic Medicine,* published in 1888, by 'the late' William A. Guy, Kings College, London. Some of the terms used in that book are still in use today.

Thomas Bale refers to laws regarding the posting of a campaign sign on someone's barn. I assumed there was a law, or at least a custom that required permission from the property owner before campaign posters could be adhered to their structures. Bridges, on the other hand, were maintained by the town or county, making them public property. They were the billboards of their time, and were adorned with notices, posters, tacked-up scripts, even painted advertisements.

The *Duncan Herald* is a fictitious newspaper, but newspapers were the key means of communication, advertising, education and generally being in the know in Carrie's time.

Local sheriff elections were held in New York State in 1899 and 1903. I fudged those dates to coincide with my story. In November of 1900, women didn't have the right to vote, but Women's Suffrage movements were widespread.

I had to drive terms like 'shutterbug,' 'snap a picture,' 'cameraman' and 'the shutter clicked' from my thoughts when writing about operating a camera in 1900. There was no shutter on cameras of that period. The photographer had to take off the lens cap, time the exposure, then put the cap back on in order to "take the picture." The removal of the cap allowed light to interact with the chemical-covered piece of glass at the back of the camera. There would be no clicking sound, no digital cropping, no multi-shots. There was an elaborate system for maintaining the integrity of the exposed plate. Any photographer of that era needed to stage her shot meticulously prior to creating a single image.

I found the term 'mudslinger' in newspaper articles ranging from the 1870s to the very early 1900s, but not the term 'mudslinging.' I made the conjugation as a literary license. "Gladhanding" is a term first noted in 1903, but it may have been in use in 1900.

The National Casket Company that Carrie visited on a pretense is real. It was organized in 1880 as the amalgamation of three large casket-making firms. It operated primarily out of Oneida, New York, and grew to have factories and showrooms all over the country.

One can find crypts in lots of very old cemeteries. The vault in this story is patterned after numerous examples I've encountered and photographed in New York and Massachusetts. I like the ones that are built into the steep side of a hill. The builders carved out the earthen embankment, laid up stone or bricks for the walls, installed benches or shelves for the caskets and built a variety of entrances. They all have iron doors. Although I'm overwhelmingly curious to see what it's like inside, I won't be so disrespectful to the dead that I would invade their final resting place. Imagination will suffice.

There really is no specific "crypt key," but I found a beautiful, complete, little brass key while metal detecting, and the entire story was inspired by it. Padlocks were as common in 1900 as they are now and the classic "skeleton key" unlocked many doors. Lock picking was probably more common (and successful) then.

The name Shun Pike and River Road are common names for routes all over my state, like streets named after Presidents and trees. Naturally, I included them in Duncan County.

Acknowledgements

I have come to rely on a wonderful bunch of people to assist me whenever I need writing tips, research help, cheering on, or a reality check. Because of this wonderful crew, I've learned so much about shoes and trains, undertaking practices, legalities, and vintage baseball. I'm forever grateful to the following people whose generosity has helped me get this book into your hands.

The Dames of Detection: Verena Rose, Shawn Reilly Simmons, and Deb Well at Level Best Books, who provided me with the opportunity to create the series.

John Mullins and Scott Keefer, my beta readers, who provide the honest perspective I always need for polishing the story. And thanks to Marlie Wasserman and Gary Earl Ross for providing the veteran read-through.

Thanks to all my writing buddies at the Schoharie Library Writers Club and the Community Library of Cobleskill. Your wise council and camaraderie gives me consistent, realistic, encouraging and supportive feedback. You all know the motto: "I wouldn't be here without you!"

Thanks to Alex Prizgintas, author, musician, historian, and preservationist who generously shared his knowledge of Orange County railroads.

I'm grateful to "Shoe-dog" Kevin McCoy who shared his profound knowledge of the anatomy of shoes.

Thanks to The Vintage Base Ball Association (vbba.org) who supplied me with the right jargon of the time.

My family and friends get my thanks for reading my stuff, asking about my progress, and feeding me! And my grandgirls and granddogs get me out of the 20th century and into reality every once in a while.

Thanks to all the Carrie Fans who continue to read, relish, and champion the series.

Thanks to my husband Dave who takes care of everything else while Carrie and I indulge ourselves.

And thank you, Muse. I'll never tire of your gifts.

About the Author

Chris Keefer began her writing career as a newspaper columnist, has published numerous magazine articles, and currently writes short fiction, essays, rants, and the Carrie Lisbon historical mystery series. She lives in upstate New York, and enjoys birding, cycling, gardening, metal detecting, town historian duties and a growing set of grandchildren. Readers can visit her online at authorchriskeefer.com.

AUTHOR WEBSITE:

www.authorchriskeefer.com

SOCIAL MEDIA HANDLES:

Facebook.com/authorchriskeefer.com

Also by Chris Keefer

No Comfort for the Undertaker. A Carrie Lisbon Novel

Tragedy's Twin. A Carrie Lisbon Novel

House Hunting. A short fiction published on *www.liquidimagination.com*

The Battle in the Bathroom. An indie published chapbook of humorous rants

www.ingramcontent.com/pod-product-compliance
Lightning Source LLC
Chambersburg PA
CBHW020622110726
47899CB00002B/617